A HARVEST MURDER

FRANCES EVESHAM

Boldwood

First published in Great Britain in 2022 by Boldwood Books Ltd.

Copyright © Frances Evesham, 2022

Cover Design by Nick Castle Design

Cover Photography: Shutterstock

A CIP catalogue record for this book is available from the British Library.

Paperback ISBN 978-1-80048-080-3

Hardback ISBN 978-1-80426-235-1

Large Print ISBN 978-1-80048-082-7

Ebook ISBN 978-1-80048-083-4

Kindle ISBN 978-1-80048-085-8

Audio CD ISBN 978-1-80048-076-6

MP3 CD ISBN 978-1-80048-077-3

Digital audio download ISBN 978-1-80048-081-0

Boldwood Books Ltd
23 Bowerdean Street
London SW6 3TN
www.boldwoodbooks.com

MAP OF LOWER HEMBROW

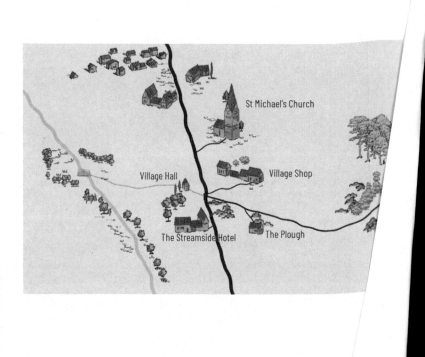

St Michael's Church

Village Hall

Village Shop

The Streamside Hotel

The Plough

To my husband who made the mistake of encouraging me to write.
I will cook a proper meal soon...

1

HARVEST FESTIVAL

Imogen Bishop, bundled up in a bright red hat, scarf and gloves against the October breeze, hurried down Lower Hembrow's main road from The Streamside Hotel to join the trickle of villagers heading for St Michael's Parish Church.

A sudden shaft of autumn sunlight bathed the church in a dramatic golden glow.

'Beautiful, isn't it?' Adam Hennessy, owner of The Plough, the village's popular inn, positioned directly opposite the hotel, joined her, panting, his breath misting the air.

Imogen shivered. 'Let's get inside in the warm.'

'Not bringing Harley to the Harvest Festival?' Adam asked. 'He'd love it.'

Harley, a cheerful mutt of unknown origin, lived happily with Imogen at the hotel she'd inherited from her late father. 'That dog's in disgrace,' she confessed. 'He dug a hole in the gardens, yesterday, just after Oswald spent the day planting crocuses. In any case, he's a real nuisance in church. I know the vicar says she's happy to have him there – Helen's a sucker for animal services with sheep and goats and so on – but even she shudders when he chases the church warden's cat. So, Harley's staying at home today.' They passed through the church porch into the nave. 'Wow, the schoolchildren have been busy.'

Imogen took a moment to admire the display. The church was a mass of colour. Bright orange pumpkins jostled green and red apples polished to a shine, while sweetcorn, tomatoes, sweet peppers and chillies overflowed into the pews, along with mountains of potatoes. The intoxicating smell of warm bread from freshly baked loaves made Imogen's stomach growl. Close by were baskets of creamy butter, yoghurt, tempting Somerset brie and Cheddar cheeses, but the hero of the display, the centrepiece that topped the pile in gleaming splendour, was a magnificent golden wheatsheaf.

Adam whistled under his breath. 'They never made wheatsheaves like that one where I used to live. It was strictly tinned goods at harvest in my run-down stamping ground in Birmingham.'

They slipped into a pew near the back of the church. 'Just as well you moved to Lower Hembrow, then,' Imogen said. 'Heritage crafts are ten a penny around here. And all the produce will be gifted this afternoon, while it's fresh.'

'That's one magnificent marrow at the back,' Adam chuckled. He pushed his horn-rimmed glasses up his nose. 'Now, hand over that hymn book, will you? I haven't sung "We Plough the Fields and Scatter" since I was a lad and I forgot the words years ago. And here's Steph, just in time.' His face lit up as Steph Aldred joined them.

'Is Dan coming?' Steph asked.

Imogen grimaced. 'No idea. You know what he's like when he's painting. He forgets everything – especially the time.'

The four friends had met when Imogen's estranged husband died in suspicious circumstances at the hotel. Adam, recently arrived at The Plough after retirement from the police force, had set about proving Imogen's innocence of the crime. Both Steph and Dan Freeman, two of Imogen's old schoolmates, had become entangled in the investigation, and they'd discovered a knack for solving crimes together. Adam and Steph had grown increasingly close since then. Imogen knew Adam could hardly believe his luck. 'I'm short, fat and bald,' he'd said, only half-joking. 'I don't know what she sees in me. But I'm not complaining.'

Imogen watched as they sang, Steph in a clear soprano, Adam in a gruff, self-conscious baritone, and a pang of envy squeezed her heart. She'd so wanted Dan at her side, today. She'd fallen for him long ago, when they were both at school, and since the investigation cleared her name, they'd spent many contented hours visiting landmarks and walking the coast path, sharing jokes and laughing until their stomachs ached. Imogen had hoped... what? She could hardly put her longing into words. So many times she'd thought Dan was about to declare his feelings but every time she'd been disappointed.

She tried to make allowances. Both of them had endured failed marriages, were in their middle years, had worked hard and were busy in their chosen fields. Photographs of Imogen's landscaped garden designs often made their way into *Country Living* and *Somerset Life*, while Dan exhibited his artwork regularly in London galleries and in the nearby Somerset town of Camilton.

Imogen realised that Dan's art always came first in his life. Deeply immersed in a painting, he would confuse appointments, often turning up at her door at the wrong time, and he'd go for days without eating properly, surviving on little more than coffee.

Sometimes, she compared their relationship with Adam and Steph's closeness, and asked herself whether she was foolish to hope for more from it.

As the organ music swelled to a climax, Imogen sang louder, trying to drown out her misgivings.

Finally, the service came to an end and the congregation spilled, chattering, across the road to the village hall for coffee and cake.

'Can't stop,' Imogen said. 'I promised Emily I'd be back early. The hotel's full to bursting.' Emily, her manager, was perfectly capable of running The Streamside in her absence, but she didn't want to stick around with Adam and Steph today, like a spare wheel.

* * *

Back at the hotel, Imogen found the lounge lively with weekend guests luxuriating on comfortable sofas in front of the roaring fire. As soon as Imogen appeared, they buttonholed her, eager for information on the best places to visit in Somerset in the autumn.

After an hour spent comparing the charms of Glastonbury Tor – chilly at this time of year – with the stunning arches of Wells Cathedral, and the smaller, more intimate atmosphere of Cleeve Abbey, Imogen heard a car squeal to a halt outside.

The vicar, Helen Pickles, swept into the hotel foyer, booming a greeting to the startled receptionist and talking nineteen to the dozen. 'Hello, hello. Now, where's Imogen? She got away before I could grab her. It took me ages to load up the produce in my car, even with Adam and Steph on the case. It's like a greengrocer's, now, and I can't stop, I'm off to the Ham Hill care home in a minute.' Like a boat with the wind in her mainsail, she burst into the lounge and dropped anchor on the one unoccupied squashy sofa, her words tumbling over one another. 'It's an emergency, Imogen. We need your help,' she gasped, fighting for breath. 'We have a catastrophe on our hands.'

'Another one?' Imogen said. One crisis seemed to follow

another ever since she'd taken on the hotel over a year ago. 'What's wrong this time?'

'I was just about to drive to the care home when I got a phone call from that waste of space, Roger Masters at Haselbury House, about the Apple Day festival. There's a week to go, the posters are up, everything's in train, and now the wretch has pulled out of the whole affair and we're up the creek without a venue. He's let us all down.' She raised her eyes to heaven. 'I don't know why I'm surprised. I never did trust the man. But I said to myself, we can't possibly cancel. Everyone's looking forward to it so much; the best carved pumpkins, the apple pie competition, the Wurzels tribute band... We can't disappoint people, now. *Nil desperandum*, as they say. And I thought, where better than The Streamside Hotel to help us out?' Helen's face radiated delight. 'Just look at the wonderful job you did with the Spring Fair.'

'Oh no.' Imogen raised a hand to fend off the very idea. 'You must be joking. The hotel's only just recovered.'

Lower Hembrow's Spring Fair, held for the first time at The Streamside Hotel in May, had been a tremendous success, but it had taken its toll on the gardens. The ornamental grasses near the stream, trampled flat by donkeys and children, had taken all summer to grow back.

On the other side of the room, Harley's head jerked up as Helen groaned. He trotted over to investigate as she begged, 'You're my last hope, Imogen. I'm relying on you.' She leaned down to the dog, muttering under her breath, 'That good-for-nothing lowlife, Roger Masters,' as she tickled Harley's ears.

Imogen winced. She'd designed the nearby stately home's garden before inheriting The Streamside Hotel from her father, and she'd loathed Roger Masters. She wouldn't mind if she never saw him again. 'Masters is a sexist thug, as I remember,' she said. 'But I thought he was happy to host the Apple Day? Didn't he say it was good for business?'

Helen's laugh was bitter. 'He did, my dear. He promised to manage the whole thing. Now, everything's ready to go; the craft marquees are rented, the food's organised and the apple press from the cider mill's already in position. But Masters has cancelled the lot.'

One of the waiters placed a tray of cakes on a table beside her and Helen's face lit up. 'My dear Imogen, you spoil me. White chocolate brownies – the absolute best. Just what one needs in an emergency.' Munching happily and spraying crumbs liberally, she went on, 'As you know, I try not to gossip, but between ourselves – and don't pass this on, will you? – between ourselves, Haselbury House is heavily in debt and in the hands of the receiver.' She flicked a crumb from her chin. 'I'm hoping The Streamside Hotel can save the day.'

Imogen wasn't sorry Roger Masters' business had failed. It felt like appropriate revenge. But it left her with a dilemma. Could the hotel possibly organise an Apple Day festival in less than a week? Helen was waiting patiently for her response, but she hesitated, problems chasing each other through her head. There was parking, and insurance, and telling the police – if she had any sense, she'd refuse.

She looked around for inspiration and caught sight of Emily, in the foyer, discussing menus with the chef. Imogen beckoned her over. 'Helen's looking for a venue for the Apple Day, but we can't possibly help, this time, can we? It's next Saturday. That's not nearly enough time.'

To her horror, Emily grinned. 'Well, it would be tricky, but if all the village helps to fetch and carry, I don't see why not. We know what's involved. It'll be just like the Spring Fair.'

Imogen bit her lip. She knew Emily loved a challenge, but still...

Sensing victory, Helen said, 'It would be such a shame to let everyone down. The Apple Day's one of the biggest events of the year. Everyone has an apple tree or two on their property and they all bring buckets of leftover fruit to press for juice to make cider...'

Imogen resigned herself to the inevitable.

2

THE PLOUGH INN

Oswald Marchmont, Imogen's gardener, levered himself onto his stool in The Plough that evening with a satisfied sigh. 'Nights be drawing in, eh?' he said. 'Autumn here already. My Freda's favourite time of the year. She made the wheatsheaf for the harvest festival, you know.'

The bar was filling up, fast, for Sunday was often the busiest night of the week.

Adam nudged Rex Croft, The Plough's barman, who was on a gap year after leaving university. 'Don't let the lads drink too much if they're driving.' He nodded towards the beer taps. 'And it's time for a new barrel.'

Rex flipped over a pad of paper, flushing guiltily. He had a bet running with Wayne, the chef, on who'd drink the most and thought Adam didn't know.

Adam grinned. His money would be on Joe, a local farmer.

'Not putting the kids to bed, tonight, then, Joe?' Oswald asked, as he did every Sunday.

'Not tonight. The wife's given me the night off,' Joe mumbled, peering sadly into his empty glass. 'Her mother's in the house, the old battleaxe.' He picked up the glass and waved it.

Adam frowned. If ever a woman deserved an evening off, it was Jenny, Joe's harassed-looking wife. When she wasn't working on their mixed farm, feeding their herd of Jersey cattle or planting barley, she was shepherding one or more of their six children around the village.

Joe went on, 'That mother of hers is an interfering old bat, always poking her nose into farm business, and that's the truth.' He heaved a sigh that seemed to come from his boots. 'Better just give us a half, I s'pose,' he grumbled.

Rex gave him a half-pint of scrumpy. 'That's not like you, Joe. On a diet?'

'I can't roll home drunk while the mother-in-law's there, can I? She's got a tongue on her could flay a tiger, that one.' Joe shook his head gloomily. 'Mind you, Jenny's as bad. She was on at me all evening. She doesn't know I'm in here tonight, though – I went out after dinner, saying I had to see after one of the cows, and sneaked off. She'll be on the lookout for me soon, one eye on the clock, so I'd better be getting back. These,' he added, showing no sign of leaving, 'are my last few nights of freedom. The mother-in-law's going to be on my case all the time soon. Jenny's going back to work.'

'That right?' Oswald said. 'Had enough of farm work, has she?'

'She's a teacher. She taught a bit, years ago, before we had all the kids. Farming a place like High Acres is a dead loss, these days. No profit in it, not now the government's got it in their sights. No more subsidies for growing food – just for making nice green places for the townies to buy their second homes. The mother-in-law says she'll help out with the kids while Jenny works. It's just an excuse to stick her nose into my business, if you ask me.' He took a long swig of cider.

Adam lined up glasses on the shelf. He'd heard the farm was struggling financially.

Rex served a couple of young farmers and Adam leaned on the bar, close to Joe. 'Good for Jenny,' he said quietly. 'You'll be glad of her mother's help, with your youngest still at home. How old is she, now?'

'Just two. Three in a week or so.' Joe's face lit up. 'Right forward little thing is Harriet, too, with her talking and all. And she knows what she wants. The mother-in-law told her off for standing on the table and she stamped her foot so hard she nearly fell off onto the floor.' He downed the last of his drink. 'Ah, well, better be going.' He dumped the glass on the bar and pushed his way out of the pub without another word.

Oswald nodded, sagely. 'There's trouble up at that farm. You mark my words,' he said.

One of the young farmers, Terry Barrington, looked up from his usual table by the window. 'I heard they're having to sell off some of the land. Joe's father-in-law gave him a fair few acres over towards the east of the county when he married Jenny, and Joe's hoping to sell some back. He thinks the mother-in-law's likely to pay a premium price now she's a widow. He's hoping she's an easy touch.' He raised his glass. 'Good on yer, Joe, that's what I say.'

Terry's mate, Eddie, a wiry lad with a shock of black hair over his eyes, muttered, 'More likely to screw Joe for every last penny, I reckon. No flies on Maggie Little, my dad says. He says there's more trouble up at High Acres than Joe lets on and Maggie won't want to buy back land that won't make a profit.'

Every head turned his way.

'Come on, Ed,' Terry said. 'Spill the beans. What trouble?'

Eddie blinked. Either his hair was in his eyes or he wasn't happy as the centre of attention. 'I don't want to say too much,' he muttered.

'You can't stop now,' Terry pressed. 'I reckon you're right about his mother-in-law. But Joe can stand up for himself. He's a cantankerous old geezer.'

Adam intervened, 'Leave it alone, Terry. And if you're wanting a game of skittles, you'd better get a move on. We've got a match booked in an hour or so.'

The young farmers left the bar balancing their drinks, pushing and shoving like sheep crowding through a gateway with a sheepdog hot on their heels, through the door to the skittle alley.

Rex, squeezing past Adam on his way to the cellar to replenish the beer, paused to murmur, 'Something there for you to investigate, if you ask me, former Detective Chief Inspector Hennessy. I wouldn't be surprised if Joe's mother-in-law is never seen again.'

3

EDWINA

A few days later, a tentative knock sounded on the door of Adam's private rooms at The Plough. He opened the door with care, remembering Harley's arrival last year. The dog had leapt at him, bursting the door's safety lock from its moorings. Adam still had no idea where he'd come from, despite his extensive enquiries. He supposed the friendly brown mutt of no discernible breed had escaped from puppy farmers, although why anyone would want to breed such a genetic mishmash as Harley, he couldn't imagine.

Harley had settled in happily at The Plough. Adam had been less enthusiastic. He'd retired to The Plough in search of a quiet life and his own company. He hadn't reckoned on a needy canine companion, especially one with Harley's boundless energy. Once he'd chewed Adam's shoes, ruined a sofa and broken half a dozen cups, Adam had offered him to Imogen, pleading inexperience with dogs and a preference for cats.

Imogen, stressed, despondent and terrified she was about to take the blame for her husband's murder, had needed help. Adam had gambled that Harley would be just what she needed, and he'd been proved right. Since then, the dog had lived in spoilt contentment at The Streamside Hotel across the road.

Today's polite tap on the door definitely didn't belong to Harley. That dog had never been known to do anything gently.

Perhaps it was Steph.

She was due at The Plough for lunch, and Adam had glanced at his watch at least four times in the past hour as he waited. He'd never understood exactly what a woman like Steph saw in him; a short, slightly overweight retired police officer with thick glasses and almost no hair. She'd be here soon and Adam's heart beat a little faster.

But today's visitor turned out to be Edwina Topsham, the keeper of the village shop. Adam forgot his manners and gaped. She'd always disapproved of him somewhat, as a recent 'incomer' to the village. Edwina had a strict definition of an incomer, that included anyone who had not been born in Lower Hembrow, or who had lived there for fewer than twenty years. Adam feared he would only become a resident when he hit his seventies.

'Mrs Topsham,' he beamed, throwing the door wide open with exaggerated courtesy. 'How delightful to see you. Please come in. Can I offer you a nice cup of tea, perhaps?'

Panting with exertion, Mrs Topsham patted at the assorted collection of pins and clasps she'd thrust in her hair at odd angles in a doomed attempt to keep her iron-grey bun in place. She must have run all the way from her small, cluttered cottage at the other end of the village, which she shared with a husband and several – Adam never knew exactly how many – cats. The cats were the only topic of conversation Adam and she shared when he visited the shop.

'Tea? I don't mind if I do,' she said now, following Adam into his living room and plumping herself firmly into the sturdiest of his chairs.

It creaked a warning and Adam held his breath. If the chair collapsed, dumping its cargo on the floor, he'd be ostracised for ever in the village.

'Well, isn't this a cosy room?' Mrs Topsham stretched her sensible brogues towards Adam's roaring fire and took a deep breath. 'Apple wood,' she declared. 'Nothing like the smell of apple logs when the weather's turning sharp.'

Satisfied that the chair would hold firm, Adam went and brewed the tea, then handed a steaming mugful to his guest and watched her stir in four heaped teaspoonfuls of sugar. As she selected one of his chef, Wayne's, cinnamon whirls from an assortment on a chintz-patterned plate, he asked, 'And to what do I owe this visit, Mrs Topsham? It's a pleasure, of course, but I don't believe you visit The Plough too often, do you?'

She chuckled, wheezed and struggled to catch her breath. 'Never set foot in here since my father died,' she said at last. 'Couldn't get him out of the place when he was alive, you see, and he died early. It was the blood pressure, you know.' She nodded wisely. 'Terrible thing, blood pressure. And you may call me Edwina since I've come to ask you a favour.'

Lost for words at the compliment, Adam offered her another cinnamon whirl.

'We all know you're a detective,' she announced.

Adam inclined his head. He couldn't deny it. He'd investigated two murders since his arrival in Lower Hembrow and, as a result, everyone in the village knew he'd once been a Detective Chief Inspector in Birmingham. 'I am indeed,' he admitted, carefully. 'Or, rather, I was.'

Once the village grapevine had hold of the news, they'd inundated him with requests to find lost dogs, investigate car thefts and follow 'suspicious loiterers'. One imperious lady had even telephoned with a demand to 'pick my Lily up from school, will you? I'm stuck in a traffic jam.'

He'd courteously declined to take on the role of a kind of unofficial 999 service, but Edwina's favour sounded different. Judging by her furrowed brow, she was genuinely worried.

'If you need the police, I'm happy to talk to them with you,' he said, kindly. Maybe she was reluctant to talk to the law. Many people were.

Abruptly, she shook her head. 'It's not really my business,' she said. Her lips snapped shut.

Adam nodded and waited. What on earth could she be about to tell him?

'It's the Trevillians, you see,' she said at last. 'Jenny and Joe. You know Joe, of course. He's in here whenever the fancy takes him, drinking and leaving Jenny to cope up there on the farm, all alone. And now, this.'

'This?' Adam raised an eyebrow. 'Has something happened?'

She spread her hands wide. 'Well, he's only gone and done a runner, hasn't he?'

'Joe?' Adam stared. 'You mean, Joe's left home?'

'Disappeared.'

'But he was here on Sunday.' Adam thought back over the chatter in the bar. Joe had seemed grumpier than usual. 'Jenny's mother was at High Acres, helping out,' he remembered.

'Huh!' Edwina barked. Adam's tea slopped over the top of his mug. 'Helping out, indeed.' She jabbed the air with a finger in time with her words. 'Interfering between man and wife, that's what I call it.'

Adam pulled a handkerchief from his pocket and dabbed at the tea stain on the knee of his trousers as Edwina went on talking.

'She's an interfering old woman, is Maggie Little. I don't know why she's taken to landing herself on Jenny and Joe, or what's been going on at High Acres, but she's been dropping in there most days. No wonder Joe left home, that very night, and Jenny hasn't seen hide nor hair of him since. He never went home. Not that I blame him,' she snorted. 'A man can't stand that kind of nosiness from his mother-in-law.' She shook her head. 'Mind you, I reckon Joe will soon regret running off. He'll be lost without Jenny. She wears the trousers in that family, running the farm and feeding all those children. It's got on top of her lately, I reckon. She's been looking tired.'

'Perhaps that's why her mother's stepped in?' Adam suggested. 'And to help out when she goes back to work. It'll be a strain on Joe.'

'That's as may be, but there's ways of managing a man without belittling him, you know.'

Personal experience, Adam guessed, glad he wasn't Mr Topsham.

'In any case,' she persisted, 'Joe will go to pieces on his own. I doubt he can even cook a decent beans on toast. He's probably sleeping on the streets already.'

'Joe's a grown man and at liberty to leave home if he chooses,' Adam pointed out. 'There's no law against it.'

Edwina scrambled awkwardly to her feet, offended. 'I'm not talking about the law,' she flared, her hands on her hips. 'I'm talking about being a good neighbour. Poor Jenny's up there, dealing with everything on the farm. She needs her husband about the place, no matter what a waste of space he might be. I'd thought you were the one to ask for help, but if you're not going to bother, I'll find someone who will.'

'Hold on a minute,' Adam protested. 'I haven't said I won't help, but I need to know the facts. Has Jenny talked to you about all this?'

With a groan, Edwina let herself fall back into her chair. 'Course she has. Worried sick, she is, and wanting him back. I told her she should come to you, but you know what she's like. Doesn't want to trouble you. But we can't let that family come to grief without trying to help, can we?'

Adam shot another surreptitious glance at his watch, wishing Steph would arrive and rescue him.

'I thought,' Edwina said, with a triumphant grin, 'your little band of sleuths might like to look into a mystery. Four of you, weren't there, investigating that murder at the races? Young Steph will help – nice little thing, isn't she?' Adam wasn't going to disagree about that. 'And then, there's Imogen at the hotel. Mind, she's busy with her own life – I've no idea what she sees in that good-for-nothing painter, but who am I to judge?' She nodded to herself. 'So, why don't you all get together and see if you can't find Joe before something bad happens to him or his wife has a breakdown?'

With that, Edwina bundled herself up once more in scarves and gloves against the autumn wind and got up to leave before Adam could protest any more. She narrowly avoided a collision with Steph.

'Just in time, my dear,' she chuckled. 'There's a job for you to do.'

'Perfect,' said Steph, waving goodbye to Edwina, shrugging off her coat and rubbing her hands together to warm them. 'Will this job help with my book? Or is it something to do with Apple Day? No one in the village can talk about anything else. I hear the apple press has already been set up in the hotel gardens, and just now a huge red tractor came charging up to the hotel pulling a trailer and nearly took the wing off my car.'

'More marquees, I suppose. It's going to be quite an event.'

'It was all over the local paper this week,' Steph said. 'I've managed to wangle a commission for a feature once it's all over. Since I haven't written my book yet, I still need to put in the odd spot of journalism. I shall bribe Imogen to give me an interview, when she slows down enough to talk.'

'I'm hoping she'll spare an hour or two tomorrow. We have a mystery on our hands, according to Edwina, and she's insisting we investigate. Against my better judgement, though.'

'Nonsense!' Steph laughed. 'I've never known a place like Lower Hembrow for mysteries, and a spot of sleuthing never does any harm. Tell me everything.'

4

MYSTERY

Spurred on by Steph, Adam had persuaded Imogen and Dan to spare an hour and meet for lunch the next day.

'It's such bliss to get away from the hotel madhouse,' Imogen admitted as Adam led them across to a quiet table in the bar. 'It's the hammering I can't stand, and Harley's wild excitement. I think he's hoping the donkeys will be there, like they were at the Spring Fair, but Oswald's put his foot down. He says the grass has only just recovered. It'll be a relief when Apple Day's over.' She shot a glance at Dan. 'You're all coming to help, aren't you?'

'Wouldn't miss it for the world,' Steph laughed. 'I love this time of year. First, there's the Apple Day festival; not that I've ever been to one of those before, but it sounds like fun and I can't wait. And then, there's Dan's exhibition in Camilton, soon. I can't believe I know a real-life artist.'

Adam exchanged a glance with Steph. 'Not to mention Hallowe'en and Bonfire Night,' he said.

Steph chuckled. 'Exactly. There's nothing better than drinking hot chocolate and toasting marshmallows around a bonfire in the dark, is there?'

'Roman candles, sparklers, burnt fingers,' Dan said. 'What a painting that will make. Better than the rather formal portraits of stately homes Henry's asked me to show at the gallery. The owners are willing to pay through the nose to see their ancestral homes glorified in oil paint.'

Adam chuckled. 'I doubt Roger Masters from Haselbury House will be sending any commissions your way. Not now his business has collapsed.'

Imogen interrupted. 'So, Adam, why don't you tell us all about this Mystery of the Missing Farmer. Any clues?'

'I hope we're not making a big mistake by poking our noses into Joe Trevillian's business,' Adam said, 'but Edwina's adamant that Jenny and Joe need our help.'

'Well, why shouldn't we try?' Steph asked. 'We did an excellent job when we investigated the murder at the races. We stopped a second murder and uncovered a whole lot of criminal activity, and your friend DCI Andrews was thoroughly grateful to us. Besides, this time it's a missing person, not a murder, so there's nothing to worry about. I mean, we won't be stepping on police toes and there's no killer on the loose.'

'So far as we know,' Adam pointed out.

'Working with all of you makes me feel like a proper detective,' Steph said. 'After all my years as a journalist trying to drag information out of reluctant politicians, it's such a pleasure to talk about clues and evidence with friends, round a table groaning with food. Which reminds me – what's on the menu today, Adam?'

'Burgers, I'm afraid. Wayne's having a day off to visit a woman in Bristol, so there's not much choice. Rex can manage Wayne's sausages and burgers, but he's no chef.'

'Talking of Rex,' Steph put in, 'I thought your Emily was looking a bit peaky when I saw her the other day, Imogen. Is that romance over?'

'I think it's fizzled out. She keeps busy in the hotel, but she's not her usual cheerful self. And yesterday,' Imogen leaned forward to whisper, 'I saw she had a chipped fingernail.'

The others gasped in mock horror.

'Isn't that a sacking offence?' Steph asked.

'Give the girl a break,' Dan said. 'She's the hardest worker I've ever met.'

The others turned in surprise.

'What?' he asked. 'I do sometimes notice what's going on, you know.'

'Especially when it's a pretty girl?' Imogen said.

Adam glanced at the pair of them. Imogen rarely criticised Dan aloud, and almost never snapped at him, but today there was an edge to her voice.

Rex arrived just then to take their order and Adam listened to his friends arguing over their lunch – though what could there be to wrangle over in choosing a burger?

Once the others had finally agreed on the sauces, salads and extra chips they required, they ordered. Rex disappeared back into the kitchen and Adam filled them all in on the details of his conversation with Edwina. 'I've agreed to visit Jenny to see what she knows about Joe's disappearance. Edwina said she's half out of her mind with worry, flipping between thinking she drove him away by saying she'll go back to work, and worrying he's had some sort of a breakdown.'

'Or run off with Maria Rostropova,' Steph chuckled. 'He couldn't take his eyes off her at the Spring Fair.'

'Shh,' Dan hissed. He was facing the door. 'Keep your voice down.'

The other three turned and watched as Maria, the 'Most Glamorous Woman in Lower Hembrow' as The Plough's regulars called her, swept inside.

Imogen groaned. 'She's always in here,' she muttered.

Steph grinned at Adam. 'Did it ever occur to you that she comes to see you?'

'She comes when she wants Adam to do something for her,' Imogen whispered. 'She's like a leech.'

Steph said, 'But a fabulous-looking one.'

Adam couldn't disagree. Widowed while living in Romania, Maria had come to England in a state she described, in her attractive and carefully exaggerated accent, as 'penniless, darlink, quite destitute'. She'd latched on to Adam, persuading him to lend her money that she'd never returned and involving him in any number of 'charitable' schemes. A little straight talking had put paid to her attempt to skim money from the charities, but neither Imogen nor Steph trusted her an inch.

Maria perched a hip on the next table. 'How lovely to see you all together,' she cooed. 'Such good friends. Are you solving more crimes?'

'Why, have you committed one?' Imogen asked, genially.

Maria's blue eyes were sharp as diamonds. She raised an eyebrow. 'Imogen, dear. What an original sweater. You have so many lovely warm things. I suppose a gardener like you needs them, out in all weathers. But this wind is so ageing, isn't it?' Without waiting for an answer, she wandered over to the bar. 'Rex, dear. May I have my usual? Better make it a double, I think. It's chilly in here.'

Dan frowned, 'She's in here a lot. Does she have a drink problem, by any chance?'

'Not sure,' Adam said. 'I've wondered. She doesn't drink more than one or two glasses of wine in here, but while she's at home – who knows.'

Steph wagged a finger at him. 'Now, don't you dare go round

there to find out. Not without me, anyway. I know that woman's your weak spot and she'll eat you for breakfast.'

'Nonsense,' Adam said, squeezing Steph's arm, 'But I think she's lonely.'

'Maybe Joe ran off with her and she's hiding him in her bedroom.'

They returned to discussing Joe's disappearance.

Steph said, 'Why don't you run out to High Acres to see the Trevillians, Imogen? You know Jenny better than the rest of us. She'll talk to you.'

'We've only chatted in the shop, where it's hard to have a decent conversation, what with her toddler demanding pizza and feeding biscuits to Harley. But I'll happily visit her at home and see if I can help. It sounds as though she doesn't know where Joe's gone, unless she didn't want to tell Edwina.' She smiled at Adam. 'More time away from the hotel's Apple Day chaos – bliss. Will you come with me? It'll be like old times, going out sleuthing together.'

He agreed, just as the door opened and Terry and his friends exploded into The Plough in a torrent of arguing and shoving. 'I wish I had their energy,' Adam said. 'A hard morning out in the fields and they're still bursting with life. And ready for one of Wayne's burgers.'

'Oh, to be young again,' Imogen said. 'And they must love The Plough to come over here at lunchtime. They don't have long breaks on the farms.'

Steph was laughing. 'Would you really want to be young again? With all the anxiety over life and our futures we used to suffer? No thanks, I'm enjoying middle age.' She turned to Dan, who was frowning. 'How are arrangements for your exhibition going? It's happening in a couple of weeks, isn't it?'

Dan nodded. 'That's right. The invitations will be going out soon.'

'Good job you have Henry to organise things at Camilton Gallery,' Imogen said.

'Well, we'll all be there to cheer you on,' Steph promised. 'And I hope Henry's charging those rich patrons of his through the nose for your pictures. Are they all finished?'

'The bulk of them are at the gallery, ready to be hung, but a few are still drying at the studio. I'm trying to stop tweaking them. I'm scared of ruining them, but sometimes, I just can't help myself. You know what it's like, Adam. You paint. You never know when a picture's truly finished.'

'I wouldn't compare my amateur daubs with your work,' Adam said, flattered despite himself, 'but I know what you mean. And exhibiting must be a strain.'

Steph picked up a knife and fork as the burgers arrived. 'So, a nice juicy mystery will be just the job to take your mind off your worries.'

5

JENNY

Later that afternoon, Adam and Imogen drove out to see Jenny Trevillian as promised. Harley sat in the back of the car, grinning at the prospect of an afternoon out. 'Take boots,' Imogen had warned Adam. 'Preferably wellies. You thought the yard was muddy when you visited Leo Murphy's racing stables, but it's nothing compared to Joe's farm. I hear he's the messiest farmer in the county.'

Imogen had made firm friends with local farming families during the racing murder investigation, and she'd managed to collect a few snippets of information about Joe and his wife to share on the journey.

'There's been plenty of talk about the Trevillians in Edwina's shop. I gather Joe and Jenny met just before they left the local comprehensive and married less than a year later. Jenny's parents owned Glebe Farm and passed almost half their land over to Joe, and that became High Acres. Joe complains he has to farm the least productive fields, and Maggie Little interferes when she thinks his work's not up to scratch.'

'Not the easiest situation,' Adam said, 'but no excuse for Joe to up sticks and leave.'

'We know he's not the most forgiving of people. His father-in-law, Albert Little, died about a year ago, and Maggie now runs their farm through a farm manager. She's a shrewd businesswoman by all accounts and was always the powerhouse behind her husband. Now the farm's all hers, I bet she has a thing or two to say about the way Joe runs his place. I bet he's gone off to grumble to some friend or other and he'll be back soon.'

'Maybe this is going to be no more than a storm in a teacup,' Adam agreed, 'with Jenny's friends winding her up to imagine some disaster.'

'Let's hope so.'

As Adam turned through a gate into the lane leading to the farm, Imogen saw she'd been right about Joe's farm management. The lane was muddy and the car had to swerve with care around a series of puddles forming in the unevenly gravelled surface.

Finally, narrowly avoiding a deeper puddle that almost approached pond status, they drew up in the yard. She was surprised to see neat rows of vegetables ranged to one side, leading to a small, well-maintained apple orchard. Jenny, she knew, was responsible for the market gardening side of the business. No doubt, she'd be bringing this year's harvest to the press on Saturday. It was free for anyone to use on Apple Day.

On the other side of the yard, however, chaos reigned. Part of a drystone wall had collapsed and a wheelbarrow half full of stones stood on a nearby patch of uneven ground, as though Joe had begun to tidy up with a view to mending the wall, but had lost interest. Grass encroached over some of the stones.

'That wall's been left for far too long,' Imogen said. 'And look at the mud around the gate of the cattle field. You couldn't wade through that, even in wellies. And we haven't had any proper autumn storms, yet.'

Adam pulled his coat closer against the sharp wind whistling around the yard. 'No wonder this place is called High Acres,' he said. 'You can see for miles.' He stood for a long moment, Harley at his side. 'I'm no farmer,' he added, 'but most of this place looks like it's going to rack and ruin.'

They had no time to talk more for Jenny had opened the door of the long, low farmhouse and was beckoning them in.

It was a relief to get inside, into the warmth of a cosy farm kitchen. A single, efficient log burned in the fireplace and a pair of old corduroy chairs stood on either side of the hearth, looking as though they'd been there for years. A strange, faintly sweet smell hung in the air.

'Always windy, here,' Jenny remarked, fussing with a kettle, her back turned to the visitors as they settled on an oak bench around the scrubbed pine kitchen table. Harley trotted happily around the kitchen, sniffing into corners. Jenny put dog biscuits in a dish, and a bowl of water by the door. She tried to shoo away a couple of the cats who'd sneaked inside, shrugged at her failure and wandered back to the table. She wore an air of dreamy detachment, so unlike her usual hyper-efficiency that Imogen began to wonder if she was on medication.

'I let the children keep one of the cats as a pet,' Jenny said, and Imogen had to concentrate to understand her. Her voice was quiet, almost muffled. 'I don't let them in the house often or the place would be full of them. When the kids take one, they have to train it and clean up any mess it makes during the process.' As she tipped a packet of biscuits onto a plate, a custard cream fell on the floor and shattered. Jenny didn't seem to notice, but Harley hoovered it up in seconds. 'I don't really like cats,' Jenny said.

'You and Harley, both.' Imogen jerked her head towards Adam. 'But Adam here's a cat person.'

'Are you?' Jenny blinked and stared at Adam through narrowed eyes, as though seeing him for the first time. She perched on an old, bent-wood chair and passed out brimming mugs of instant coffee, her hands shaking slightly.

Imogen and Adam exchanged a look. Something was wrong, but Imogen couldn't quite put her finger on it.

She said, 'Edwina told me you wanted to talk to us.'

Jenny frowned. 'Did she? Was it about the cats?' Had she forgotten her conversation with Edwina?

'About Joe,' Imogen replied. 'She said he's gone missing,' but Jenny didn't appear to hear.

'There are kittens on the way,' she mumbled, tugging at the front of her cardigan. The buttons were incorrectly fastened, leaving an empty buttonhole at the bottom and a spare button at the neck.

She looked dishevelled. With a jolt, Imogen realised what was wrong. She bit back an exclamation and concentrated on Jenny, who was still talking. 'That old blue-coat cat sitting under the porch is expecting.'

Adam's eyes, behind his specs, were alight with a spark of excitement. 'Kittens? When are they due?'

'Any day now. But we have to wait six weeks before taking them from the mother. Do you want one?'

'Um. I-I'm not sure,' Adam sounded vague. 'I mean, maybe, if they need homes. Although...' his voice faded.

Imogen nudged him. 'Go on, you know you'd love a cat. Oh.' She bit her lip, remembering the reason for his hesitation. He'd told her once how he'd lost a much-loved cat during a police case and sworn not to adopt another. How could she have forgotten? She hoped he'd left that experience at the back of his mind and was ready to move on.

Jenny had turned away and Imogen seized the opportunity to whisper in Adam's ear. 'Are you thinking the same as me?'

He nodded. 'I suspect she's been drinking.'

That was the smell Imogen had noticed in the house – faint and sickly-sweet. Stale alcohol.

Jenny was back with another plate of biscuits. Digestives, this time. 'Oh, dear,' she muttered, looking at the custard creams as though wondering how they'd arrived there.

Imogen exchanged a worried glance with Adam and stood up from the table. 'Jenny,' she said. 'Are you sure you're quite well? Has the doctor prescribed tablets or something?'

Jenny's expression changed and she raised herself to her full height. She was tall and sturdy, but her hands were still trembling. 'I am perfectly well. I don't need a doctor,' she said, with immense dignity.

'I meant, with the worry of Joe—'

Jenny sniffed. 'Joe can do what he likes. He'll come back, he always does, like the bad penny.'

She gave a sudden shout of wild laughter that turned to hiccups.

Imogen and Adam weren't going to tease much information from her while she was in this state.

'I think,' Imogen said, 'we should stay here a while. Where's your little girl, by the way?' Surely, there should have been a two-year-old running around? 'Is Harriet at nursery?'

Jenny blinked and shrugged, looking around with an air of surprise at not seeing her daughter. 'No idea. Oh, wait. My mother's looking after her.'

Imogen gazed around the kitchen. Apart from a basket overflowing with toddler toys in the corner of the kitchen and a highchair folded against the wall, there was no sign of any of the Trevillian offspring.

Adam said, 'Where does Mrs Little live? Could she come over?'

Jenny blew her nose, noisily. 'The bungalow down the lane. My parents were going to retire there, but just after they moved in, Dad

died. Now, Mum keeps it all going. She says she likes to keep busy.'
She took a step forward, overbalancing a little so she had to grab at
the table to steady herself.

Imogen took her arm. 'I think you could do with a lie-down,'
she said. 'This business with Joe must be worrying. Let's get you to
bed.'

She helped Jenny through a low arch from the kitchen into the
lounge, where an old fireplace occupied almost an entire wall, logs
heaped inside the fender. On the other side of the room, a half-
open door led to a flight of steep stairs.

She steered Jenny, drowsy and unprotesting, through the door
and helped her mount the stairs that twisted in a spiral to a
bedroom on a semi-landing. She eased her into the bed, tugged off
her indoor slippers and covered her loosely with a quilt.

'There, you'll feel better after a sleep,' she murmured.

Adam was waiting when she returned to the kitchen.

'Should we call the doctor?' Imogen asked. 'My nursing skills
are non-existent, I'm afraid. I think it's alcohol to blame, but I could
be wrong. She might be on some tablets that disagree with her.'

'Maybe we should check in with the formidable Mrs Little first.
If she's helping to look after Harriet, she must have an idea of
Jenny's state of mind, and she'll tell us about any medication. The
doctor won't. And I'm more than curious about Joe's mother-in-
law.'

Imogen said, 'What are you grinning about?'

'Well, while you were upstairs, I had a brief snoop around. The
place is full of photos of their endless brood of children; mostly
school photos, which makes it hard to distinguish one from the
other, what with the school uniforms and tidy hair. There are a few
photos of them on horses, with rosettes.'

'The eldest girl was in the Pony Club,' Imogen remembered.

'But I did find this.' Adam pointed to the enormous, surprisingly modern, American-style fridge. Held in place by a magnet in the shape of a Highland cow was a stiff card, with gold edges. He read out, 'An invitation to an At Home at Haselbury House to celebrate their year of opening to the public.'

'Interesting,' Imogen said. 'I didn't get one, which is annoying and rather rude since I designed the garden. I see the event took place a few weeks ago. I suppose the Trevillians move in grander circles than we do, if they were invited to the big house. I wonder if they went.'

'And,' Adam said, 'I wonder how close Joe might be to Roger Masters, who's recently put his failing business into administration.'

6

MRS LITTLE

Adam and Imogen left Jenny, fast asleep and snoring gently, and chivvied Harley away from the cats. They'd been teasing the poor dog mercilessly with a typical feline tactic; creeping slowly within a few centimetres of the target animal before racing out of danger behind a handy sideboard.

Panting with excitement, Harley leaped into the car. 'You'll never outwit a cat,' Adam said. 'But I applaud your determination to keep trying.'

'He'll have plenty of practice if you take one of the kittens,' Imogen said.

'Actually, I was thinking of asking for two. They could keep each other amused. Steph said she had a pair of kittens when she was growing up.'

'That sounds wonderful,' Imogen said. Envy tugged at her. Her rooms at the hotel were comfortable, almost luxurious, but they had nothing like the charm of Adam's sitting room. She thought of Adam and Steph, cosily happy together in front of the fire with a pair of kittens chasing balls of paper around the room, and bit back a twinge of jealousy. Adam deserved his happiness.

The car lurched back through the exit from High Acres and turned left, down the steep hill.

Adam said, 'In The Plough, Joe mentioned that Jenny was planning to go back to work.'

'As if she doesn't do more than enough with the farm and the family. Why don't they – what's the expression? – diversify? Take in summer visitors or make cheese? That's what all the other farmers are doing.'

Adam shrugged, as much as was possible while steering the car around potholes. One was so wide, it stretched full across the road and, wincing, he steered through it. Rainwater rose in waves around the car. 'They're certainly not spending much on the upkeep of this lane,' he said. 'And if Jenny's daytime drinking's a real problem, will she be able to cope with a new job?'

'I expect it's Joe's disappearance that caught up with her, today,' Imogen suggested. 'The house is clean and tidy enough, as though she's usually able to cope.'

As the lane continued, the road turned into a neatly kept, tarmacked drive. The car swung in and stopped outside a small, modern red-brick bungalow. 'This must be the place.' The driveway was wide enough to take a tractor, never mind Adam's car, and no other vehicles were parked there, so he left the car near the front door.

A child's voice rang out as they approached the house.

'That's coming from the back garden,' Adam said and set off around the side of the house, Imogen in tow.

In the small back garden, a toddler was digging in a wooden sandpit to one side of a neat lawn, chattering happily to herself as she upended a bucket of sand and whacked it with her spade. The lawn was surrounded by angular flowerbeds, where autumn dahlias and Michaelmas daisies lined up in regimented rows in front of carefully maintained hedges. Not a single weed had dared to raise its head.

Carefully, the child levered the bucket away, exposing a neat sandcastle.

Imogen recognised Harriet, Mrs Little's granddaughter. She'd been at the Spring Fair, perched precariously on one of Dan's donkeys, a hard hat wobbling on bright blonde hair, while Grab paced carefully up and down.

Imogen caught her breath. She'd felt so close to Dan that day when he'd turned up with the donkeys. He'd kept them a secret from her, conspiring with Oswald to spring the surprise, and the donkey rides had turned out to be the main attraction at the Fair. She smiled, remembering. Then she bit her lip. Recently, Dan and she had drifted apart. She'd been busy with the hotel and he'd spent every moment painting, preparing for his exhibition, and had seemed to forget about her.

She didn't have time to think about that now. Rising from a row of dahlias, a weeding fork in her hands, was a tall, sturdy woman. Her long brown coat flapped in the wind against a pair of solid boots. 'Can I help you?' she challenged, in the kind of voice designed to see off double-glazing salesmen.

Adam stepped forward and held out a hand. 'You must be Mrs Little,' he said, warmly.

Imogen swallowed hard, fighting the urge to giggle, for *little* this lady was not. She towered several inches over Adam, and her coat was stretched tightly across her stomach.

For a long moment, the woman stared at his hand in silence, one eyebrow raised, her mouth pursed. Imogen had seen that expression before at the hotel. Harley had once brought half a dead mouse in from the garden and, tail wagging with pride, dropped it at the feet of a Royal Navy captain's wife. The woman had stared in silent fury, just such a look of disgust on her face, while her husband roared with laughter.

While Imogen collected herself, Adam said, 'I'm Adam Hennessy, a, er, friend of your daughter, and this is Imogen Bishop. We've just come from Jenny's house. She told us one of the children was here, with you.'

Mrs Little took his hand in a fierce grip and shook it vigorously. 'Have you come to take her back? Thank the Lord. Another verse of "The Wheels on the Bus" and I'll have to lock her in a cupboard.' Her voice was deep and resonant and her accent impeccably upper-class.

Was she joking? Imogen was almost, but not quite, sure she was. 'No, actually,' she said. 'We think perhaps you should go to your daughter. Mrs Trevillian's feeling a little, er, unwell.'

The woman peered more closely at Imogen. 'You're Councillor Jones's daughter, aren't you? I knew him well, of course. Before he disgraced himself, that is.'

How dare she? Imogen raised herself to her full height, reaching only to Mrs Little's chin. She controlled herself. Now wasn't the time to defend her father's reputation, but what a tactless woman this was. She took a calming breath. 'We called in to see Jenny because she'd asked for our help. However, she isn't at all well,' she repeated, with emphasis.

'Well? Well?' Mrs Little's voice rose on each word. 'Of course she's well. She's a Little.'

Imogen smothered a gasp, but Adam's police experience seemed to kick in. 'Perhaps we could all go inside and talk about this.'

The toddler was now chasing Harley enthusiastically around the garden. Mouth open, tail waving like a pennant, he was having the time of his life. 'Harley,' Imogen called, sharply. No need to give this woman another reason to sneer.

To Imogen's surprise, Mrs Little guffawed cheerfully. 'Grand fellow, that dog. I like a nice mutt. Plenty of hybrid vigour in a multiple cross-breed, you know. I've no time for all these Cruft dogs, with their Labradoodle this and Shih Tzu that. What's the fellow's name?'

Adam told her.

'Harley, bring the child in with you,' Mrs Little called.

* * *

Harley trotted obediently indoors, Adam and Imogen following in his wake.

'You have a way with dogs,' Adam said.

'Exercise, that's what dogs and children need.' Mrs Little announced, hands planted on her hips. 'Fresh air, exercise and good wholesome food. That's the way to keep things shipshape.'

The bungalow was immaculate, every table polished to within an inch of its life, the brown leather chairs and sofa set at right angles to each other. A vacuum cleaner buzzed in one of the other rooms.

'Have a seat.' Mrs Little waved vaguely towards the two-seater Chesterfield. 'I'll just tell the cleaner to stop that dreadful noise. One can't hear oneself think.'

Adam and Imogen sat obediently as they waited for her return. Adam murmured, 'I think our Mrs Little considers herself a cut above us. I bet she comes from a county family.' He pointed towards a photograph on the mantelpiece; a man in a naval uniform and his wife. 'It looks as though her father was in the Navy. And in a senior position – those are a captain's epaulettes.'

Mrs Little returned but did not offer refreshment.

Imogen said, 'I'm really rather worried about Jenny. Is she on medication? Maybe prescribed by the doctor? We know her husband's, er, away. She's asleep at home at the moment.'

'Asleep?' the woman barked, 'At this time of day? I don't know what she's thinking.'

Adam put in, 'But you know she's not well, don't you? That's why you're looking after Harriet.'

The child was sitting on the floor, tickling Harley's tummy.

Mrs Little stood still in the centre of the room, a muscle in her cheek twitching. Then, as though making up her mind, she sank into one of the chairs and gave a long sigh. She clasped her hands – big-boned, capable hands – tightly together as though fighting to regain control of herself. 'You're quite right, of course.'

Adam said, 'And it's not medication from the GP, is it?'

Silently, she shook her head.

'How long has she been drinking?' he asked, in a conversational tone.

Mrs Little's hand travelled halfway to her mouth before she returned it to her lap.

'I think,' Adam added, 'you should tell us exactly what's going on. Jenny asked for our help, through a friend. We went to visit her, hoping to help find her husband, but she wasn't in a fit state to tell us anything. It's clear she's very upset that Joe's gone missing, and perhaps that might explain her state today, but I suspect she has a problem that you've been trying to hide. Is that why Joe's left? Because of Jenny's drinking? Or is she drunk because he's left?'

Mrs Little winced. 'I suppose it will be all over the county, soon,' she said, in a low voice. 'Well, let people talk. I'm tired of trying to hide it.' She glanced towards the photograph of the Navy captain. 'What would Father have said,' she muttered to herself.

While the adults talked, Harriet was pulling leaves off a nearby pot plant.

Mrs Little rose and tapped her on the shoulder, not unkindly. 'Why don't you go into the garden and collect up all your toys.' She nodded at Imogen and murmured, 'We can watch her from here.' She sat down again, and raised her voice as the child trotted back into the garden, Harley at her heels. 'Yes, my daughter is a drunk. She married a wastrel and the strain of keeping him on the straight and narrow has driven her to drink. Now he's out of her hair at last and good riddance, that's what I say. She's far better off without him.' She took a long breath. 'And none of this would have happened if my daughter hadn't let us all down by getting herself pregnant while she was at school.'

7

HAM HILL

'Adam realised straight away that Jenny had been drinking,' Imogen told Steph and Dan the next day, flopping down on the soft grass on top of Ham Hill. The four friends had taken advantage of a perfect October day to climb up through the trees, kicking through the first fiery autumn leaves to fall from the beech, ash and horse chestnuts. Steph had collected a pocketful of smooth brown conkers.

'I don't know if Jenny drinks because Joe's such a layabout, or whether he got like that because she drinks,' Adam said.

Imogen shuddered. 'Jenny's mother told us all about it in the end. Adam was at his sympathetic best – and you know he could winkle a secret out of a slab of concrete.'

'It's rather a sad tale,' Adam said. 'I don't think it's common knowledge or I'm sure Edwina would have told me when she visited, but it turns out that Jenny's eldest child isn't Joe's at all.'

Steph stopped admiring one of the conkers. 'Wow. Didn't see that coming,' she said.

Adam went on, 'Mrs Little admitted she and her husband were furious when Jenny told them she was pregnant. The father was someone she'd met at a party to celebrate the end of A levels and they'd had a one-night stand. When she told him she was pregnant, he didn't want to know and Jenny didn't want to marry him anyway, so Maggie Little sent her off on an extended holiday to her grandparents in London and managed to keep the pregnancy a secret from most people. Joe, though, had always been keen on Jenny, and she liked him too. She wrote and told him about the baby, and he offered to marry her.'

'Really? And bring up someone else's baby? Who would have thought it of Joe?' Steph said.

'He's not such a bad lot, then,' Dan said.

'The Littles were so relieved that Joe wanted to marry her that they passed much of their farm, Glebe Farm, to him, hoping he'd make a go of it, helped by Jenny. Everything was fine for years, and all the other little Trevillians came along in due course. But recently, farming's become harder and Glebe Farm was teetering on the brink of financial disaster. By that time, Jenny's dad was showing signs of one of these lung diseases that farmers get – Mrs Little reckons it was due to chemicals in the water, and she might be right. Those were the days when farmers spread chemical fertiliser everywhere and threw poison around to control pests. If only they'd known, eh?'

'No wonder he was still quite young when he died,' Steph said.

'Exactly,' Adam said. 'He never made it to seventy. The farms are going organic, now, both Glebe Farm and High Acres. Mrs Little won't allow chemicals near the place, not after her husband's illness, but farming organically makes it more expensive and time-consuming. That's why she didn't want to buy back any of the Trevillian land. She has enough on her plate, although she's quite a formidable lady, that one. She employs a couple of men on the farm, and has a cleaner and so on in the house, so there's no lack of money there.'

'Definitely out of the top drawer, is Mrs Little.' Imogen took up the story. 'She could see Joe wasn't going to set the world alight, but she and her husband were glad enough that he married Jenny. I think she never quite recovered from what she saw as the shame of an illegitimate daughter. People still saw it as a problem, then.'

Dan said, 'That explains the big gap in ages between the Trevillians, then.'

'That's right,' Imogen said. 'Shona's twenty-three, but the next child, Hermione, is only sixteen. Then, there's a twelve-year old, Donald, Irene's nine, Jack's four and Harriet is almost three.'

'Well done for getting the names right,' Adam put in. 'I lost track of them all.'

Steph said, 'One thing I've heard about big families is that they almost bring themselves up. I wouldn't know, myself, as my daughter, Rose, is my only child. My husband and I didn't stay together long enough for any more.' She sighed and shook her head. 'But that's a story for another day. To get back to the Trevillians, I suppose Shona helps to look after the younger ones. But it must all be a strain, just the same.'

Adam agreed, 'Too much of a strain for Jenny. She trained as a teacher years back while her mother helped look after Shona, but she never got a teaching job as there was so much to do on the farm. Maggie Little told us she's poured mountains of cash into the farm over the years, but it's losing money hand over fist. That's why Jenny was going to start work. Although, with Joe away, that's all come apart. She told the school she'd changed her mind.'

'Can't see how she can teach anyway,' Imogen said, 'if she's struggling with alcoholism.'

'What a mess.' Steph shook her head. 'Who knows what sends someone over the edge. I don't know who needs more sympathy – Jenny, struggling and exhausted, or Joe, out of his depth, unable to cope and legging it.'

Dan pulled up handfuls of grass, piling them up in a tower. 'It's worst of all for the children. None of it's their fault.'

Adam added, 'And then, there's widowed Mrs Little, trying to help, praying the neighbours won't notice her family falling to pieces in front of their eyes and too afraid of what people might think to ask for help.'

'Well,' Dan said at last, 'I suppose there's really no mystery to Joe's disappearance, after all. He just couldn't stand it all and so he left. He's probably in a hotel or with a mate and he's entitled to his privacy. It was a cowardly thing to do, if you ask me, but the family's probably better off without him.'

'I don't think Jenny sees it like that,' Imogen objected. 'She needs help, which is possible, once people know what's going on. We suggested Maggie Little talk to the vicar at least. Helen's brilliant at sorting out people's tangled messes.' She scratched her head. 'I suppose there's no need for any further investigation. I mean, we know why Joe left, now, so there's no real mystery for us to investigate, although I think he should be ashamed of himself. You can't just walk away and leave your family, especially when you own a farm. The cattle don't milk themselves. Maggie Little's sure he'll be back soon enough, and she's sent her cattle man to help out in the meantime.'

'Still,' Steph said, 'I don't see why we shouldn't go on asking around. See if anyone in the village has an idea where Joe might have gone.'

'But let's leave it until next week,' Imogen begged. 'Apple Day's almost here and the hotel staff are rushed off their feet. I need to be there.' She smiled at her friends. 'And any help will be gratefully received.'

8

DONKEYS

Apple Day arrived with an autumn chill in the air, but a clear blue sky. The preparation for the great day had caused quite a stir at the hotel. There were fewer young holidaymakers in Somerset, now the children had gone back to school for the autumn term, but the older couples who'd already booked into the hotel had been delighted when Emily emailed them to tell them the hotel was hosting the festival during their stay. 'What could be nicer,' one couple had replied, 'than a proper rural festival.'

Dan and Imogen had been in the office when Emily had read out the email responses to her messages.

'They're thrilled,' Emily had said, 'we could have charged them extra.'

Her assistant, Michael, had chuckled. 'We'll double the price of cider in the beer tent.'

'No, we won't,' Emily had said severely. 'Our reputation is built on wonderful service, great food and value for money – and the gorgeous gardens, of course.'

'They're looking good, I must admit,' Imogen had remarked.

'Look at the colour in the Japanese maples. And the hawthorn's full of berries.'

'Not to mention the grapes on the vines,' Dan had agreed. 'Although, those starlings have had the best of them. You won't be making wine this year, more's the pity.'

After much heart-searching, they'd decided against offering rides with Smash and Grab at the event. 'It was wonderful at the Spring Fair,' Imogen had said, 'but Oswald begged me not to repeat it this time. The donkey hooves churned the grass up terribly, even though we kept them down by the stream, away from his manicured lawns. But at this time of year, a few hooves will turn the grass into mud and it'll stay like that all winter.'

Dan was disappointed. Smash and Grab, his old friends, had been the highlight of the Fair, and he'd been hoping to make it up to Imogen for his recent neglect.

As the day dawned, Dan woke to the plaintive sounds of his ancient alarm clock clanging five o'clock and the smart watch on his arm buzzing insistently. He padded across to the bathroom as the grandfather clock he'd inherited from his late parents began to chime.

He'd set up all the alarms he could. There was no way he was going to be late today. He wanted to prove to Imogen that he was reliable.

He didn't even need to ping the elastic band on his wrist as a reminder.

Imogen had been quiet and thoughtful, recently, and Dan felt guilty. He'd been so busy preparing for his exhibition at Camilton Gallery. He knew that when he was painting, everything else took second place, but in the past few days, most of the work done, he'd been able to help a little to prepare the hotel for Apple Day.

Imogen and Emily had worked their socks off during the past

few days under the guidance of the vicar, Helen Pickles, and Dan had promised to arrive at the hotel early, to help with any last-minute problems. He knew he wasn't great at putting his feelings for Imogen into words, but actions spoke louder, didn't they?

Now, with half an eye on the clock, he examined his face in the bathroom mirror, trying to decide whether or not to shave. Imogen liked a little stubble, she'd said, but not a full-grown beard. Where exactly did today's growth fit in with her hierarchy? He should have asked her to draw a picture of the exact amount of stubble she liked. He always preferred images to words.

Chuckling, he checked the time again. Everything was going well. He was going to be at the hotel in good time, ready to hang bunting, hammer nails, stagger under crates of cider and man the cider press, which needed plenty of muscle.

He'd do any of those things.

He would be on his very best behaviour. And maybe, afterwards...

His stomach churned and he swallowed as he pulled out the drawer beside the bed and retrieved the tiny, blue box. It was time for the ultimate gesture. He slipped the box with its precious contents into his pocket, refusing to think about his first, foolish step into matrimony that had ended so quickly.

Or about that other thing.

He'd thought he was done with marriage, but maybe he'd been wrong. Imogen was special and he wanted her beside him for the rest of his life. He was sure of that, now. He would make her happy if it was the last thing he did.

Meanwhile, it was time to feed the donkeys. He could already hear them calling. At least, he could hear Grab, always the hungrier, cheekier and louder of the two. He peered through the kitchen window that overlooked the paddock and rubbed at it with the sleeve of Imogen's favourite sweater, a dark blue, heavy oiled wool, knitted in a pattern she'd described as cable stitch. Whatever that was.

The fog on the window wasn't condensation, just early-morning autumn mist. Drops of water spangled the trees beyond the paddock so that they glistened like chandeliers, but his house remained beautifully warm.

Dan loved his home. He knew artists were supposed to freeze, preferably in a garret, but success had enabled him to build a centrally heated architect-designed single-storey house (ridiculous pride prevented him calling it a bungalow) with a bespoke studio constantly flooded with light from three sides of glass windows. The place was perfect.

It had taken almost all of his savings from his first successful exhibition, during which every painting had sold, even at the sky-high prices Henry had set, but it had been worth every penny. His breath caught as he imagined Imogen here, with him – and Harley. Would she want to live here? He shrugged. The only way to find out was to ask her.

Meanwhile, he had to keep the donkeys fed and watered. And that meant stepping out into the morning's chill, breathing in faint traces of burnt wood from last night's fire and sniffing the last whiff of smoke in the air.

He warmed a bucket of water to take the chill off, for Smash was getting older and disliked cold water. As he clanked towards the donkeys' shelter, Grab trotted towards him across the paddock, ears pricked. As soon as he saw Dan, he opened his mouth to reveal two rows of enormous, tombstone teeth, and brayed.

'Good morning,' Dan said, as he did every day. Grab nuzzled his pockets, searching for treats. 'Have a carrot,' Dan suggested, offering a couple. He looked around. 'Where's Smash?'

It wasn't like the big grey to stay inside the shelter while his friend snaffled all the treats. The animals were inseparable, always together, their faces usually close together as though they were talking. When Dan had visited the Donkey Sanctuary, almost on a whim a couple of years ago, the earnest teenager showing him around had insisted he take both donkeys or none at all. 'Donkeys pine if they live alone,' he'd said.

Dan had succumbed to the donkeys' charms and never regretted his decision. In his eyes, donkeys made perfect pets. 'Less needy than dogs, friendlier than cats,' he'd said one day, standing at the bar of The Plough with Imogen and Steph while Adam pulled pints. During the heated argument that followed, he'd almost had to run for his life.

But where was Smash?

Heart thudding, Dan set off towards the shelter at a run, water sloshing from the bucket. No need to fear the worst, he told himself, trying to be calm. But donkeys rarely showed they were ill until they were really poorly. If Smash was lying silently in the shelter, he might be truly sick. Or worse.

But he wasn't there. The shelter was empty.

He must be behind the building.

Dan left the bucket and hurried around the back, calling Smash's name. The donkeys liked to rest under the broad panoply of the old oak tree. That was really the only other place Smash could be hiding.

But he wasn't there.

He'd gone.

Stupidly, his stomach clenched as though he'd been punched, Dan turned in a circle, hoping Smash would magically reappear.

Grab was at his shoulder, nuzzling him.

'Where's your friend?' Dan asked.

Grab trotted into the shelter and out again, braying loudly, calling for Smash.

Fighting panic, for surely the animal couldn't have gone far, Dan ran to the gate. It was tight shut.

Could Smash have jumped over the fence? He'd never seen him try. Besides, if one donkey had gone, the other would have followed.

Dan retrieved the bucket, rattled it and shouted for Smash.

Silence.

He turned to Grab, his heart hammering. 'Where is he?'

* * *

Dan rang every farmer he could think of who lived near enough for Smash to reach. None had seen him on their property. 'But I'll keep an eye out,' they said. 'He can't have gone far.'

Grab criss-crossed the paddock, restless, unable to settle without his friend.

Dan jumped in the white van he'd hired for ferrying his paintings to the gallery and drove up to the village. He buttonholed the postman, stopped Mrs Cox as she loaded a couple of reluctant children into her car and knocked on Mrs Hammond's front door. Mrs Hammond came down to the studio every week, to keep it clean. She was a huge fan of the donkeys.

'He's never disappeared?' she said, horrified, and called back to her elderly brother who shared the cottage. 'Smash went missing last night. Have you seen him?'

A disembodied, tetchy voice answered, 'How would I have done that? We haven't been outside the house since *Pointless* came on at teatime yesterday.'

Mrs Hammond clicked her tongue. 'Don't mind him. He's ornery in the morning. But, don't you worry, young man. If Smash comes up here, we'll let you know. And he knows which side his bread's buttered, that one does. He'll be back safe and sound before you know it.'

She was leaning by the open door, ready for a chat. 'Won't you come in for a cup of tea? The kettle's on. You can tell me about that nice Mrs Bishop. I hear she's running the Apple Day, and we'll be along later today. Wouldn't miss it for the world.'

Dan gulped and glanced at his watch. It was nine o'clock already. He'd promised to arrive at The Streamside Hotel before now to help with the preparations.

He was going to be late again.

Well, it couldn't be helped. 'I have to find Smash,' he said out loud.

'I'll see you this afternoon, dear,' Mrs Hammond said. 'We love a harvest supper. We had one at St Michaels, over in Lower Hembrow the other day – quite an evening, that was, but it's Apple Day that counts in this part of the world. We'll be taking a bucket of apples from our garden, all ready to be pressed. And don't you go fretting about Smash. He's a wise old fellow. Maybe he just felt like a change of scene.'

* * *

Hours later, Dan had driven up and down what felt like every lane in the county, stopping to peer over hedges into any field that might attract a roaming donkey.

Finally, he admitted defeat.

Returning to the studio, he searched the paddock again, fruitlessly, as though Smash might be hiding behind a two-foot-high bush.

He'd have to go. Time was passing fast and he needed to show up at the hotel before events began at twelve. He tried to call

Imogen, to explain, but she didn't answer her phone. Too busy, he supposed.

'Sorry to leave you alone,' he told Grab. 'But he'll turn up. He'll be fine. Everyone says so.'

Reluctantly, he drove away, leaving Grab with his head hanging over the fence, gazing sadly at the rear of Dan's car.

9

APPLE DAY

Imogen, putting the finishing touches to yards of bunting on the tea tent, ground her teeth in fury.

This was the last straw.

Just for once, couldn't Dan have arrived on time? He'd promised to help and she needed him. This Apple Day had already taken all her energy, even though Helen Pickles had kept her word and sorted out the posters, the local newspaper and the apple press. 'Never again,' Imogen muttered.

'You always say that.' Adam had overheard her as he staggered past, loaded with trays of cups and saucers.

She winced. She hadn't meant to speak out loud.

'Mind you,' he went on, pausing for a moment, 'I'd say "never again" too. I'm just glad The Plough's too small for an event like this.'

'Look at your smug face,' Imogen accused, laughing despite herself. 'At least, you're here and helping.'

Adam took the trays to a white-clothed table in the tea tent and returned. 'He'll be here, soon,' he said.

Imogen sighed. 'Once the hard work's done.'

'Don't jump to conclusions.' Adam was on his way back for another load.

Imogen muttered under her breath, 'I will if I want,' not caring that she sounded like a spoilt child.

Unfortunately, Dan chose that very moment to appear, flushed, flustered and full of contrition. 'The donkeys,' he said. 'I tried to get here sooner.'

Imogen glared at him. 'It doesn't matter,' she lied, her voice crackling with fury.

'Of course it matters. I'm so, so sorry. I really meant to be here early to help.'

'You always do.'

Dan visibly flinched, but she didn't care. The past few days had been frantically busy, and she was heartily wishing she'd never agreed to host today's festivities. Dan letting her down was the last straw.

She was in no mood to listen to a load of apologies.

'Good intentions,' she muttered, 'best laid plans, bright ideas. They butter no parsnips with me.' Whatever possessed her to say such a stupid thing; the kind of cliché her grandmother used?

Imogen felt angry tears prickle her eyes as she thought of her adored hard-working, sharp-tongued, care-worn grandmother. Rage rose in her throat and overwhelmed her. 'I'm tired of it all,' she said, gesturing at the garden, the preparations and, most of all, Dan. 'I'm tired of waiting around until you bother to show up. Tired of coming a bad second to... to a pot of paint and a brush. I've had enough of expecting – hoping...' she stopped. What was it she'd been hoping for? She wouldn't even put her foolish dreams into words. 'I've had enough of you,' she ended.

There, she'd said it. She hadn't intended to; the words had just popped out.

She took a deep, shuddering breath, half wishing she could

unsay them. But she'd meant it, hadn't she? She'd truly had enough.

She stood her ground, glaring at Dan.

Dan's eyes, those beautiful, dark eyes that she'd loved for most of her life, glittered. He folded his arms across his chest.

'Not everything's about you,' he said, ice crackling in his voice. 'I try my best. Okay, I'm not perfect – not the kind of man you want. I am who I am, Imogen, and it's just not good enough for you, is it? I can never meet your standards.'

Imogen felt the force of his cold anger and gasped. 'You could if you wanted to,' she wailed. Her nails dug into her palms. A stone had found its way into her chest, so she could hardly breathe, but she couldn't, or wouldn't, take back her words. 'Maybe if you cared enough,' she whispered. 'Enough to sometimes, just sometimes, put someone else – put me – first.'

Dan's hands, clenched into fists, fell back by his side. He shrugged. The anger ebbed from his eyes. 'Okay. Maybe you're right. Maybe it's all no good.'

She hadn't expected that. She was pumped up, ready for a fight – the kind that ended with shouting and finished with tears and reconciliation. She needed Dan to show he cared; that he had real, deep feelings for her.

But that wasn't going to happen. He didn't even care enough to raise his voice.

Well, she wasn't going to back down.

She turned away. She could sense Dan, waiting, but she wouldn't give in. It was up to him, now. Did he care, or not?

She took a step away, leaving him behind.

Then, as the enormity, the finality of what was happening hit her, she stopped, scared.

Maybe she'd been hasty.

Her anger had ebbed, leaving her cold and shivering. She turned back, but she was too late.

He'd gone.

Just walked away. He really didn't care about her, did he?

Imogen couldn't see. Her eyes stung too much, and tears slid down her face, tickling her nose. She blinked, scanning the field, seeing tents, braziers full of wood, the apple press on its wooden platform, villagers passing to and fro, laughing, chattering.

But she couldn't see Dan anywhere.

She longed to hide away. Maybe she could leave, go upstairs to her rooms, curl up and cry on her own where no one could see her. She wanted to be alone with her misery and nurse the end of the relationship that, she realised now, had never been real, anyway. She'd wanted Dan, and assumed he wanted her, too. But she'd been wrong.

She wouldn't stay here a moment longer.

But before she could move, Harley was there, his tail wagging, panting with excitement. He dropped his disgusting, much-loved toy rabbit at her feet.

Reluctantly, she picked it up. He made a grab for it and they set to in a tug-of-war. Harley growled in mock-anger while Imogen pulled and twisted the toy, fighting, letting out her anger.

Deep inside her, a heavy, dull ache set in, as though she'd swallowed pebbles. It was bottomless; a pain she'd never felt before, one she believed would never go.

Some of Dan's words came back – words that hadn't registered in her consciousness at the time, while she was angry.

Something about the donkeys?

A crawling, clinging sense of shame crept over her. Had something happened to Dan's treasured donkeys? Was that why he was late? He'd looked terrible – flushed and jumpy. Had she leaped to conclusions, and spoiled their relationship for ever over a mistake?

If only he hadn't just walked away.

She dropped Harley's toy, letting the dog shake it from one side to the other, grunting, disappointed by such an easy victory. As he cast it at Imogen's feet once more, she forced her hand against her mouth, squeezing her lip against her teeth so hard it hurt, trying and failing to make it hurt more than her heart.

* * *

How long she stood, struggling to keep her emotions under control, Imogen didn't know.

'Are you all right?'

She peered, blearily, at the face in front of her.

'Steph?'

Steph's hand was heavy on her arm. 'What's the matter. You look as though you've seen a ghost. You're not ill, are you?'

Imogen shook her head. her tongue moistened her lips. 'No, it's nothing.'

'I can see it's not,' Steph said. 'Come on, let's get a cup of tea. You need one.'

Meekly, Imogen let Steph lead her inside the tent, to a tiny chair at one of the plastic tables. Soon, she was sipping hot, brown tea full of sugar. She grimaced.

'That's better,' Steph said. 'Now, you don't need to give me details. I saw you and Dan, um, talking.'

Imogen gave a soft laugh that turned into a hiccup. 'Did everyone see us?'

'I don't think so. People are busy. It's all about to kick off. Can you cope?'

'Of course.' Imogen stood. The pebbles were still there, inside her, weighing her down, but she could walk and talk. She was still here, if only half alive. She shrugged her shoulders back, suddenly bewildered. 'What should I be doing?'

Adam appeared, looked into her face and said, 'You're needed by the apple press. The younger lads are getting overexcited and I reckon their parents could do with some help.'

Children. They were the last thing Imogen wanted to deal with. But, oddly, their pushing and shoving, their childish jokes and threats to 'pee in the apple juice' cut through her mood. As usual, Adam had seen what she needed. Not pity. Not sympathy. A job.

10

CIDER

The afternoon passed somehow. The air was warm now the mist had drifted away. Everyone from the village had come to the Apple Day festivities, plus a host of others Imogen had never seen before. One of the young farmers lit a brazier as the sun began to sink and the night to draw in. Parents handed out sparklers as the light dimmed, and children clutched them in gloved hands, writing letters that hung in the air for long moments, just as Imogen had done when she was a child.

The last of the apples tumbled from baskets and sacks into the maw of the apple press, the air was filled with sharp, sticky sweetness, and bottles of apple juice passed from one hand to another.

Jugs of last year's cider stood on every table, alongside full glasses and heaped plates of pork pie and ham, as the villagers toasted the apple harvest and each other.

A tribute band of would-be Wurzels struck up 'Combine Harvester' and the air rang with the chorus.

At the edges of the grass, Oswald sat with his cronies, a group of old men and their wives, laughing with the ease of many years of marriage, of happiness, of sadness, of just keeping on going and never giving up on each other.

They drank strong, cloudy scrumpy. They'd be rolling home, merry.

Imogen's eyes filled again. She'd never be one of them; part of a happy old couple who'd been together for years. She swallowed and looked around for something to cheer her. Emily was at the barbecue, gazing adoringly at Wayne, the chef from The Plough. Rex wandered from one table to another, his face sour. Imogen wasn't the only one with relationship problems. Emily, it seemed, had transferred her attentions back from him to Wayne. Apparently, she couldn't make up her mind.

Imogen felt a spurt of envy for Rex's youth. He was upset just now, but he had his life in front of him. He'd finished university and a job somewhere exciting beckoned – he could do whatever he wanted.

'And so,' Imogen whispered to herself, 'can I. I'm not done yet.'

With new determination, she strode across the grass to Shona, the eldest of the Trevillian children, who was shepherding a couple of her siblings.

'I'm glad you came,' she said. 'You've been wonderful, looking after the young ones since your dad went. Adam told me he's still missing.'

Shona grunted. 'The little ones are easy. It's Donald and Hermione that give me bother.'

'Teenage hormones?' Hermione was sixteen. She was ostentatiously gulping cider, casting sharp glances at Shona, daring her to object.

'I'm going to have to take her home,' Shona muttered.

A pair of lads raced past, shrieking. She raised her voice, 'Donald, stop that stupid fighting or I'll beat you up myself.' Donald grinned and went on chasing his mate. Shona groaned. 'They never listen to me.'

'But you're holding the family together. You should be proud.' There was no sign of Jenny Trevillian. Imogen grasped the bull by the horns, 'Is your mum coming tonight?'

Shona's face burnt brick-red. 'She's... um, having a rest. Gran's staying with her. To look after her.'

Imogen slid down onto the empty seat next to Shona. 'I'm sorry you're having so much to deal with.'

Shona's eyes glinted in the firelight. 'It was all right when Dad was here. People think he was, like, a bit thick and that, but he's fun, most of the time. He loves the farm. He even cries when we send the pigs to the abattoir. I bet people wouldn't believe it. He pretends he's got a cold, but we all know how he feels.' She sniffed. 'I wish he'd come home.'

Imogen pulled a small pack of tissues from her waist-belt. Why did young people never carry their own tissues? Or pens? Or coins? Imogen had never been allowed out of her parents' house without a handkerchief and coins for the phone.

Shona blew her nose.

Imogen turned as an angry voice rose above the music. 'Where are you, then, woman?' it bellowed.

The band fell silent.

Imogen gulped. She knew that voice.

Shona leaped to her feet as Joe Trevillian lurched into the garden, tripped over a bump in the grass and stumbled towards her. 'Where's your mother, girl?' he slurred.

'Dad!' Shona was crying, big tears pouring down her cheeks. 'Dad, you're all right? We all thought—'

'All right? Course I'm all right. It's that mother of yours who needs locking up and I'm going to tell her so.'

He half-fell into a chair. It teetered on spindly legs. 'Where is she, then?' He turned his head from side to side, his eyes unfocused. His chin was bristly, his face greenish, his T-shirt stained and one of his trouser legs was carelessly tucked into a sock.

'Dad, she's not here.'

'Then where is she? The—'

Imogen jumped up. 'Joe, that's enough. We're glad to see you back, but if you're going to shout and swear you can get on home.'

Adam arrived and dropped a heavy hand on Joe's shoulder. 'Come on. I'll take you home. You can't drive in this state.'

'What state's that? What you talkin' about.' Joe's words were now so slurred, Imogen could hardly understand what he was saying. 'I ain't taken a drop. It's her what does the drinking. Jenny. Didn't know that, did you?' His speech became an incoherent mumble.

He tried to stand, but fell back on to the chair.

'Dad, what's wrong?' Shona grabbed his arm.

Imogen took his other side, but it was too late. Joe was sliding, falling, his eyes rolling up into their sockets.

Shona screamed. 'Help him, someone. There's something wrong,' but Joe slid slowly to the ground and lay there, quite still.

Adam knelt beside him. 'He's not breathing.'

The doctor came running, pushed Adam aside and leaned over Joe, pumping his chest. A crowd gathered, horrified, pulling out phones to call for an ambulance, the police and anyone else that occurred to them.

'There's a defibrillator,' Imogen cried. 'Emily, fetch it.'

Emily was already halfway to the hotel.

Shona, shivering, grabbed at Imogen. 'What's the matter with Dad? Is he ill?'

Between them, Adam and Imogen pulled her out of the way, sobbing, while the doctor worked.

The defibrillator arrived and the doctor waved everyone aside as he used it. 'Stand back. Clear.'

Joe jerked, fell back and jerked again as the current shot through his body, but Imogen could see it was no use.

The doctor worked on, sweat forming on his brow, until the wail of an ambulance siren sounded.

The crowd that had gathered round, horrified, were whispering, hardly daring to raise their voices.

Parents held their children close.

Shona trembled so violently Imogen could hardly hold her. Nearby, Edwina Topsham and her friend, Barbara Croft, threw their arms around Joe's weeping children.

Finally, the doctor shook his head. 'Imogen, look after Shona, will you. I'm afraid Joe's dead.'

11

TRAGEDY

In a packed Plough Inn next day, the only possible topic of conversation was Joe.

Oswald toasted him. 'It's a sad loss of a good man,' he said, raising his glass.

The young farmers tried to guess Joe's cause of death. 'Maybe he had some kind of heart condition?' Penny suggested.

'I wouldn't have thought so,' Ed objected. 'He's been heaving hay bales around all his life. Why would he suddenly drop down dead after a pint or two of cider?'

'Aha,' Terry grinned, more excited than upset by the tragedy. 'The cider. Bet that had something to do with it.'

'Nonsense,' Rex snapped. 'Why would that make a difference? Look how much Joe could put away in an evening here. More likely he had a stroke.'

'Nah,' Terry insisted. 'My money's on the cider. My gran had a stroke and you could see it in her face – all lopsided, it was.'

'Not all strokes look the same,' Ed pointed out.

Penny said, thoughtfully, 'I thought Joe looked pretty ill when he arrived. His face was sort of pale and yellow, like a baby with jaundice. My little sister had it when she was born, and they had to put her under a special lamp.'

Terry snorted. 'Joe's no baby.' He looked around at his friends and thumped the table. 'I reckon someone topped him. You mark my words. And it's not just me that thinks so. The police agree. They've set up a crime scene.'

'A *possible* crime scene,' Adam cautioned. 'They're just being careful. They won't be jumping to conclusions and nor should we.'

'You said that before, when Imogen Bishop's husband died,' Terry objected, 'but it turned out that was murder, wasn't it? See?'

Some of his mates nodded wisely, but Adam held back and carried on serving. They'd all know, soon enough, why Joe had died. Until then, the best he could do was try to prevent hotheads like Terry from flinging wild accusations in all directions.

Terry and his cronies had made several trips to the hotel that Sunday, hoping to squeeze information from the constable guarding the area, without results. Scene of crime officers in white overalls passed in and out at intervals, heaving mysterious cases of equipment, their lips firmly sealed.

Even Edwina Topsham's gifts of doughnuts had been politely refused. 'Which is odd,' she said later, 'because in crime series on TV it's all the police ever eat.'

Just as Adam began to hope the speculation in The Plough had died down, Oswald said, 'I wonder how his poor wife's taking it.'

That set the lads off again. 'She might be with the police,' Ed suggested. 'They might have arrested her.'

For what felt like the fiftieth time, Adam asserted there was no reason at all to suppose foul play. 'You can't expect the poor woman to appear in the village next day as though nothing's happened.'

Penny said, 'I saw the vicar's car heading that way this morning; I reckon Helen Pickles went to see the family after Church. You know, I feel really sorry for them all. Joe loved his kids. I went to some parties at High Acres when I was at infant school with Shona, and he used to organise all the games. He liked to crawl around the floor, pretending to be a lion, so we'd all run away.'

'Well, maybe so,' Terry said, more quietly. 'Old Joe wasn't too bad. But I bet I'm right and someone did him in. Just you wait and see.'

12

STEPH

As the young farmers ordered another round and the chatter in The Plough died down, Steph arrived, slipping through into the bar. 'I thought you could use an extra hand in here,' she murmured in Adam's ear. 'I pulled pints, years ago, when I was a barely paid hack learning journalism. If I'm going to live here, I'd better get some practice. And,' she smiled, 'I'm as curious as anyone else about Joe's death. What a dreadful thing to happen. I suppose it's too soon for any information?'

Adam's spirits soared. What have I ever done, he wondered, for a reward like Steph? She was tiny, energetic, and full of life, and he dreamed about her even when they weren't together.

What's more, they'd recently agreed they would soon be together for good, here in The Plough. He imagined her sitting at her desk in the corner of his living room, writing the novel she'd been planning for years, a pair of kittens trying to sleep on her laptop, and he had to blink twice and clear his throat.

'Glad you're here,' he said. 'You've missed most of the speculation, and folk are sympathetic, on the whole. Even the ones who argued most with Joe.' He nodded towards Terry, who'd turned his attention to the serious business of draining his pint.

'You know,' Steph said, 'it's almost worse when someone dies if you don't like them. I mean, everyone hates to lose friends and acquaintances, but you mourn them with a kind of unalloyed sadness. It's so simple and straightforward. But with a man like Joe, you feel a great heavy burden of guilt. Should I have been nicer to him, that kind of thing?'

'He was a strange man,' Adam said. 'Do you remember when he came to the planning meeting for the Spring Fair? Grumpy as could be, until he watched Harley playing in the garden.'

'Yes, he turned into a different person, then. He did love his animals.'

Adam watched Steph as she polished a glass, her face a picture of fierce concentration.

'Any idea how he died?' she asked. 'Or where he went when he left home? We never got to the bottom of that, did we?'

'It seemed just a simple domestic quarrel. Everyone thought he'd turn up again – which he did, of course. I'm trying to keep a lid on speculation in here, which isn't easy. Those lads have already jumped to a dozen conclusions.'

'The more lurid the better?' Steph suggested.

'The post-mortem will tell us why he died and until then we can't know. Meanwhile, the police took the names and contact details of everyone at the Apple Day, which will keep them busy. They haven't got around to me yet.'

'Nor me. They'll start with the family, won't they? They'll have their hands full. Maybe...' her voice faded away.

Adam frowned at her over the top of his glasses. 'Are you suggesting something?'

'Can't fool you, can I?' she said, innocently. 'But they're going to be so busy, sifting through everyone who knew Joe.' She waved her arm in a gesture that took in the whole of the busy Plough. 'Maybe they'll need a little help?'

'I doubt it. If this is a non-accidental death – and there's no reason to suppose that – the police will set up a full-blown murder investigation. They won't want us butting in.'

'Well,' Steph said, and Adam recognised the insistent note in her voice, 'I've been a journalist all my life. That makes me a professional nosy parker, and you're an ex-detective, so you're just as bad. The police didn't do so well when Imogen's husband died, or the jockey at Wincanton. It was you and Imogen who sorted those out – with a bit of help from Dan and me, if you don't mind me saying so. I think we should do what we can.' Her eyes were alight with excitement.

'I think we should keep our noses out,' Adam said, firmly.

Steph pouted, theatrically. 'I knew you'd say that. We'll see. We thought we knew why he'd left home, when you and Imogen found out about Jenny's drinking. And, by the way, I haven't quite forgiven myself for missing that little investigation.'

He clasped her fingers, keeping their joined hands below the level of the bar. There would be enough gossip about Steph moving in soon enough.

'But in the light of Joe's possible murder—'

Adam interrupted. 'We have no idea how he died and you're jumping to conclusions, like the lads.'

'Maybe we all jumped to conclusions when we decided he'd left because of Jenny's drinking.'

Adam couldn't deny it. 'That's true. We might have been wrong. In any case, I suppose we should tell the police we're already involved, if they find any funny business. Although they won't be too pleased.'

'Nonsense. DCI Andrews would be falling over himself to

involve you unofficially. He thinks you're a genius. And so, by the way, do I.'

Steph's warm kiss on his cheek ruined Adam's attempt to keep her under The Plough's radar. The young farmers hooted and cheered.

'Come and have a drink with us,' Ed called. 'You're far too gorgeous for Adam. Shove up, Terry. Make a bit of room.'

'Leave it,' Terry said.

'Pining for Penny's mate, Jane, are you?' Ed grinned. 'I hear she's working tonight. They're behind with the yoghurt on her farm.'

Terry just shrugged.

Adam whispered in Steph's ear, 'I love that they're jealous.' His heart was thudding with pride, for he couldn't recall a single time in his life when men in their twenties, with biceps the size of coconuts, had ever shown the slightest sign of envying him.

He was happy simply to bathe in the glow of the young farmers' envy, but Steph had something else on her mind. 'What should we do about Imogen and Dan?'

'Do?' Adam forced his thoughts back from the pleasant land in which they were roaming. 'Nothing, of course.'

'Nothing?' Steph's squeal fell into one of those strange pauses that happens in a room full of separate conversations and a range of inquisitive heads turned their way. She blushed and waved a hand in the air as though to say, 'nothing to see here.' As conversations started up again, she hissed, 'We can't leave them like they were yesterday. They're like a pair of – I don't know – a pair of lost lambs.'

Adam laughed. 'And you think we should be a pair of Bo Peeps, leading them home to each other.'

'They can't seem to manage it themselves,' she retorted. 'And they're so perfect for each other. After all, they've been in love since they were at school. I know, I was there.'

'As I wasn't at that exclusive private school with the rest of you, I wouldn't know,' Adam said.

'All I can see is that as soon as they get close to being in a proper relationship, it all goes wrong.'

Adam thought about that. It was true. Adam was sure they were crazy about each other. He'd never seen Imogen more devastated than she'd been yesterday, after their quarrel. Dan had left the hotel grounds and not been seen since.

Steph was still theorising. 'They sabotage themselves. I think they're scared of commitment.'

Adam scoffed. 'They're both grown-ups, you know.'

'Are they? Is anyone? I mean, I won't see forty again, but I still feel eighteen, inside.'

Adam was silent. Her words struck home. He'd behaved like a teenager when he met Steph. He'd been nervous and jealous and if she hadn't taken the initiative, maybe they'd never have got together.

'Fair enough,' he said. 'What do you suggest?'

'I have an idea.' Briefly, she outlined her plan.

He grimaced. 'Do you really think we should interfere?'

'Of course we should. Give me a moment. I need to make a phone call.'

She disappeared into Adam's private sitting room and returned shortly with a smile on her face.

'I spoke to Imogen.' She beamed with triumph. 'I said, "Let's meet up for coffee, somewhere that isn't Lower Hembrow, because Adam's refusing to do any investigating over Joe's death and I think we should go it alone."' She paused for breath and crossed two fingers on each hand. 'You hadn't actually refused, had you? Imogen thinks it's all up to the police. She sounded dreadful, as though she had a cold. She kept mumbling about how much clearing up there will be to do when the police leave, and how she's never going to let another local event anywhere near the hotel grounds. But she did agree to meet up with me at the Bishop's Palace, in Wells, tomorrow.'

Adam smiled. 'She'd always rather be outdoors.'

'And it's the perfect place to interest her in my plan, while you tackle Dan.'

Adam sighed. 'Very well. But don't blame me if Imogen bites your head off. She's very independent.'

'Don't worry. I know how to handle her.'

'Meanwhile, I'll tackle Dan.' He shook his head. 'I don't know why I let you persuade me into things.'

She squeezed his arm. 'You love it, really,'

13

BISHOP'S PALACE

Steph and Imogen met in Wells on Monday morning and walked through the cold autumn air to the Bishop's Palace. They stopped to lean on the wall beside the moat for a while, watching for the swans. Soon, a ghostly white form glided into view out of the morning mist, followed by her three smaller, less elegant offspring, baby brown down still sprinkled through their white feathers.

'Still a bit *ugly duckling*, aren't they?' Steph said.

The mother of the brood was first to close her beak around the rope that hung on the wall on the far side of the moat. With a swift, practised movement, she tugged on the rope and the bell swung, clanking cheerfully. She swam a few yards away, watching as one of her cygnets followed her example.

'Every year,' Steph said. 'Every year, she teaches the babies.'

'It's worth their while,' Imogen was determined to be cheerful. 'They're hungry.'

Sure enough, the signal worked, and the swans were fed.

Imogen said, 'Quite a day, last Saturday.'

Steph nodded, thoughtfully. 'Joe Trevillian murdered, or so it appears. Adam tells me not to jump to conclusions, but I'd bet a pound to a penny someone killed him. Who'd have expected that? There's quite a mystery, there. More to it than it seemed at first. I mean, he disappears and everyone worries about him, and then he reappears and promptly dies. If that isn't odd, I don't know what is.'

Imogen groaned. 'You're as bad as half the village. It's as though they want to find out there's been foul play. But I can tell you, from bitter experience, that it's no joke when someone's murdered. I just hope it was natural causes.'

Steph wrinkled her nose. 'You're right, of course. I wasn't trying to play it down. But there's still the mystery of where Joe went, and did he really leave home because of Jenny's drinking, or because of her mother invading his house, or because of something else? And why did he die?'

'I can't help wishing,' Imogen said, 'and I know it's selfish, but I really hate that it happened at the hotel. We've had more than enough disasters, there. In fact, I've been wondering, lately, whether I should stay on there at all. I feel like a lightning rod, attracting drama.'

'None of it's been your fault,' Steph protested.

'Still, Emily certainly doesn't need me – she's perfectly capable of running the hotel and the staff without my input, and her deputy Michael's starting to calm down and behave. He's even agreed to stay in the hotel with Harley on Bonfire Night in a couple of weeks, so he's not spooked by the fireworks. I've been wondering whether I should find somewhere else to live. A real place of my own.'

'Seriously? You won't leave Lower Hembrow, will you?'

Imogen shrugged. 'I'm starting to think there's bad luck attached to the place. Or to me. What with Greg and my father—'

'Neither of whom died because of you, or the hotel,' Steph was quick to point out. 'Come on, you've made a great success of the place. It's thriving. You and Adam have put Lower Hembrow on the foodie map; there's your swanky chef and the fabulous gardens you've created, and The Plough's the most popular country pub in the county. Lower Hembrow is benefiting from all the work you and Adam have put in over the past two years. The locals won't let you leave. They'll riot, first.'

Imogen stared at her, for a long moment, before bursting into giggles. 'Now, that's a sight I'd like to see. Maybe Edwina will glue herself to the road outside the village shop.'

'And the boys from the village can throw eggs, and Harley will chase you down the lane, stopping you from leaving. You can't take him with you, you know – he's part of the hotel, now.'

Imogen said, 'Okay, you've convinced me. I was just feeling sorry for myself. You know... About Dan. We've sort of broken up. Although there wasn't really much to break. I'm beginning to think it was all in my head. Dan doesn't need a real relationship.'

Steph nodded, acknowledging the problem. 'Or so he thinks, perhaps. But I think you're a perfect pair, and you never know what may happen. But instead of doing anything as drastic as moving, perhaps you need a new project to keep you busy.'

Imogen laughed.

Steph said, 'I mean, even busier. There won't be so much to do in the garden at this time of year.'

'Apart from planting hundreds of bulbs?'

'That's Oswald's job, and his team of village lads.'

They walked through the gateway into the Bishop's Garden.

Steph said, 'What do you think of this place, from a professional point of view?'

'I think it's lovely. Peaceful. With plenty of water. I come here for ideas, sometimes.'

'Talking of ideas,' Steph continued, 'I had one the other day.'

'Not about solving Joe's mysterious death?'

'I'll get on to that. No, this one's to do with the hotel. You see, when I move into The Plough—'

Imogen interrupted. 'So, you're really going to do it? That's wonderful news. Congratulations. No wonder Adam looks like the cat with the cream.'

'I know. And I'm going to love it there, on the whole. With a few reservations.'

'Because...'

'Well, the living quarters are tiny. They're cosy, of course, and big enough for Adam and me to live in, but I have to work. I'm nowhere near rich enough to retire, so I've made a start on my book, at last.'

'Have you? Good for you. What are you writing? True crime?'

'Not quite. I don't want to upset the people involved – I think I've had enough of that as a journalist. I don't want to rake up people's bad memories. I'm going for mystery fiction. I'm having the most amazing fun thinking up gruesome murders and Adam can help with police procedure and so on. But the trouble is, I have hundreds of books, so I need loads of shelf space. I could fill all Adam's walls with shelves, and it's not fair to push his painting stuff aside. He loves his hobby. In any case, I need total peace and quiet when I'm writing. I can't bear music, or voices on the radio, and I certainly can't write when the bar's full of customers. I end up listening to their conversations, which is great for ideas but doesn't get the words on the paper.'

'Does Adam know you feel like this?'

'He does. We talked it over and he can see my point. Then, we had a brilliant idea which would be wonderful if you agree.'

'Me? What do I have to do with it?'

Steph's cheeks were a little pink. 'Well,' she muttered, sounding suddenly less sure of herself. 'You have some outbuildings behind the hotel.'

'You mean, the potting shed?'

'Not just that. There's a sort of folly thing near the boundary with the village hall. I was thinking, what if I could rent a bit of it, get it fixed up and use it to write in? I could have peace, quiet and a space big enough for all my mess. And it's a big place, so you could make it into a craft centre and charge rent to struggling creatives like me.'

Imogen was frowning, deep in thought. 'That folly isn't being used just now, and it's very big. It used to be stables, once, rather than just a folly.'

'Exactly. You see, you could open it up, have a small studio for me – don't overcharge me, I'm a starving writer – but you could have a couple of other studios there as well. For spinning, or weaving, or turning wood – whatever.'

Imogen grinned. 'To tell you the truth, I've been wondering about that building. I can't let it crumble away. For one thing, it could soon be a safety hazard. Emily and I have talked about it and she mentioned something similar, but I was so busy designing the gardens that I didn't have time to think it through. It would bring more income into the hotel and it shouldn't annoy any of the village.'

She shot a glance at Steph. Her friend was beaming, a triumphant grin spreading over her face. That was suspicious. Was the idea cooked up just because she was looking for a place to write or was there some other motive behind it?

Oh well, she'd find out soon enough, and the more Imogen thought about the idea, the more excited she became. A decent-sized project was just what she needed to distract her from the mess she had got herself into with Dan. 'Why don't we adjourn to the restaurant,' she said, 'have a big lunch, and talk it over.'

* * *

Imogen took Harley out to the hotel garden, later, in search of Oswald. She found him digging up a row of pumpkins.

'You didn't enter these in the "Best Pumpkin" competition,' Imogen said.

He laughed. 'Not these baby-sized creatures. Did you see the winner? One hundred and forty stone? Not the UK record, but it needed a big wheelbarrow to get it here.'

'So, what will you do with these?' Imogen was curious.

'They're all going out to folks in the village who paid for them at Apple Day. They'll be carving faces for Hallowe'en.'

'Great idea – any left over for the hotel foyer?' Imogen asked.

'Aye, Emily already reminded me to spare one or two for that Michael to carve.'

Imogen remembered why she'd sought out the gardener this afternoon, and as he threw tennis balls for the dog to chase, she outlined Steph's suggestion for the old folly. 'Do you think it could work?'

Oswald leaned on his spade, grunting. 'Not really about gardening, is it?' he said. 'Not my province.'

'Well, it is. At least, regarding the design of the area. You see, the folly's very picturesque at the moment. The trees over there,' Imogen pointed to a copse of oaks, 'they frame the outbuilding beautifully. But we need to do something with it before it falls down. There's plaster coming off the walls and the brickwork needs repointing.'

'Ah,' Oswald grunted. 'Suppose you're right, then, Mrs Bishop. But you won't want to spoil the look of it. Maybe you need to ask one of they architect fellas. They'll maybe design some workshops, keeping the front – what do they call it, now, the front...' he screwed up his face in thought.

'Elevation?' Imogen suggested.

'That's it. The front elevation. Keep it looking good. Mind you, they'll cost an arm and a leg. These overeducated professional chaps always do, if you ask me.'

'You're right. But wouldn't it be great to have thriving craft work-shops on the land? Maybe a pottery? There are a couple of potters around the county. I bet Dan will know one or two—' She broke off. She wasn't seeing Dan any more, was she? For a short while she'd almost forgotten their quarrel, caught up in the excitement of new developments for the hotel. The dull ache in her stomach returned, along with a headache.

Oswald didn't seem to have noticed anything strange. He was nodding, already half-turned, keen to get on with planting alliums and bluebells under the trees. 'Aye, there's plenty of folk would like to rent a place to work. Good luck to you, miss. Your father would be pleased to see you making such a success of the place. And now, if you'll excuse me, there's bulbs to plant under the trees and those lads from the village will be sitting around doing nothing if I leave them alone for too long.'

If Oswald approved, the craft venue sounded like a good propo-sition. But she wouldn't jump into anything without a properly costed plan. She needed to talk to Emily.

If nothing else, this idea was definitely going to stop her pining after Dan. Of one thing she was very sure. She wouldn't be approaching him for advice. She'd lived most of her adult life without him and she really didn't need him to be part of the rest of it.

Saying these words over and over in her head, she took Harley back indoors to search for Emily.

14

STUDIO

While Steph was meeting with Imogen at the Bisho's Palace to work on her craft studio plan, Adam set out for the village of Ford to broach the other part of their idea to Dan. That wasn't his only motive for the trip, of course. He'd overheard something on Saturday while Dan and Imogen were quarrelling; something about Dan's donkeys, that aroused his curiosity. Was there a clue there to the problems between Imogen and Dan? Steph was determined to do something to bring Dan and Imogen together, but Adam wasn't convinced. Was it wise to interfere? Probably not.

Adam shrugged as he drove between hedges turning to gold in the low, slanting sunlight. It would do no harm to talk to Dan, and gauge his feelings.

Near to Dan's studio, the lanes narrowed, the trees standing tall and stern, as though reluctant to admit visitors.

Dan, though, threw the door open in seconds, as though he'd been waiting on the other side.

'Oh, it's you,' he said.

'Sorry.' Adam had never hit it off especially well with Dan. When they'd met, they'd each been wary of the other. Adam suspected Dan had been jealous of his relationship with Imogen – at least, until he'd grown close to Steph. They'd called a truce, though, some months ago, so why was Dan unwelcoming?

'Expecting someone more interesting?' Adam said.

'What? Oh, no.' Dan's eyes looked beyond his visitor. 'I thought you were the vet.'

'Ah. Something wrong with Grab over there? He seems a bit fed up. And where's Smash?'

'Come inside and I'll tell you. It's freezing out here.'

Adam was glad to find the stove alight in the studio where Dan painted. Canvases leaned against the walls. An oil painting stood on an easel, drying.

'The last of the country house paintings,' Dan commented.

'But that's not why you're expecting the vet – unless he's offering you a commission?'

Dan shook his head. 'Sadly, that's not it. And there's nothing wrong with Grab – well, there is, but there's a reason...'

Adam raised an eyebrow. The man was talking nonsense. 'Maybe you should start at the beginning?' he suggested.

Dan took a deep breath. 'Saturday – in the morning, before the day turned into a nightmare – I went out to feed the donkeys, and I couldn't find Smash. At first, I thought he was in the shelter, because the nights are getting colder. It's warm in there, you see.'

Adam nodded.

'But he wasn't there – he'd disappeared. I looked around, up and down the lane, bothered a few farmers I know, but there was no sign of him. I spent most of the morning searching. He's not a young fellow and he's a rescue donkey, so he's a bit fragile. Oh, he's fine for kids to ride, so long as they're not too heavy, but he needs a careful diet to stay fit. Some supplements along with the straw.'

'Oats?' Adam asked.

Dan winced. 'Definitely not. They're too rich for donkeys.'

'Really? I'd no idea they were such delicate creatures.'

'Exactly. They need plenty of TLC and the two of them have to be together. Believe it or not, they pine if one goes missing.'

Funny, Adam thought, the effect your animals have on you. Unconditional love, he supposed. He thought briefly of his old, much-loved cat and his grief at the animal's death. But then, wasn't grief the price you pay for love?

Dan continued talking. 'Then, this morning, Grab woke me at the crack of dawn. That animal bellows loud enough to wake the devil, when he chooses. I shouted at him from the window, but he ignored me and kept on braying at the top of his voice, so I went outside to see what was going on, and there was Smash standing on the other side of the gate, waiting to be let in. He looked exhausted, hardly able to stand, but as pleased as Punch to be home. That's why the vet's on his way. Something weird must have happened to Smash. Someone took him, rode him or worked him, I've no idea why, and then brought him back.'

Adam tried to make sense of that. 'So, he's arrived home as though nothing happened?'

'That's right. The gate was fastened all the time, so he didn't get out by himself. Someone took him out and brought him back. But what did they want him for?'

'I'm on shaky ground, here,' Adam admitted. 'All I know about horses I learned over that racecourse business, and I don't know donkeys. But at least Smash is back safe and sound.' He thought for a moment. 'Maybe you left the gate unlocked on Friday night, and he walked off and then couldn't get back in?'

Dan shook his head. 'Leaving his mate Grab all alone? No chance. They're inseparable.'

Adam pointed at a painting on the wall. 'Is that a portrait of Smash? He's the grey, isn't he?' The donkey seemed to be laughing at him, full face, his mouth wide open.

Dan chuckled. 'That's how he looks in the mornings. Not today, though. He's like a little old man, all shaky legs and a mournful expression.' He focused on Adam for the first time and his brows drew together. 'But you're not here about my donkeys. Sorry, I've been running on. Have you come about Joe Trevillian? Has there been a development? Do we know the cause of death, yet?'

'Not yet,' Adam said. 'I came here about something else. You see, there's a lad in the village I've got to know. Young Alfie Croft. Have you seen him?'

Dan's eyes narrowed as he thought. 'Isn't he the lad who named, er, the hotel dog, Harley?'

It seemed Dan didn't want to say Imogen's name. So, maybe Steph was right and those two really did need help if they were going to get back together. Adam suppressed a chuckle at the thought. He really wasn't cut out to be a marriage counsellor.

Instead, he said, 'He's quite a character, is Alfie. He's the younger brother of my barman, Rex.'

Dan nodded. 'Got him, thin little fellow, young Alfie.'

'That's right. Well, it turns out he's a bit of an artist. Likes to draw and paint. He's been in to my place, had a go with a picture of The Plough. And he put my nose right out of joint, to be honest. You remember I painted the place, once.'

'You didn't make a bad job of it, as I recall.'

Adam, taken aback, grinned. 'Good of you to say so, but young Alfie's drawings made me blush. He's got real talent, but they don't teach much art at school, these days – it's all STEM subjects, whatever they are, and I was wondering—'

'Science, tech, engineering, maths.' Dan explained. 'Useful, in fact, in art. Perspective, and so on.' He looked directly at Adam, summing him up. 'And you were wondering – what?'

Adam shifted on the spot as a spark of amusement lit Dan's eyes. 'Well,' Adam swallowed but ploughed on, 'if you remember, you gave me some tips and I wondered if you'd like to look at young Alfie's work and see if you could do the same for him. Maybe talk about painting? Give him a spot of encouragement?'

Dan took his time to answer. He touched a finger to a sketch that lay on the table, looked at the canvases on the walls, his eyes resting on the painting of Smash.

Finally, he spoke quietly, almost to himself. 'I don't teach much. It seems presumptuous, like I'm an expert, which I'm not. I just got lucky by painting the kind of pictures people like.' He gave a tiny nod, as though making up his mind. 'But I won't be doing Alfie any harm, will I?' He drew a deep breath. 'I'd be pleased to help if his mother's okay with it. But can he get out here? It's a bit out of the way, too far for a bike ride and he's not old enough to drive. Could we use The Plough? A back room, maybe?'

Adam had a sense that Dan had made a big decision; far more important than agreeing to help a teenager. He wondered what was going on behind those dark eyes and that floppy fringe. Adam had a theory about men who let their fringes fall over their faces. Shyness, sometimes, or feeling uncomfortable with other people. Adam let his eyes roam around the studio. It was so personal; every inch devoted to Dan's creativity. But only through the paintings. There were no family photos anywhere. Just Smash and Grab on the walls. The vast majority of the pictures, of course, were already at the gallery, ready for the exhibition, but still, no family. It seemed that Dan went out of his way to guard his privacy.

Dan was waiting for an answer.

'The Crofts don't have a car, so it would have to be in the village.' Adam smiled. Steph was going to be pleased with him.

The donkeys interrupted with a burst of loud and lugubrious noise.

Dan's chin jerked up and he stepped over to the window. 'I can hear a car,' he said. 'And so can the donkeys.'

'Your vet, I imagine?'

He was right.

'Morning, morning,' the vet, Derek Jenkins, said as he burst into the studio, bringing a blast of cold air and bonhomie.

He shook Dan's hand enthusiastically, pushed aside the drawing on the table and dropped his black bag in its place. 'Fine autumn day – my favourite season. Mists and mellow whatnots – perfect. Mind you, winter's even better. Christmas, you know, the kids can't wait. Already started on the carols at school. Soon be glitter on the carpet and Sellotape stuck to the chairs. Now,' he grinned from Adam to Dan, 'what can I do for your donkeys? And how's that dog of yours, Adam – Harley, isn't it?'

Dan offered tea as Adam reported on Harley's rude health.

'Splendid, splendid,' the vet said. 'No tea yet, best have a look at the prodigal son, shall we?'

'I'll get going.' Adam rose.

Dan said, 'Stay, if you've time. We'll talk painting.'

Surprised, Adam hesitated. Steph would be out for most of the day, describing her bright idea to Imogen. Rex would be behind the bar and Wayne was cooking lunch today. A free day stretched ahead, and there was nothing Adam would like more than talking painting with a professional. 'Tell you what,' he said, 'I'll put the kettle on while you see to the donkeys.'

* * *

The vet gave the donkey a reasonably clean bill of health, given his age and recent adventure. 'Nothing your care won't cure,' he grinned. 'But it's best to check your gate, since he probably escaped that way.'

'Maybe he jumped?' Adam suggested, over tea and biscuits, but the vet shook his head.

'He'd never make it. In any case, he wouldn't leave Grab alone.'

'So, someone took him?'

'Or, someone came in, left the gate open and the donkey wandered out. You might have closed the gate automatically, Dan, without thinking about it, so he couldn't get back in.'

Adam shook his head. 'No. We all know you're absent-minded, but that's too far-fetched.'

'Well,' Derek Jenkins said. 'At least he's back safe and sound. Just keep a padlock on the gate in future.' He thought a moment. 'Funny though, Joe Trevillian going missing and turning up again, just like Smash. At least your donkey seems to have a strong heart and lungs.'

'You think Joe died of a heart attack?' Adam asked.

The vet shrugged. 'I know no more than anyone else who was there. But that's the most likely thing. Although his face was a bit yellow-looking.'

'From the drink, do you think? Or something else?'

'No idea. I like to stick to animals.'

Dan put in, 'Yellowish skin – isn't that jaundice?'

Adam said, 'Let's wait and see what the post-mortem suggests. Joe was in good health, as far as anyone knew.'

'Quite right,' the vet agreed. 'One hint of possible foul play and Lower Hembrow will be pointing the finger in all directions. Best to leave it to the authorities.' He swallowed his tea and left for a string of other visits, while Adam and Dan talked painting.

Later, when Adam left, Dan made his way across the paddock to check on Grab. Both donkeys were there, now, nuzzling each other and chuntering happily. Dan's head ached from attempts to solve the mystery of Smash's disappearance. He knew he'd kept the gate shut. Members of the public occasionally found their way down the lane to the studio and tried to feed Polos and other inappropriate rubbish to the animals, but even if they ventured into the paddock and left the gate ajar when they departed, the donkeys had never before tried to wander. And one would never, Dan was quite certain, go off without the other.

Which left him wondering. Someone, he was sure, had taken Smash. But who, and why?

He stood back, eyes roaming around the shelter. To one side was a feeder, which Dan refilled every day with fresh straw, moving the previous day's remains to the floor as bedding. The vet had taken some straw away for testing. He'd also suggested an extra bout of cleaning and disinfecting the shelter, just in case Smash was bringing in viruses from wherever he'd been. 'Can't be too careful,' he'd said.

Dan fetched a barrow and shovel from the lean-to beside the stable and shooed Smash and Grab out into the paddock. The grass was hardly growing at this time of the year, but there was still enough for them to graze happily, and the sun was shining. He'd give the shelter a thorough clean. A spot of strenuous exercise was exactly what Dan needed.

Soon, he had stripped off his sweater to work in his T-shirt. He turned, to hang it on a hook on the wall of the shelter.

'What's that?' he muttered. A scrap of paper was taped to the wall. He hadn't noticed it before. One of the donkeys had chewed its corner.

He pulled it off the wall, and flattened it out.

The words he read chilled him to the bone. 'SEE HOW IT F...' it read, in printed capitals. The rest of it had been chewed away.

Dan stood, motionless, for a long time, his brain racing. Someone had taken Smash. Kept him for a couple of days and then returned him. At least they hadn't hurt him. But they'd left a note. Was it some sort of warning?

Dan bit his lip. Surely not...

But the donkeys were vulnerable. His house was fitted with

alarms, ever since his cleaning lady, Mrs Hammond, had been attacked during a burglary, but the attached cameras focused on the house. They didn't include the paddock. He could get that changed, but short of bringing the donkeys inside the studio, he had no idea how else to protect them.

Should he call the police?

He snorted aloud at the idea. Expect the overworked rural police to spend time on a vague threat?

He finished mucking out the shelter, refilled the feeder, took the old straw to the heap at the side of the house and called the firm who'd installed the cameras. He could protect his own.

15

CAUSE OF DEATH

Huddled in their seats in The Plough that evening, the young farmers were still speculating about Joe. Terry, biceps threatening to burst out of his rolled-up shirtsleeves, kept returning to the subject, finding ever-wilder reasons for claiming Joe had been killed deliberately. 'What do you reckon, Rex? Who dunnit? Start a sweepstake, shall we?'

'Sorry, mate,' Rex said, glancing behind him towards the cellar. 'It's against the law in here. No licence.'

'Only if the law knows about it—' Terry broke off as Adam appeared from the cellar. He cursed. 'Forgot we have our own cop spies around here.'

Adam smiled sweetly. 'You don't have to drink here. In fact—'

'Nah, only kidding. Jeez. Just came in for a quiet pint.'

'Keep it quiet, then,' Adam said. 'And let's have no more gossip about poor Joe. No one's suggested he was killed.'

As Terry rolled his eyes, Adam grinned at Rex.

'Sweepstakes aren't actually illegal in a pub, as you know, but they're not a great idea,' he said, quietly. 'Especially while everyone's on edge. Who won your bet with Wayne?'

Rex grunted. 'Huh. Wayne, of course. Always a winner, that one. Anyway, there's enough trouble around here at the moment. Joe's death's shaken everyone up. My mum was in church and Shona came in with the two youngest and they were in a right state. It's not fair on Shona. She told me all about her mum drinking and all. She's taking time off from the solicitors in Camilton where she works to look after the family.' He sounded furious on Shona's behalf.

Adam said, 'They'll give her compassionate leave.'

Rex burst out, 'Well, she should have someone looking after her, not have to be mum and dad for the rest of the family.'

'Funny what goes on in families,' Adam said. 'And, talking of families,' he changed the subject, 'how's your brother, Alfie, doing?'

'He's great. Still planning on getting a motorbike as soon as he can.' Alfie had named Harley after his motorbike passion, when the stray dog first arrived in the village. 'Mum's trying to stop him, but he thinks he'll look cool and get all the girls. He saves up everything he earns in the shop at weekends and holidays for his bike, and he wants to be an artist, like Dan Freeman. He wants to go to art college and all. Though, how he's going to do that on one art class at school, I dunno.'

Adam's phone rang, interrupting their conversation. Seeing the caller was James, a police forensic pathologist he'd known for years, Adam left the bar to take the call. 'James. How's the house-hunting going?'

'Don't ask, mate. The wife's got a list of must-haves as long as your arm, and the girls are complaining about leaving their friends and moving out of Birmingham. I thought they'd be thrilled to get out into the countryside.'

'Teenagers? Thrilled?' Adam scoffed. 'When does that ever happen?'

'Exactly. Anyway, I have news for you. This neighbour of yours,

Joe Trevillian? His death was on the news. They sent some poor journalist to report, stood in a field where nothing at all had happened, but where the camera could just about see a police car if the operator leaned sideways.' He chuckled. 'I rang around a few contacts today, told them I was coming to live near Lower Hembrow itself, and got them to gossip about the locals.'

'And?'

'Well, there's talk of poison.'

Adam groaned. 'Alcohol poisoning?'

'No, afraid not. They found some other substance, but it hasn't been fully analysed yet. I thought you'd want to know I'm on the case. Haven't I met Joe in The Plough? A farmer, wasn't he? Big lad, swallowed his pint without it touching the sides?'

'Not any more, I'm afraid. He's leaving a family of six kids,' Adam murmured, his brain in overdrive, revisiting Joe's dramatic reappearance at the Apple Day in the light of a possible poisoning. Where had the man been? 'This is going to set the cat among the pigeons.'

James was still talking. 'So, there's my favour for you.'

'And there'll be a couple of drinks behind the bar for you next time you visit The Plough.'

* * *

The Plough was quiet that evening, with just a few of the young farmers in their corner.

A good time to pump them for information, Adam decided.

'Have a beer on the house?' he offered, improvising. 'You've just made it to the top of my league table for regular visits.'

'Right? Cool.'

Adam grinned. These lads really weren't cool at all – whatever cool was, these days. They were some of the hardest workers he'd ever met. Their language was foul and they squabbled incessantly, but their hearts seemed to be in the right place. And tonight Penny and Jane, a couple of young women fresh from agricultural college, were with them, so the swearing was subdued.

The women had no difficulty keeping up with the men when it came to beer and cider, though.

Adam fetched half a dozen pints. 'Mind if I join you?' he asked.

'More the merrier,' said Ed, the smallest, wiriest in the group. 'Get all the best intel here.'

Adam shot him a look. The lad grinned, his eyes bright. There were no flies on him.

'Right, then, cards on the table,' Adam said. 'What's the talk about Joe on the farms?'

Ed chuckled. 'A potted history of the Trevillian family coming up.'

Before he could say anything more, Terry interrupted, 'Bet you didn't know Shona isn't Joe's daughter.'

Adam kept his face blank, letting them talk freely.

'It's true,' Penny said. 'My sister was at school with Shona. She said her real father was a teacher. He taught Jenny – she was Jenny Little, then, of course, not Trevillian – and they had a fling, but Mr Little found out and threatened to feed the teacher into his combine harvester if he didn't get out of the county.'

Adam matched the information with Maggie Little's story. Shona's version of the facts, more exciting that her grandmother's, rang true.

Penny went on, 'So they got married and lived happily ever after. Not. Jenny had another five kids as well as doing most of the farming, since Joe was such a loser. No wonder she turned to drink. I'd have kicked Joe out years ago.'

Terry leered. 'Not if what I've heard about the size of Joe's—'

Penny's glare stopped him in his tracks. 'Of his family, I was going to say.'

'Yeah, right,' said Ed.

'Anyway,' Terry continued, 'the other Trevillians are all Joe's. Or so they say.'

Penny leaned forward a little, so her voice didn't carry. 'You see Maria, over there?'

Adam nodded. The local beauty was holding court at a distant table, surrounded by three men from the local orchestra; the handsome first violin, a weedy man who played the bassoon, and a huge, ham-fisted giant who played the flute with the delicacy of an angel.

Penny whispered, 'Maria and Joe had a fling in the summer.'

Terry sniggered. 'Yeah. All over each other at the Taunton Show, they were.'

Adam rose to get another round for the young farmers. He murmured his findings to Steph, who was holding the fort with Rex at the bar. 'It seems there were more problems than we knew at High Acres, but I don't see any motive to kill Joe. After all, he came to the rescue of the Littles' reputations.'

'I wonder who Joe might have upset – another farmer, perhaps. And where did he go when he left The Plough on the previous Sunday? We never found that out,' she said.

'You're right. We need to know where he went.'

'So, we're on the case, are we?' Steph grinned. 'Have you spoken to your DCI mate?'

'Well,' Adam hesitated, 'I don't want to interfere. DCI Andrews will have everything under control, I'm sure. But I'll have a quick chat with him on the phone. He's been grateful for our help, before. I'll see what he thinks.' Adam sighed. 'Joe was one of my regulars. We'll all miss him in The Plough, the grumpy old so-and-so. I'm going to make sure the police get to the bottom of this case.'

16

PROJECT

While Adam thought through possible reasons for Joe's poisoning, Imogen was busy with her plans for the renovation of the hotel's old folly.

Emily had, with her customary efficiency, arranged for a series of consultants to inspect the building on Tuesday, so they could put in bids to turn it into a series of workshops. Imogen ate sandwiches in the office with Emily before they arrived, to work through the information she'd put together on the three firms.

The first applicant, a supercilious young man with skin tight trousers and leather shoes without socks, swept up to the front door in a red Porsche, narrowed his eyes in disgust when Harley dropped a tennis ball at his feet and stepped over it with exaggerated care, taking no notice of Harley's wistful eyes. He whisked around the folly in half an hour, muttering constantly into his iPhone, refused Emily's offer of tea and biscuits – 'Can't possibly stop, three more projects to visit today,' – promised a quote for the work within a week, said, 'My advice is to knock that dump down and start again. Get rid of those old trees while you're at it,' and disappeared.

'Over my dead body will he get the contract,' Emily muttered.

'He doesn't care about the beautiful stone of the folly or your lovely hawthorns. We'd end up with brick boxes. And I bet he'd charge the earth.'

The second candidate arrived in a Land Rover. 'That's more like it,' Imogen murmured.

He coughed into a large white handkerchief. 'Bit of a cold,' he muttered. 'Still, you have to keep going, don't you? Mustn't grumble.'

Emily rolled her eyes.

He ate three biscuits and drank a cup of coffee at a snail's pace before they could persuade him out into the grounds. Finally, he tramped outside in a worn, muddy pair of wellies, pulled a scarf around his neck, rubbed his gloved hands together and muttered unhappily about the weather, coughing as he walked.

'Now, what were you planning?' he asked, as the three of them stood outside the folly.

Imogen explained. 'Three – or four, if possible – workshops for local craftspeople.'

The man sucked his teeth. 'Going to cost you, I'm afraid. Look at this wood around the door.' He kicked at the frame and a chunk of wood fell off. 'And it's going to take a year or so.' He sneezed.

'Are you sure you should be at work?' Imogen asked.

'Small firm. Can't afford to be off sick.'

Emily's shoulders slumped and she raised her eyes to the heavens. Imogen agreed inwardly. They weren't about to trust this man with their precious project.

'This is going really badly,' Emily said, later, as the walking virus-incubator snuffled his way back to his car. 'Let's hope number three's more likely. Brian Arbogast's the name and he seems to be part of a London-based firm. I'm not sure if that's a good thing, though. Is it more risky, do you think, being based so far away? Although I believe they have a branch in Devon.'

'Let's give him a chance.'

They didn't see the third candidate's car, for he parked it unobtrusively at the back of the car park and walked into the foyer of the hotel, carrying a leather case and smiling warmly at the receptionist, who blushed and flicked at her hair.

Emily, watching from the office with Imogen, gasped, 'It's a George Clooney lookalike!' pulled down the hem of her skirt and straightened her jacket before leaving the office to greet him.

He wasn't, Imogen thought, really in Clooney territory. He was younger, for one thing, and his smile was lopsided. His hair was mostly grey and less expensively cut, so that a few strands refused to lie down on the top of his head. If it weren't for a little wax, his fringe would have fallen over his forehead. Like Dan's. Imogen pushed the comparison to the back of her mind. This was the best-looking man she'd seen for months. Not only did she like his face, but he also towered at least three inches above Imogen. She liked tall men. She could stand up straight when she was with them. What's more, this one wore sensible, stout walking shoes, perfect for an autumn garden.

'I can't wait to see your grounds,' he said. 'I've heard a lot about them. In fact, I've seen your other garden, over at Haselbury House. The owner sings your praises, you know.'

'Have you done some work there, too?' Imogen asked.

'We were going to. Unfortunately, the contract fell through recently.' He didn't mention his lost client's bankruptcy. Discretion was another point in his favour. 'So,' he went on, 'let's see if we can develop something in keeping with your garden, shall we?'

* * *

The contractor admired the honey-colour of the folly's Hamstone. 'We must keep the facade,' he said. 'That will save demolition costs, as well, although we'll need to make it safe. And three units will work better than four; much more spacious. You could always add another at a later date, but you don't want to build anything that you can't rent out. Potters and spinners need plenty of space to work.'

Imogen breathed easily as they strolled back to the hotel. This man had managed to restore her faith in the whole project. The first two candidates had thrown her off balance, and she'd begun to think the whole idea might be foolish. This man, Brian Arbogast, seemed to understand exactly what she wanted.

'And, if that offer of coffee's still standing,' he said, 'we can talk more about your ideas. If you have time, that is?'

Emily looked at her watch. 'Sorry, I have to check that afternoon tea's all organised.' With a regretful smile, she was gone, leaving Imogen alone with the consultant.

They spent a long time sketching out ideas on paper. That was the way Imogen approached her own design work and her spirits rose even higher.

Finally, they'd agreed on a series of possible adaptations to the folly, ensuring they'd keep the character of the building.

'With any luck, we can use the builders that were let down over Haselbury House. I'll talk to my firm about that. They'll be looking for a good project to take its place. We might even get a special deal from them,' he said. 'But you need to think it all over and be quite sure about what you want. I'll send in my bid in the next few days, once I've agreed it with the partners.'

Imogen stole a glance at the business card Brian had given her. Newbury, Smith and Harnsworth. She realised she knew a little about the company. She'd seen one of their designs on a TV programme. It was a London-based firm with branches in the West Country and a good reputation for clever renovations. Second-home owners adored their innovative work and knack for providing the light, airy spaces and modern touches city dwellers treasured, within rural, chocolate-box locations.

Brian was still talking. 'You need the new buildings to be an asset to the gardens and not spoil the hotel's ambience. It's such a fabulous place. You must get plenty of business from celebrities who come down here to be incognito for a while.'

'We're doing okay,' Imogen said. It would be bad business practice to boast about the small group of actors who'd begun to make the hotel their home from home, especially in the winter. 'People love the big fireplaces and the grounds, and we have one rather grand suite that we use.' On the spur of the moment, she said, 'Would you like to see it? It's not booked until the end of next week. We often upgrade people when the room's free, but there's no one in there at the moment.'

What on earth had come over her? she wondered. But she was enjoying talking to this man. After Dan's distant behaviour, the attention from someone like Brian was intensely flattering.

Not, of course, that they would be having any more than a professional relationship. The man was probably married.

The lift took them to the fourth floor, to the Oak Suite.

'Here we are.' She unlocked the door and showed Brian inside.

'Very, very nice,' he said. 'I wish I could afford to stay here.' He stood for a moment, his eyes ranging around the room. 'I love the paintings. Is that one of The Streamside Hotel garden?'

Imogen turned away to hide a blush. Brian was looking at the painting Dan had started for her father but not completed. Adam had given it to her, having bought it for a song from Henry, the gallery owner in Camilton. Dan had painted it years before he'd gained his current reputation and Imogen thought it was beautiful, even without the finishing touches. Dan winced whenever he saw it but she'd refused to let him change it.

She would take it down, later. It reminded her too much of its artist.

Brian squinted at the signature. 'D Freeman? I don't know the name, but painting's not my thing. I'm just a businessman, I'm afraid.' He smiled that lopsided smile. 'Boring, I know.'

'Not at all. I'm in business, too.'

'But you're very creative, I can see that. Your gardens are beautiful. Haselbury House was in the county magazine, wasn't it? The owner showed me.'

Imogen said nothing. She didn't want to spread gossip, but even when she was working there she'd been aware that the owner was cutting corners, and she'd had a strong feeling he was involved in the financial scam that had shocked the area, although the police had never charged him.

'At least, with your craft studios, you're planning for the future,' Brian said. 'Good for you.'

Imogen's spirits soared. *There are plenty more fish in the sea than Daniel Freeman*, she told herself.

'I'll send over a quote in the next few days.'

It took all Imogen's determination not to offer him the contract, there and then.

17

PIERRE

By Tuesday evening, Dan had a set of new cameras installed, at huge cost, to cover the shelter, the gate and various areas of the paddock, as well as the front of the house. He could paint alone to his heart's content, confident that the donkeys were safe. He'd forget about Smash's adventure. It had just been a local lad or two, playing a stupid practical joke. And the note? A childish attempt to scare him. He wouldn't waste more time on it.

Except, he discovered, he couldn't paint at all. He set up the easel and sorted out sketches he'd already made of an assortment of horses, donkeys, trees and lakes, for he would be happy never to paint another stately home. The upcoming exhibition had drained his interest in overblown architecture quite dry.

Failing to find inspiration in the sketches, however, he turned to photos he'd taken of Somerset scenes. Glastonbury, Dunster, Exmoor, Watchet; all lovely places, but too familiar, too often photographed or painted, to inspire him. He had nothing new to offer on any of them.

He flipped open a sketch pad and idly doodled faces. But he could only remember Imogen's. The way she turned her head on that long neck; the involuntary lift of one eyebrow when she pretended not to mind that Dan had arrived late to a meal; the width of her sudden smile, in that expression of trust and openness that crossed her face occasionally. He'd encountered it most often when she'd been working in the hotel garden, cheeks flushed with digging and Harley at her feet, scrabbling at the disturbed earth in a search for old bones.

Imogen smiled too rarely. Was that his fault? He knew he'd been a disappointment to her. He turned his attention to the sketch but couldn't capture the expression properly. It was easier to draw the frequent wariness in her face, the other smile that didn't quite reach her eyes.

He threw his pencil down. What was the point, anyway? There was unlikely to be any future for him with Imogen. He should have known better than to expect it.

He hid the sketch pad in the bottom drawer of a cabinet. It was time to stop the self-pity and move on.

Coffee, that was what he needed, and plenty of it. He wouldn't sleep until he'd broken his duck and found something – anything – to paint.

He returned from the kitchen bearing a steaming mug and half a packet of chocolate digestives. The sudden thud on his front door startled him into dropping his mug on the floor.

'Coming,' he called, sweeping the broken shards under the table and mopping up the coffee with a painting rag. He remembered his new, expensive entry camera. Time to try it out. He peered at the screen. 'Pierre?'

His son waved, mouthing, 'Let me in.'

'What are you doing here?' Dan ran to the door and threw it open. Pierre lurched inside, dropped his backpack in the middle of the floor and, towering over his father, enveloped him in a hug that threatened to choke him within an inch of his life.

Dan searched his memory. Had Pierre warned him he was coming? Surely he hadn't forgotten? Pierre had completed his university course in photography and disappeared across the world taking pictures, but he hadn't mentioned an autumn trip to England.

Dan felt his smile expand into every muscle of his face.

'How long can you stay?' he asked.

'Long as you like,' Pierre said. 'I've had it with France, to be honest. Oh, good timing.' He helped himself to a handful of biscuits. 'Anything stronger than coffee around here?'

'Red wine?'

'Of course. I'd have brought you some decent stuff from over there, but...'

'But you would have drunk it before you arrived.' Dan laughed and led the way into the kitchen. He pointed at his prized, self-indulgent, temperature-controlled wine 'cellar'. 'Help yourself.'

'Thanks, Dad.' Pierre took his time to choose, squinting at labels and rejecting most of the bottles with a Gallic sigh, finally selecting one and pouring generous measures into two large glasses. They returned to the studio and he swirled the wine, sniffed appreciatively, his nose deep in the glass, and took a mouthful. 'Works with the biscuits, anyway,' he pronounced, taking another. His grin teased his father, as it always had. 'I saw your last exhibition did well. I get the online versions of the newspapers.'

'You texted me. I think you were in Colombia at the time. Your mother emailed, by the way. She thought you were dealing drugs or being trapped into acting as a mule for one of the gangs. I think she wanted me to rush over and rescue you.'

Pierre snorted. 'I wasn't born yesterday,' he said, draining the glass. 'But now,' he nodded towards Dan's remaining few canvases around the walls, 'What are you painting at the moment? There aren't many pictures here. Where are they? Another exhibition?'

As Dan filled him in on the Camilton gallery plans, Pierre stopped to admire the portraits of Smash and Grab on the wall. 'Glad to see the donkeys are still around,' he said.

Dan grunted. 'Come on, let's see your work. You must have some in that huge rucksack.'

Pierre rummaged in the bag and pulled out a lever-arch file. He opened it up and waited, tapping one finger nervously on the table.

Dan took his time examining his son's work, his heart beating faster. Pierre liked to photograph people. Old and young, poor and rich, some in national costumes, most in work clothes.

Dan sighed with relief. 'They're good – some of them are brilliant.' What would he have said if they'd been no good? He noticed a brown envelope from the bottom of the file. 'What are these?'

Pierre shifted on his chair. 'I managed to photograph some war zones...'

'What?' Dan stopped, horrified, the envelope half-opened.

'I got an internship in a newspaper and went out to a couple of smaller wars – if you can call any war, small,' Pierre said, calmly.

Dan swallowed. The images showed children running, panicking, desperate.

'These make quite a statement,' he managed. 'Does your mother know what you've been doing?'

Pierre shook his head. 'Not yet. She was bothered enough about Colombia.'

Dan cleared his throat and grinned at Pierre. 'If I wasn't a reserved, middle-aged Englishman I'd give you a big—' But Pierre had already thrown his arms around his father and hugged him tight.

'A good job I'm half-French, then,' Pierre said. 'Oh,' he went on, releasing Dan from the hug. 'I had one photo published in a local paper.' He burrowed into his backpack and brought out a sheet of newsprint, folded into a small square. 'I went with some volunteers from Somerset, handing out food parcels in Africa.'

Impressed, Dan asked, 'Have you framed a copy?'

'Not yet. The photos are all on my laptop. It's all done digitally, these days. I thought, maybe I could stay a while in your studio and frame this and some other photos.'

Dan said, 'It will be a pleasure. When was it published?'

'Yesterday.'

Dan peered at the paper. 'I see you just call yourself Freeman.'

'It's a great name for a roving photographer.'

'So it is.'

'By the way, according to the paper, there's been another murder nearby. It's getting to be a habit around here,' Pierre said. 'Did you know this man?'

'I've met him once or twice. But I'm innocent,' Dan said. 'Now, while I sort out bed linen, like a good father, you can pour us both a nightcap.'

18

VILLAGE SHOP

Imogen set off with Harley for their usual walk to the village shop the next day. Preoccupied with the proposed craft workshop idea, she'd spent many hours closeted in the office with Emily, working on their plans.

'It's as well we can diversify,' Emily had said. 'It's hard to make a hotel do more than break even. The running costs are enormous.'

Imogen had agreed. 'If we can make the folly work for its keep, I think we should be okay, and, luckily, the bank seems to agree.'

The village shop was busy that day with a constant stream of customers, still swapping theories about Joe's death.

Barbara Croft, checking the prices of sausages, paused. 'I reckon it was stress made Joe keel over. Money worries – it's the same for everyone, these days. I was only saying so to my old man the other day—'

Edwina, sitting in state behind the counter at the rear of the shop, interrupted, 'Harley,' she cried, 'my favourite customer.' She poured dog biscuits into a bowl and lowered it to the floor, grunting with the effort, 'I expect you've been busy, what with poor Joe and then this new business venture of yours.'

'You don't let the grass grow under your feet, do you, dear?' Barbara said. 'My Rex heard all about it in The Plough.' The village grapevine never failed.

'I'd love you to spread the word,' Imogen said. 'We think we have room for three workshops, although they'll be quite small. We thought of woodturning and perhaps a potter. If you know any likely candidates?'

'And a space for that artist of yours,' Edwina said with a wink.

Imogen swallowed. 'I'm... I'm not sure about that,' she mumbled.

She would decide who was allowed to use the studios, and she certainly wouldn't be approaching Dan. Besides, he had his own purpose-built place in Ford.

'You look after that Dan,' Edwina was saying, to nods of approval from her customers. 'He's a good man. A bit artistic, if you know what I mean, all distracted and absent-minded, but none the worse for that. His heart's in the right place. I was sorry to hear about his donkey. One of those that came out to the Spring Fair.'

Imogen's head jerked up. 'His donkey?'

'He must have told you. I heard it from Peter Hammond, who had it from his sister, her that cleans Mr Freeman's house, so I know it's true. Someone stole one of those donkeys – the big grey, Peter said – out of its field and hid it for a couple of days and then took it back safe and sound. Some stupid practical joke, I suppose, but your Mr Freeman was beside himself. Still, all's well that ends well, I always say, and the animal's none the worse for its adventure.'

Imogen bit her lip. How could she not have heard? Why hadn't Dan told her?

She winced. He'd tried, hadn't he? At Apple Day. And she'd taken no notice.

The shop's customers had moved on and were discussing the donkey rides at the Fair.

'They were the highlight of the day for my youngest, Amy,' said Barbara. 'First time she'd been on horseback – well, donkey-back. Now she's begging for a horse for Christmas, but who can afford to keep a horse, these days? Even Jenny Trevillian was talking about selling that old bay pony her Shona used to ride.' She leaned her elbow on Edwina's counter, inches away from a precarious jar of tomato puree, preparing for a good chinwag.

Edwina moved the jar out of danger. 'She won't be letting the horse go. Not now Joe's dead,' she said. 'What a tragedy that is. I don't know what that poor family will do now.'

'Especially,' added Barbara, 'with Jenny's...' she hesitated, delicately, 'her little bit of trouble,' she finished.

Two other shoppers nodded, knowingly.

'What a life she's had,' Freda Marchmont, Oswald's wife, said. 'At least her mother's still around to help out. I hear Joe was trying to sell some of the farmland back to her—'

The clatter of the bell above the shop door stopped her in mid-sentence. Maria Rostropova had entered. As always, she paused just long enough to be sure all eyes had turned her way. Then she wafted across the room and smothered Harley in a mix of affectionate kisses and strong perfume.

Barbara wrinkled her nose.

Edwina, her voice cool, said, 'And how can we help you today, Mrs Rostropova? Another jar of caviar, perhaps?'

Imogen winced at the sarcasm, but Maria said, 'I still have a little left from the one I bought here. I'm afraid it's not the very best caviar, but I think Harley may like it. Perhaps I'll send it over to your hotel, Imogen.'

The atmosphere in the shop dropped to zero.

'My word, is that the time?' Barbara paid Edwina, shoved her sausages hurriedly into her shopping bag and bolted for the door, almost colliding with Shona Trevillian.

Freda Marchmont hugged Shona. 'How are you, my dear? Is there anything we can do to help?'

Shona shook her head. 'Thank you. That cake you sent over was lovely. We're really grateful.' She smiled briefly at Edwina and Imogen. 'Everyone's being so kind.'

'Of course, they are,' said Edwina. 'Your dad was a pillar of the community. And your mum too, of course.'

Shona gave a shaky laugh. 'I just came in to buy more pizza. You know what Jack's like – he won't eat anything else. Oh, and more tomato ketchup, please.'

'Do you have a date for the funeral?' Imogen ventured. 'We'll all want to be there.'

Shona shook her head. 'Not for a while. The police are still investigating. There are some forensic things...' She pulled a packet of Rice Krispies off the shelf, her hands trembling, and dropped it. It split, cereal spilling across the floor. 'Oh, I'm so sorry...' she hiccupped, bursting into tears.

'Never you mind, my dear.' Edwina bustled across and led Shona to the wooden chair at the side of the counter. 'Just you sit down and I'll make you a nice cup of tea. Mrs Bishop and Harley will clear up. Won't you?'

Maria slipped silently out of the shop.

'Of course,' Imogen said, retrieving the box while Harley snaffled the cereal.

'It's just,' Shona sniffed, loudly. 'It's just so horrible at home. Mum's... she's not well at all, and Granny comes in and starts telling her off and searching the house for bottles, and there aren't any because I've been throwing them out. And Mum says she needs a little drink to get through the day, and Jack and the others are all fighting, and I just don't know what to do.'

'Well,' said Edwina, 'you've come to the right place, hasn't she, Imogen?'

Imogen thought for a moment. 'Why don't we ask a few people to pop in and give you a hand with things at home? Would that help?'

Shona sniffed. 'It's not so much the housework, or the farm.' Edwina pushed a box of tissues towards her and she blew her nose. 'People are being very kind. You've been sending meals from the hotel, Mrs Bishop, and Mr Hennessy sent Wayne over with a pile of burgers, and the vicar's been in every day. And Fred, who helps with the milking, has been putting in extra hours on the farm. But it's Mum I'm worried about. She cries all the time and it gets worse when she has a drink.'

'Does the doctor know?'

Shona shook her head. 'Mum said we weren't to tell him.'

'Well,' said Edwina, 'we can't let you children manage this alone. We'll make out a rota.' She had the light of battle in her eyes. Imogen could see that the Trevillian family was going to want for nothing, if Edwina had anything to do with it.

* * *

While Edwina made lists and settled down with her phone to call in reinforcements, Imogen, Shona and Harley returned to the hotel, Imogen wheeling the bike, while Shona gripped the dog's lead as though it were a lifeline. Imogen popped her head into the office to tell Emily where she was going and led Shona around to the back of the hotel. She jettisoned the various tools and large wheelbarrow from the back of her pickup truck, replacing them with the bike. Harley leapt aboard and they set off for the Trevillian farm.

'This is very kind of you,' Shona muttered. 'I didn't mean to cause trouble.'

'It's no trouble. I'm sorry you have so much on your plate,' Imogen said. 'I take it your grandmother's visits don't really help?'

Shona groaned. 'She keeps on about Dad, what a bad lot he was and so on. She says if Mum hadn't behaved like a slut she'd never have had to marry him.'

'Woah!' Imogen gasped. 'That's harsh.'

'That's Granny's way.' Shona managed a shaky laugh. 'Did you know Dad isn't my real dad? I mean, Joe?'

Imogen searched for a diplomatic answer. No need to tell Shona the tale was common knowledge. 'There's certainly a big age gap between you and the others in the family.'

Shona told the story. 'But my biological father never sees me,' she ended forlornly.

Imogen clicked her tongue. Selfish beast. No one would care that he was Jenny's teacher, after so many years.

'Granny's always helped out, but she just makes it such a thing. It wasn't so bad when the farm was doing well. Mum loves the farm work – she grew up doing it. But it's been difficult lately. The bills and so on. Granny had taken to popping in. A lot. Especially on Sunday evenings, and every time she came, Dad and Mum would argue and Dad would go out – down to The Plough, I suppose – to get away from her. Like on the night Dad left. Then Granny would grumble about him and when she ran out of things to criticise, she'd go home and Mum would pour herself another drink.'

Imogen swerved to avoid a car speeding in the other direction.

'Isn't that Dan Freeman?' Shona said. 'And there's someone in the car with him. Is he heading for the hotel?'

Imogen's stomach contracted. 'I don't expect so.'

Shona turned and looked at her. 'I heard you two have broken up.'

Imogen caught her breath.

'Sorry, but you know what Lower Hembrow is for gossip,' Shona said, with just a hint of a watery smile. 'Maybe he's going to see you to make up.'

Imogen clenched her teeth. The grapevine might be the lifeblood of the village, but being the subject of rumours could hurt. 'I very much doubt it,' she said.

19

ART LESSON

The squeal of bicycle brakes outside The Plough roused Steph from work on her book. 'It sounds like someone's gasping for a drink.'

She'd set up her laptop precariously on a rickety table, next to a printer, and she was alternately typing and printing.

She threw a screwed-up sheet of paper into the bin.

Adam groaned. 'I forgot. I invited Alfie round for a spot of painting with Dan.'

'What?'

'Part of our plan to get Dan over here more often, see if Imogen and he can't sort out their relationship. You remember? I persuaded Dan to come over and give Alfie an art lesson.'

A quiet knock on his private door interrupted.

'He sounds timid,' Steph hissed.

Sure enough, Alfie looked ready to turn and run when Adam let him in.

Steph said, 'It's all right, don't mind me. I'm just packing my things up. I'm going nowhere fast with this book. I'll get out into the bar, ready for the first customers.'

'Don't worry about clearing up.' Adam grinned. He wanted the room to look busy when Dan arrived.

A car drew up.

Alfie gasped, 'Is that Mr Freeman?'

'Don't look so worried,' Adam said. 'It's the same Dan who ran the donkey rides.'

'I know, but he's a professional artist,' Alfie said, in starstruck tones. 'I mean, he'll think he's wasting his time with me.'

Adam stopped on the way to the door. 'Now look here, young man,' he said, pointing a finger at Alfie. 'He wouldn't come if he didn't want to. I've shown him a handful of your drawings and he thinks they're good. So don't run yourself down.'

Alfie blushed, as Adam brought Dan and a stranger into the living room.

'I hope you don't mind,' Dan said. 'I've brought my son, Pierre.'

'Welcome to The Plough,' Adam said, hiding his surprise. He'd known Dan had a son from his short, ill-conceived marriage to a French woman, but he'd forgotten. He shook the young man's hand. He was a chip off the old block, even taller and better-looking than his father. 'Don't hit your head on that beam over there. People were smaller when they built this place. Luckily, I fit in perfectly.'

Pierre said, 'Dad said he's giving an art lesson. He used to do that for me when I was small.'

'Really?' Alfie's eyes glowed. 'Are you an artist, too?'

'He's a photographer.' Dan glowed with paternal pride.

'Yeah. I've done some painting, but I haven't Dad's talent. I used to come over to England to visit – I grew up in France, you see. Dad would lend me an easel like this one.' He easily manhandled Adam's easel from against the wall, as though it weighed almost nothing, and assembled it in the middle of the room.

Dan set a big, black box down on the floor and pulled out

brushes, paper, glass jars and vast quantities of rags. 'Now then, let's have some fun, Alfie. What do you like best in the world?'

'Motorbikes,' Alfie said.

Dan chuckled. 'Then, motorbikes it is.'

Adam left the three of them to it and followed Steph into the bar. 'They don't need me.'

'So, that nice young man is Dan's son? I knew he had one. A photographer, too. He must have inherited his father's creative gene as well as his looks.' She sighed. 'I hoped I had a creative gene myself, but this book I'm struggling with is going nowhere fast. I thought it would be easy. It seems writing a whole book is a different kettle of fish from thousand-word articles. I can't decide whether to plan out the whole story, or just start writing and see what happens.'

'I can't help you with that, but I know you'll manage just fine,' Adam said. 'Meanwhile, here come the first customers of the day – Terry and Ed, of course, gasping for beer.'

'If only Imogen would drop in and find Dan being so kind.' Steph stopped in the act of collecting glasses from the overhead rack. 'You know, I suspect Dan hides behind this cover of vagueness and forgetfulness. He comes up trumps when it matters. Like the way he brought the donkeys to the Fair and donated one of his paintings. I think there's more to Dan Freeman than most people realise. I just hope Imogen doesn't freeze him out, and then regret it.'

* * *

An hour later, Alfie wobbled away on his bike clutching a handful of drawings of motorbikes, complete with neat pencil lines showing how to calculate the right proportions for the road they were travelling.

'He'll be good,' Dan said, coming into the bar with Pierre, still wiping paint from his hands, 'and he's certainly enthusiastic. We've cleared up, I think. No damage to anything expensive, and thanks for letting us use your room.'

'You can't make a worse mess than Harley when he first arrived,' Adam pointed out.

Dan ordered wine for them all. 'Young Alfie's keen to do more and I'd like to help him. In fact, he said a couple of his friends were really jealous. He's at school with Donald Trevillian and he wants to come along, too. It seems they get precious little time at school for art. To be honest, I haven't enjoyed myself so much for ages. I'd forgotten what a buzz you get from working together.' He grinned. 'But we need to find a bigger place to meet, where it won't matter if we spill paint. Somewhere that isn't a living room. The boys would be welcome at the studio, but Ford's really too far out of the village when you're travelling by bike.'

Steph and Adam exchanged glances.

'What?' Dan asked. 'What are you two up to?'

'It's an idea we had,' Steph said. 'About a workshop.'

'Really?' Dan looked around the room, and then peered out of the window. 'There's not much space, here. Did you mean in the village hall?'

'Not unless you want to share the space with the playgroup, the knitting circle, the line-dancing group, the Zumba class—'

Dan held up his hand. 'Heaven forbid. What's this idea of yours?'

Steph said, 'The hotel has that old folly in the grounds and Imogen's going to convert it to a set of craft studios.'

Before Dan could object, Pierre said, 'That's a brilliant idea. It'll get you out of your cave.'

Adam raised an eyebrow. 'You mean your father's beautiful studio?'

Pierre nodded. 'I do. It's full of light but very isolated. And painting's a solitary enough business at the best of times. If it weren't for the donkeys, Dad would be on his own for days. And you told me you'd had a break-in earlier this year.' He broke off. 'What's wrong, Dad?'

Dan hesitated, as though making up his mind whether to speak. Finally, he told Steph about Smash's disappearance. 'He went missing on Apple Day, and then on Monday he just turned up again.' He looked from Pierre to Adam. 'It was odd. Adam and I talked about it at the time.'

Steph said, 'Pierre, why don't we go back and finish tidying Adam's room. These two can have a drink together and Adam can solve the Mystery of the Disappearing Donkey. Although it sounds as though somebody left the gate open.'

Pierre said, 'Good idea. You can fill me in on all the things Dad's not saying, including more about the hotel and this Imogen Bishop my mother told me about; the woman Dad's gone out of his way to avoid mentioning?' As they left the bar, Pierre's voice floated back. 'He thinks I don't know what's going on in his life.'

'Right,' Adam said, ignoring Dan's embarrassment. 'What didn't you want to say in front of your son? Who looks like a fine chap, if I may say so.'

'He is, isn't he?' Dan beamed. 'He's already getting his work taken up by the papers. But I didn't want to worry him about the donkeys. You see, there was a development. Well, it wasn't new, but I didn't see it at the time.'

'Come on. Steph will strangle me if I don't get all the details.'

Dan grimaced, reached for his phone and showed Adam a picture of the note he'd found in the donkeys' shelter.

Adam read it through and nodded, thinking. Finally, 'This is a threat,' he said.

'It's very vague.'

'None the less, you should be taking it seriously. How secure are you at the studio?'

Dan detailed the new cameras. 'It feels safe enough. The cameras can't see every inch of the place, but they should catch anyone approaching the donkey shelter. I just don't want Pierre worried.' He hesitated, then opened his bag and pulled out his newspaper. 'While I'm being the proud father, here's a copy of Pierre's first paid professional work. Good, isn't it?'

Adam admired it for a long moment. 'He's a chip off the old block,' he said. 'Funny to find this in the local rag. Does Pierre know the editor?'

'He says not and I don't want to upset him – you know, make him think the photo's only being used because of his contacts, not because it's good. But I'm wondering why my local paper would be using an unknown photographer's picture.'

'Quite a coincidence, isn't it?'

'I thought so. Do you think it's intended for me to see? As another... kind of warning? A sort of, "we know your family"?' He shook his head. 'Sounds crazy when I say it out loud. Maybe I'm imagining things. Growing a paranoia.'

Adam shook his head. 'There's a saying – just because you're paranoid, it doesn't mean they aren't out to get you. After that business with the donkey, I'd be careful, if I were you. There's not enough to take to the police at the moment, I'm afraid. It would just be filed.'

Dan gave a short laugh. 'And brought out later if anything dire happens to me.'

'I don't expect it will get that far. Keep the evidence – the dates of the donkey's disappearance and a copy of the paper. Meanwhile, I think it's time we did some gentle investigation.'

'Thanks, Adam. I think you're right. But let's not tell Imogen. We're not seeing each other at the moment so there's no need for her to know. I want her to get on with her life.'

Even as he spoke, Dan's throat constricted. He was going to miss her.

20

GALLERY

The Gallery in Camilton occupied the middle house in a Georgian terrace that arced gracefully around a grassy square in the nearby town.

'It's almost as grand as Bath,' Pierre said, as Dan steered the old van round the square and through a covered entrance that led to the rear of the terrace.

'Beautiful, isn't it? I still find it hard to believe Henry puts on exhibitions just for my work.'

He knocked at the rear door of the gallery, but no one answered.

'That's funny. Henry said he'd be here,' Dan muttered. 'Friday morning, eleven o'clock, he said. To hang the paintings.'

Pierre swung to face him. 'What did you say?'

'Eleven o'clock, Friday— Oh no.'

'Dad,' Pierre chuckled. 'It's Thursday today. Honestly, you need a nursemaid.'

Dan shrugged. 'That's what your mother used to say. Still, no harm done. Henry gave me a key to the back door.'

'He's dealt with artists before,' Pierre said. 'Come on, let us in. Please tell me you haven't lost the key.'

'Course not.' He fumbled in his pockets. 'Here it is.'

With a flourish, he unlocked the door and pushed. It moved a few inches and stuck. He pushed again.

'There's something in the way...'

He shoved harder, and the door flew open.

Dan's jaw dropped.

The door had been blocked by a console table lying on its side, and Dan's final push had sent it skidding across the floor. A shattered vase lay on the marble floor, its flowers crushed and mangled in a puddle of water.

Dan stepped over the vase, motioning for Pierre to stay back in the doorway. He held a finger to his lips. 'Burglars,' he mouthed. 'Call the police.'

As Pierre jabbed at his phone, Dan silently inched open the door to his right and listened, motionless. All was silent.

He held his breath as he padded into the room. It was an empty office. Nothing disturbed the workaday atmosphere of calm efficiency. Office chairs remained tucked neatly behind desks, computers, lamps and pens set out on the surface. No burglar had been inside.

Dan released his breath, backed out, shook his head at Pierre and trod softly towards the stairs that wound up from the hall.

He could just hear the murmur of his son's voice below in the hallway, talking to the police.

Then, a hush enveloped the building.

Dan trod lightly along a passage towards a door at the far end.

A touch landed on his shoulder.

He swung round, fist raised.

'It's only me,' Pierre hissed.

'One of my nine lives gone. Don't do that again. I don't think anyone's here, though.' Dan nodded at the door. 'This is the gallery.'

He pushed open the door.

Pierre gasped. 'I don't believe it,' he whispered.

Facing them, on the longest wall, were two paintings, already hanging in place. Two elaborate country houses, owned and lovingly restored by celebrities, all turrets and gables, hung side by side. The first remained intact, just as Dan had painted it, but he could hardly recognise the other. Daubs of red paint splattered the surface, sliding glutinously downwards, dripping slowly, inexorably, onto the floor. A single painted chimney remained visible above the mess.

'Dad. Are you okay?'

Dan shook his head, swallowing hard. How many hours of effort had he put into the picture? But that hardly mattered.

'Who?' he murmured. 'Who would do that?'

Pierre tugged at his arm. 'Come away. Leave it for the police to see.'

Dan tried a smile. 'Not my best painting, anyway.'

'Where are all the others?'

'Oh, no!' Stomach lurching, Dan ran across the room and rattled the handle of the door into the storeroom. It was firmly locked. 'We disturbed them,' he said, his heart rate slowly returning to normal, 'before they could do any more damage. They must have run out through the public entrance at the front of the building when they heard us at the back.' He pointed. 'There's more paint spilled on the floor over there.' A trail of red splashes disappeared through the open door at the front of the room.

Pierre grabbed his arm. 'We'd better not touch anything. We don't want our fingerprints all over everything, do we?'

'In case the police suspect us? As if I'd ruin my own work. Are you sure they're coming?'

'I told them this is a posh art gallery and the burglars might still be here. In fact, I think I can hear a car, now.'

They retraced their steps down the gallery's back stairs and burst out of the door just as a car arrived. Two officers ran towards them.

'That was fast,' Dan said.

'There's a silent burglar alarm on the building. We were already on our way. Now, you two stay here while we take a look.'

The smaller of the two police officers, a delicate-looking girl with a blonde ponytail, entered the gallery. Pierre and Dan sat on one of the steps as the other officer, a fresh-featured lad barely old enough to have finished A levels, flipped open his notebook and listened as they told the story.

'You see, we came on the wrong day,' Dan said. 'We were meant to meet the owner tomorrow to hang the paintings. I... er, got the day wrong.'

The officer looked down at his notebook, writing studiously, but Dan saw his grin. 'You're the artist, I take it, sir?' the officer said.

Dan nodded. 'The owner or his assistant will be back later, I imagine. Whoever did this must have watched the building and came in when he saw it was empty.'

'At least no one's been hurt, I suppose,' Pierre said.

That was little comfort to Dan. The destruction of his work sickened him. It felt personal – personal and vindictive. First, his donkey stolen, and now his art ruined. He closed his eyes, briefly, thinking. Who could hate him that much?

The blonde officer returned. 'You can leave everything to us, sir. This is a crime scene now and my colleagues will be here at any moment. We'll contact the gallery owner. You've already contaminated the area enough by wandering about, so we'll need samples from you both and a detailed statement.' She turned. 'Mike, take these two down to the station. I'll join you when I can.'

The young constable's face fell as he was dismissed. He frowned at Dan and Pierre. 'Follow me to the station, please,' he said and climbed into his own car.

'They're not very sympathetic,' Pierre said as Dan started the van.

'They'll need to make sure it's not an insurance scam, I suppose. Henry insures the paintings while they're here.'

At Camilton police station, a burly sergeant took their details. 'I gather you interrupted the villain or villains,' he glared, as though they'd committed a crime simply by being there, 'so we need to take your witness statement.' He rolled his eyes at the young police officer. 'More paperwork.' He heaved a deep sigh. 'Right at the end of my shift.'

21

OSWALD

The snap of autumn crisped the air the next day, with the first touch of frost on exposed leaves and patches of shady grass slowly melting.

The news of the break-in at the gallery had quickly spread to Lower Hembrow. Wayne had phoned Emily, and she'd passed it on to Imogen.

Imogen's heart bled for Dan, but there was nothing she could do, as they were no longer seeing each other. Instead, this morning she was seeking out Oswald to talk about Joe's death. Now they knew he'd been poisoned, the idea that he'd been deliberately killed seemed less ridiculous.

Oswald had no malicious bones in his body, she was sure, but he knew Joe's ways better than most. He'd lived in the village for ever. Surely he would have a theory or two.

But instead of finding Oswald drinking tea in the potting shed, as she'd expected, she found him down by the row of hawthorn trees. 'How's the bulb planting going?' she asked.

'Not so bad.' He stopped work and leaned on a long-handled implement with a cone-shape at the bottom and a horizontal footrest. 'This 'ere planting contraption makes a big difference. No kneeling. I dig the holes and drop in the crocuses and narcissi. Don't hardly have to bend down at all.'

'I'm glad it's making a difference. This part of the garden's going to look fantastic in the spring. And it's not so bad right now, with the berries.'

'Aye, those the starlings have left us,' Oswald groaned. 'Now, what can I do for you, Mrs Bishop?'

'It's not about gardening, this time. Let's go and warm up in the potting shed.'

Once in the shed, with the kettle boiling, Imogen felt a shiver run down her spine.

'This place saw some action at the Spring Fair,' she said.

'And that's a fact,' Oswald said, stiffly.

'But all's well that ends well.' Imogen bit her lip. Somehow, she always ended up talking to Oswald in clichés. It was something to do with his lilting Somerset accent. She hoped she hadn't offended him. He was standing as rigidly to attention as a man in his eighties who'd spend most of his life digging and kneeling could manage. 'Is everything all right?' she asked.

'That's up to you, Ma'am.'

'Ma'am?' Puzzled, Imogen frowned. Then, the penny dropped. 'Oswald, I don't have a complaint. I just wanted to ask you something.'

The wrinkled face relaxed and Oswald lowered himself onto a chair as Imogen poured boiling water over teabags in a couple of mugs. 'That's all right, then. I did think you were about to give me my marching orders. I know I'm not as sprightly as I used to be – what with a touch of arthritis or two, but I reckon I can still do my job.'

'And so do I, so let's put that idea to bed straight away. You'll be head gardener here as long as you want to be. The young lads you've been training over the past few years are learning fast and they can do the heavy work while you supervise.'

He grinned, his ruddy cheeks like little round apples. 'That's nice of you, miss. And my Freda'll be relieved. She's terrified I'll give up work and spend my days getting under her feet,' he chuckled.

'No chance of that.' Imogen stirred a teabag with one of Oswald's ancient, worn spoons, pressed it gently against the edge of the mug, extracted it and dropped it onto a saucer. 'I wanted to talk about Joe Trevillian.'

Oswald was nodding. 'Silly young fool, he always was. Bad-tempered and cantankerous, but he had a good heart underneath it all.' He took a sip of tea. 'I'm a-going to miss our run-ins, over in The Plough. Banter, the young people call it on this 'ere Instabook, or whatever it's called.'

'You say he had a good heart?' Imogen prompted.

'Took on another man's child, didn't he? And a nice little thing she's turned out to be, that Shona.'

Imogen smiled. Of course, Oswald would know the truth of Shona's birth. Nothing in the village got past him. 'How many people know she's not his biological daughter?'

Oswald scratched his head. 'Pretty much everyone in these parts, I reckon. All the village and the farming folk. Some do say he only took on Jenny because her father gave him the farm, but my eldest lad knew them both at school and he reckoned Joe always had a soft spot for Jenny Little, despite her bossy ways.'

'Is that your son who works with you here?'

'No, my other lad. He moved away when he left school, to Camilton. He's the brainy one, is Phil. He runs the – what do you call it? – the PR or HR department in that big glove factory there. Him and his wife, Milly, have a nice little house and a couple of youngsters. Bright as buttons, both of them. Not much good at gardening, though. Just grass and a few bushes.'

'I bet you're proud of your family,' Imogen interrupted. She'd love to while away the morning talking gardening with Oswald, but she needed to hear more about Joe. 'And, as you say, Joe did a good job with his children. They were all at the Apple Day and that made it even worse when he died.'

'Good kids, all of 'em. Even that Hermione will grow out of her sulks, one day, although Freda says they've been hit hard by his death – and Jenny's drinking, of course.'

So, the Trevillians' closely guarded secret was common knowledge. Imogen wouldn't have expected anything else, with a grapevine like the village's at work.

'When did Jenny's problems start?'

Oswald tossed the last of his tea out of the potting shed door. 'Built up over the years. Six children and a farm to run, you see. My missis says it wore her down. She'd never take any help that was offered, neither, and that's a mistake.' He nodded sharply to emphasise his words. 'Young Jenny tried to do everything, and then she started to have a drink at night to relax. White wine, that was what she liked. Just to wind down at the end of the day, she said. Joe told us she didn't see why she shouldn't, what with Joe going down The Plough.' He shook his head sadly. 'Recently, though, the farm's been doing badly. Sheep and cattle used to be mainstays of that place, but they haven't turned much of a profit for years. Joe said you can't give away sheep wool, these days, and the supermarkets take all the profits from the milk.'

'Did they diversify? You know, start other businesses on the farm?'

'Aye, they tried making yoghurt and cheese – young Shona's keen on these funny cheeses, Somerset Brie and whatnot – but she's working in town nowadays and the rest of them are at school.'

'So it all fell on Jenny's shoulders?'

'Joe did his best, but he wasn't the brightest lad in Somerset. He couldn't handle the accounts and so on, so yes, Jenny did all that – until the drinking got bad. I did hear something about her messing up the accounts...' He leaned his head close to Imogen's as though someone might be listening, even though they were alone in the shed, 'I heard Joe telling that Maria Rostropova one night in The Plough. You know he had a fancy for her – though I never could see why. Out for herself, that woman, if you ask me.'

'What did you hear?'

'He told her that Jenny had made some big mistake or other, had the tax people or suchlike down on her. Joe said, if they paid up, the farm would go broke and if they didn't, he'd be going to prison.'

Imogen sucked in her cheeks. Maybe it was time for another visit to Jenny Trevillian.

* * *

Emily waved at Imogen as she passed the office. 'The bids are in for the craft studios.'

Imogen's pulse quickened. She must be more excited about the work than she'd realised.

Emily had printed out the bids, and the two women read them through in silence over coffee.

At last, they looked up and Emily grinned. 'No contest, is there?'

Imogen couldn't keep the grin off her face. 'Well, Mr Porsche is off the table – I knew he'd want to destroy the folly and build brick sheds. And he's expensive, too.'

'What do you think about our friend with the head cold?'

Imogen shook her head. 'Worthy but dull and the price is low – too low. I think his firm's desperate for the work, cutting too many costs, and a bit shady.'

Emily was chuckling. 'So, we're left with the gorgeous Brian, who seems to have put his heart and soul into this bid. A reasonable price and some lovely drawings.' She shuffled the bids into a file. 'So, shall I email him with the good news? No, wait, I have a better idea.' She looked at Imogen and chuckled. 'I'll phone the unsuccessful candidates and you can phone Brian. He'd love to hear your voice.'

'Don't be silly,' Imogen said, but her heart was still thudding in a most unusual way, and her hand shook as she tapped her phone.

Brian's reaction was everything she could have wanted. 'That's wonderful news,' he said, warmly. 'I can't wait to get started. Can I come and talk to you about it? Sort out all the details?'

And before she knew it, Imogen had agreed to spend the afternoon with him. Her trip to see Jenny could wait for a day or two. Suddenly, the sun seemed to shine more brightly and the grey autumn world looked more colourful. Of course, Brian was bound to be married, but even so, she was going to enjoy talking with him again. She didn't need a man to look after her – just some sensible conversation with a man who thought about things the same way she did.

22

FRANCE

In the few days since Pierre had arrived at the studio, Dan had grown comfortable, having him around. 'You make good coffee,' he said.

'I'm half French, don't forget. *Maman* still talks about your dreadful brew. She says no Englishman should be allowed in the kitchen. No wonder you eat at The Plough so often.'

'I bet that's not all she complains about.'

'There are other things,' Pierre chuckled.

'Go on, then – tell me.' Dan thought for a moment. 'Or maybe not.'

'Well, she says you swept her off her feet, but when she landed, she realised the two of you were chalk and cheese.'

'Sounds bad...'

'Actually, not. But,' Pierre said, shrugging, 'I don't think you could ever live together. And, she's happy with Michel. He cooks.'

'Good for Michel.' Dan was laughing. 'Your *maman* is quite a woman. I hope she runs Michel ragged.'

Pierre snorted. 'I think he's a bit – what's the English expression? – hen-pecked. And I can't imagine anyone telling you what to do.'

The laughter died in Dan's chest. He thought of Imogen. She was the opposite of his ex-wife, Elise, in so many ways. Black-haired, fiery, demanding, Elise had wanted more and more from Dan until he'd felt his life disappearing into a cloud of domesticity. Elise had strict rules for everything, from the exact way to heat a croissant, through the only way of stacking the dishwasher, to the clothes Dan wore. 'You English are so un-chic,' she used to say.

At eighteen months old, Pierre had been banished to a *Jardin des Enfants* every day, so Elise could keep the house tidy and entertain her friends to coffee and patisseries. Dan had returned from the school run one day to find Elise had moved all his painting mate-rials out of the tiny room he used as a studio. 'This would make a beautiful garden room,' she'd said.

'No,' Dan had said. 'Or *non* if you prefer. That's the room I need.' Galleries were beginning to take an interest in his work and he was excited. He'd been beginning to think he could make his living as a painter.

She'd wrinkled her nose in the way he'd once found delightful and stamped her foot.

The fight had lasted for hours. 'Selfish, English philistine,' she'd sneered.

Finally, exasperated, Dan had said, 'If my studio goes, I go.'

'Then go,' Elise had said. 'Go back to your fat English woman – what's her name? – the one you were at school with, whose photo-graph you keep in your wallet. Imogen something. Huh. Like she'll ever look at you.'

And in that moment, Dan had realised the crazy infatuation at university that had led to his marriage to Elise had never been more than an illusion.

He'd packed up his things, collected Pierre from school, explained as best he could to the uncomprehending toddler that his father had to go back to England but *Maman* would look after him, and left.

Father and son had stayed on good terms and Dan was grateful to Elise for that. She'd soon found a French man, Michel, who indulged regularly in the *cinq à sept,* the nationally recognised late-afternoon ritual when French *affaires* between a man and his mistress took place. That had suited Elise just fine, leaving her to clean the house to her heart's content. The two seemed happy enough.

Pierre pulled on a woollen beanie. 'I need pastries for breakfast,' he said. 'I'll bring you some. We can celebrate your exhibition going ahead.'

'At least there's only one painting ruined. Henry's happy because the insurance claim's going through but I haven't heard anything from the police to suggest they've found the culprit. I suppose one break-in's not much of a priority, now the police have announced they're looking for someone in connection with Joe's death.' He smiled. 'You don't need to go out, you know. There are croissants in the freezer.'

Pierre wound a scarf around his neck. 'No, I need more than that. I need a pain au raisin, with plenty of that proper creme in the middle. Or cinnamon. I love cinnamon.'

'Well, good luck finding that around here.'

Pierre winked, 'I've already found a little café where the baker is a genius. And they sell proper chocolates. It's on the seafront at Exham. I might be a while, but you'll be glad when you taste the food.'

'You're definitely your *maman*'s son.'

'Funny,' Pierre stopped in the doorway. 'She says I take after you.'

* * *

Dan, starting a portrait of Pierre, hardly noticed that it was almost two hours later when his son returned toting bags full of cakes and chocolates.

He tossed a chocolate box down on the studio table. Intrigued, Dan investigated. The smell of chocolate filled the air.

'It's like a Parisian chocolate shop,' Pierre said. 'And on the way home, I bought this.' He opened a newspaper, with great care, onto the table, smoothing the pages lovingly.

Dan was too busy enjoying the beautifully decorated chocolate that melted on his tongue, to care about the paper. 'What is this?' he asked.

'Vanilla and lemon.'

'It's different,' Dan said. 'Nice.' He helped himself to a pain au raisin. 'Mm. So's this.'

Pierre rustled the newspaper. 'Stop guzzling and look.'

Something about his tone made Dan sit up. Pierre was pointing to a photo.

'Yemen,' he said. 'It's one of mine.'

Dan all but choked on his pain. 'Your photo?' he said.

'My first in a national,' Pierre said. His cheeks glowed. 'And they paid me well!'

Dan leaped to his feet and grabbed his son. 'You're a real professional now.' He beamed.

He read and reread the caption aloud. Freeman, the by-line proclaimed.

'This is wonderful,' Dan said, when they'd calmed down. 'You'll need a copy to send to your mother.'

'I bought six,' Pierre admitted. 'And a bottle of champagne.'

He leaned across and gathered up the paper, holding it as fondly as if it were a new-born baby.

Dan said, 'Ring her now. And your girlfriend. I'm assuming you have at least one waiting for you at home… What's the matter?'

For Pierre had stopped, the broad grin dying on his face, like the tide draining away from the beaches along the Bristol Channel.

'Oh, nothing,' Pierre said. 'Just deciding who to call first,' and he wandered away, his phone already at his ear, his eyes on the newspaper.

Girl trouble, Dan diagnosed. Like father, like son.

23

FOLLY

Imogen was relieved to be able to immerse herself in the arrangements for the folly conversion for the next few days. She didn't want time to think. When she wasn't busy, the scene with Dan at the Apple Day still played in her head, over and over. Each time, it left her feeling small and depressed and wishing she hadn't made a fuss about nothing. He'd been late, but that was Dan. He was often late. He'd apologised, but she'd ignored that and blamed him – for what? – for arriving late at a village event? Hardly a hanging offence.

Still, it had happened. They'd quarrelled and he'd walked away, and she'd let him go, but she told herself, with a rhetorical flourish, Dan was not the only fish in the sea, nor was he the single pebble on the beach.

She envied Adam's bond with Steph. When she first knew him, he'd seemed the least likely to ever find love, until he'd met Steph. Now, the two were so happy with each other, it almost hurt Imogen to watch them. She found herself shying away from the visits to The Plough she used to enjoy so much.

Her heart raced ridiculously fast, however, when Emily handed the phone to her in the office with a call from Brian Arbogast.

'I'm wondering whether you've made a decision about the doors. We need to start ordering so they're ready in time,' Brian explained.

'Doors, yes.' Imogen felt ridiculously flustered. 'We thought oak would be nice.'

'It would – but expensive.'

Emily had already pointed that out.

'Tell you what,' Brian said. 'Have you got an afternoon free soon? I wondered if we could spend an hour or so going over those kinds of details. Maybe have lunch first?'

Imogen took a deep breath and counted to five, pretending to consult her diary. She didn't want to sound too keen.

'How about Wednesday?' she said, remembering beef wellington was on the hotel menu that day.

'Perfect.'

As the call ended, Imogen caught sight of Emily's face. 'What?' she asked.

'Nothing. Just nice to see you looking cheerful. I don't mean to be rude, but you've looked a bit... tired, lately. I think you should enjoy yourself for a change.'

Emily sometimes behaved like a mother hen, even though she was almost twenty years younger than Imogen.

'I'm fine. But it will be nice to get the project under way. Why don't you join us for lunch?'

Emily shook her head, grinning. 'I don't think Brian would be too pleased. You can give me instructions after he leaves.'

'Well, he'll be working for us, so it's not up to him,' Imogen made a valiant attempt to sound dignified. 'I'm going out for an hour or two. I want to see how the Trevillians are getting on.

Shona's employer is letting her work half-days, so she has time at home with the children but she's still struggling.'

'It must be dreadful, knowing your father was deliberately killed.'

'And still no one knows where he went or what he was doing after he left The Plough. Poor Shona.'

A visit to Shona was just what Imogen needed, and with luck she'd be able to find out more from Jenny. If Oswald's assessment of the state of the Trevillian family finances was true, that may throw some light on what Joe had been doing before he was killed.

* * *

Shona was not at home when Imogen called in to the farm. Instead, Hermione, her sixteen-year-old sister, threw the door open and fixed Imogen with a belligerent frown. 'Yeah?' she grunted.

'Is your mum in? Or Shona?'

Hermione gave a theatrical sigh. 'Mum's in bed with a headache. And we don't need Shona here all the time. I'm not a baby.'

'No, of course not. Is, er, school out today?'

The ghost of a smile flitted across Hermione's face. 'The boiler broke down, so they sent us home.'

Imogen decided not to interrogate that too carefully. 'Well, I've brought some things from the hotel. You know, those toiletries we put in the bedrooms. I thought your mum might like them.'

Hermione stood back. 'You'd better come in, I suppose. I'll see if Mum's awake.'

She waved vaguely at the living room and Imogen went inside, while Hermione stomped upstairs. At least the room was neat and tidy. A teen magazine lay on the table, probably tossed aside when she rang the doorbell.

Hermione returned. 'She's asleep,' she said. There was a pause. 'I can make some tea,' she muttered, ungraciously.

'That would be lovely.' Imogen sat in an armchair, looking out into the back garden. The borders were weed-free, and the hedge clipped. 'Beautiful garden,' she said, as Hermione returned.

The teenager blushed. 'Thank you.'

Surprised, Imogen said, 'Do you like gardening?'

'Yeah. Gets me out of the house.' Hermione pointed. 'See that shed? Me and Dad built that. Donald was supposed to help, but he's hopeless. Dad says he's got two left hands.' Her voice faltered. She clenched her hands by her side.

Imogen said, 'Sounds like you and your dad were good friends.'

Hermione's face crumpled and she slumped onto the battered brown cord sofa, her hands pressed against her mouth.

Imogen handed her a tissue. 'It's all right to cry, you know,' she said.

Hermione nodded and shuddered. 'That's what Mrs Pickles said. The vicar. She told me Dad would know I'm sad at the moment, and that was fine, and he'd want me to get on and have a happy life.' Her voice had faded away by the end.

Good to hear that the vicar was still visiting. She always knew exactly the right thing to say.

'And you will,' Imogen said. 'Have a happy life, I mean.'

'But at the moment, all I can think is that Dad left us,' Hermione stammered. 'That's worse than him dying. He ran away on purpose.'

'Don't forget, he came back. He hadn't left for good.'

Hermione sat up a little straighter. 'Mum said it's all her fault.'

Imogen bit her lip, not knowing how to reply. 'We don't know people's reasons—' she began, but Hermione interrupted.

'And she's right. Her and granny. On at him, all the time, they were, nagging about the farm, like it was Dad's fault the supermarkets won't pay for the milk and the cows got TB. Everything was always his fault.'

'But your mum and he have always managed before. I'm sure they would have again, if he hadn't... if nothing...' Imogen had tied herself up in knots. What had happened to Joe? How could this family ever find peace if they didn't know?

She heard a noise and turned to see Jenny, in a dressing gown. 'Imogen. Thank you so much for coming,' she said. 'I'm sorry I was asleep...'

Imogen nodded. 'You don't need to apologise. Hermione's made me tea.'

'Mrs Bishop brought you some things,' Hermione said. 'To make you feel better.' There was an edge to her voice.

Imogen looked from one to the other. There was animosity there, but wasn't that often the way with teenage girls and their mothers? 'If there's anything we can do,' Imogen said, 'you just ask.'

Jenny sat down. 'We're managing quite well, thank you. My mother's helping out.'

Hermione clicked her tongue. 'So she should.'

'That's enough,' Jenny said.

The girl glared, stood up, grabbed her magazine from the table and swept out of the room.

Jenny raised her eyes to the ceiling. 'Hermione and her grand-mother are always at daggers drawn. Hermione's just like her dad, bless him. She takes everything my mother says to heart. She has a tongue on her, does Mum, but she doesn't mean anything by it.' She tucked a strand of uncombed hair behind her ear. 'Anyway, I'm going to sort everything out. I know my little problem's all around the villages, everyone knows about it, but I'm going to fix it. The vicar's given me the name of a therapist she knows. My kids need their mother.' With a nod, she stood, and Imogen took the hint.

Whatever the undercurrents in this family, it was clear that Jenny didn't want her help.

But that wouldn't stop her. She was on a mission today.

'Before I go,' Imogen said, keeping her voice light, 'there's just one thing I want to ask. You see, no one seems to know where Joe went when he left The Plough that day. But I haven't heard you asking about it, or wondering. Which makes me suspect you already know.'

Jenny's sharp intake of breath meant she was right.

'He had a mobile phone, didn't he?' Imogen asked.

'He did, but it wasn't on him when he – he died at the Apple Day. It was lost...' Jenny's voice faded and she bit her lip.

'But before it was lost, did you look to see where he was when he failed to come home? I bet you have one of those tracking apps on your own phone.' She paused, her pulse racing with anticipation.

Jenny fixed her gaze on her hands and whispered, 'He was with that woman.'

Imogen nodded. 'Maria Rostropova?' So, that's where Joe went that night. She wasn't surprised.

Jenny muttered under her breath. Imogen couldn't catch the words.

'You knew all the time, didn't you?'

'Joe must have thought I was stupid. He's never been able to resist a good-looking woman, and he's been seeing her on and off for months. My Joe was such a fool. Like a baby. He couldn't stop himself. If he saw something he wanted, he just went for it. I don't think he even wondered if I knew. And I never said. I thought, better that Maria than anyone else. She wouldn't want anything permanent.' Suddenly, Jenny looked up. 'The thing is, Joe's phone disappeared the night he left. He went to Maria's, and then it was gone. So I don't know how long he stayed with her. And I won't give that woman the satisfaction of asking. Joe's gone, now. What does it all matter?'

'It matters a good deal. Don't you want to know what he was doing? Why he died?'

Jenny shrugged. 'I'm past caring. Joe was my man, but he wore me down over the years with his women and his shoddy ways on the farm. If he hadn't left, we might have lost the farm...' she bit off the last word, shooting a quick glance at Imogen.

Imogen waited, but Jenny said no more.

Well, she'd learned a little, but there were still missing days between Joe's disappearance on that Sunday and his reappearance the next Saturday.

Jenny pulled her dressing gown closer, as though gathering the remaining shreds of her dignity, and said, 'I've told you all I know. Now, if you don't mind, I must hurry into Camilton. I have a life to live, and so do my children.' She hesitated. 'Thank you for the toiletries, by the way. Shona will be delighted,' with a twitch of the lips in a tiny smile. 'She's been a treasure during all this. I don't know what we would have done without her. Or my mother. Mum's helping out, today.'

Imogen made her escape.

News of Imogen's visit to the farm had, through the mysterious channels of communication in the countryside, immediately leaked to the residents of Lower Hembrow. The moment the shop door clanged at her entry that afternoon, heads turned, faces bright with anticipation.

'And how is Jenny today?' Edwina paused from adding a packet of lentils to a top shelf. 'Don't get much call for these around here,' she murmured. 'Meat and two veg, that's what most like. With plenty of potatoes.'

'She's feeling better,' Imogen said, and clamped her mouth shut, determined not to say more. The news of Joe's whereabouts was going to Adam first.

'She'll bounce back. She always does.' That was Mrs Evans, from the farm half a mile beyond High Acres. 'I've known her for years. What she's put up with from that man doesn't bear thinking about, and I don't care who hears me say it.'

'Now then.' Edwina frowned. 'Mustn't speak ill of the dead, you know. Whatever Joe was, his kids loved him, and so did Jenny, though she used to grumble.'

The door chimed again and Maria Rostropova swept in. Imogen turned away. This was no place to question her about Joe.

'Hello, ladies,' Maria said. 'I'm just popping in for some smoked salmon. If you have any?' she smiled sweetly at Edwina.

'As it happens, I do.' Edwina, in triumph, retrieved a pack from the chilled cabinet and handed it to Maria.

Maria left and Edwina grinned at her customers.

'She comes in to test me. Last week it was the caviar, and once she wanted some highfalutin champagne.'

'But how does she afford things like that?' Mrs Evans scowled. 'It's not as though she works for a living.'

'Private means, I reckon,' Edwina said. 'Still, mustn't gossip, must we? There's none of us better than the rest, that's my opinion.'

Mrs Evans looked put out, her eyes narrowing until they almost disappeared. She collected her shopping, paid the bill and left without further conversation.

'Can't stand that woman,' Edwina said. She pottered across to the back of the shop where a curtain led to a tiny kitchen. 'Time for tea. Join me in a cup, my dear?' From the kitchen, she popped her head back into the shop. 'I expect you're sorry about the exhibition being spoiled.'

'Sorry? Exhibition?'

Edwina emerged, carrying mugs of strong brown tea. 'Have I spoken out of turn? Oh, dear. Me and my mouth. It just runs away with me, sometimes. Well, I'm sorry about what happened at the gallery. Your Mr Freeman must be disappointed. It seems he's having quite a run of bad luck.'

'Oh,' Imogen collected herself. 'Yes, the exhibition. But only one painting was ruined. It's all going ahead.' She swallowed a mouthful of burning hot tea and made a show of looking at her watch. 'I've just remembered. I have an appointment. Must run,' and left, before anyone could see her sudden fury.

For Edwina's words had reminded her she'd had no invitation to Dan's exhibition. Was Dan deliberately shutting her out? Really? She'd thought they could still be friends. She stomped along the road back to the hotel.

'No,' she stopped. 'I'm not letting it go.' She was tired of putting up a shield, pretending her feelings were intact.

She turned into The Plough. Adam would understand.

He ushered her into his living room. 'Hey, good to see you. How are the renovation plans going?'

Imogen burst out, 'Did you have an invitation to the opening of Dan's exhibition?'

Adam said nothing for a second. That was long enough.

'You did, didn't you? How could he send one to everyone and not to me?'

'I expect,' Adam said gently, 'yours hasn't arrived yet.'

'Yet? He's cutting me out, that's what it is.' She shrugged dramatically. 'Well, if that's the way he wants it. I hope everyone hates it and he doesn't sell any paintings.'

Adam shook his head. 'You don't mean that.'

Hot tears prickled Imogen's eyes. 'Yes, I do.' She flopped into a chair. 'Of course, I don't,' she said, wiping her eyes with the back of her hand. 'I'm not that vindictive. But he's like a selfish little boy, always wanting his own way...' She broke off. Adam's eyes were twinkling. 'Don't you dare laugh. I know what you're thinking – that I do, too.' She thought for a moment. 'Anyway, it's too late in life for either of us to change. We're too set in our ways.'

Now Adam was grinning like a Cheshire Cat. 'I remember saying that about myself.'

'And now look at you and Steph.' Imogen managed a watery smile. 'I'm very glad for you, Adam. You deserve someone like her.'

'She's wonderful,' Adam said, so simply that more tears gathered behind Imogen's eyes. 'I know I don't deserve her. But love isn't about what we deserve, is it?' He grinned and pushed his glasses farther up his nose. 'Now, let me feed you coffee and cinnamon buns – fresh today, you know.'

'That will be lovely. And I won't think about Dan any more,' she said, knowing that wasn't true. 'Because I've been to see Jenny and I have news for you, about Joe...'

24

BRIAN

On Wednesday morning, Imogen woke with a light heart. Her invitation had arrived the previous day, leaving her embarrassed to think of the fuss she'd made in front of Adam. She sighed. She'd made a fool of herself so often in front of him that she'd learned to forgive herself. 'Of course,' she realised, 'the invitation came from the gallery, not Dan. It was just the post. Late, as usual.' And she'd at least managed to stop herself driving over to Dan's studio to berate him in person.

Her stomach twitched when she thought about visiting the exhibition, but she tried to ignore it. She was getting over Dan, wasn't she? She needed to move on.

How much the prospect of lunch with Brian contributed to this optimism, she wasn't sure. But there was no denying the little spurt of excitement she felt.

When Brian arrived, she felt as nervous as a teenager. He looked very dashing. He was a little taller than Dan, and there was less grey in his hair. Not that she minded grey hair in a man. It looked distinguished. Brian had dressed soberly in a jacket and tie. This was, she reminded herself, a working lunch. He was only here to discuss the finer details of the folly conversion.

They visited the site before lunch. 'It's going to look terrific,' Brian said. 'Rural, but sophisticated.'

Imogen laughed. 'I'm not sure Lower Hembrow's ready for sophisticated.'

'Well, if you're the example, I'm right.'

Imogen couldn't hide her pleasure. She'd always blushed easily, and the habit hadn't lessened as she got older. If anything, it was getting worse.

But Brian was smiling. 'Let's have a cocktail before lunch,' he suggested.

Despite the presence of the hotel staff, who seemed to be taking turns to serve Brian and casting regular surreptitious glances at their table, lunch was a pleasure. Before long, the conversation turned from the building project.

'Tell me about Lower Hembrow,' Brian said. 'You're lucky to live in such a small place. There must be a great community spirit.'

'There is. In the spring, the fair raised enough money to fix the roof of the village hall, so the playgroup can meet more often, with plenty left over to add some swings to the play area. I'd no idea how expensive a child's play area could be – what with special flooring, and non-splintering wood, and all the safety regulations – but it's great for the village children.' She realised she was babbling and stopped talking.

He topped up her glass with wine. She hesitated for a second. She didn't like drinking in the middle of the day. Still, this lunch was going so well. She felt happier than she had for days.

Brian said, 'And, what about the adults? This man who died. Joe, wasn't it? I suppose you all knew him.'

'Absolutely. He leaves a widow and six children, not to mention a farm. And farming's tough, these days. But everyone in the village is helping out. If only we knew the facts. You see, Joe was poisoned, but we don't know how. It couldn't have been the cider at the Apple Day – we were all drinking from the same barrels. But there were traces of something in his blood and we'll just have to wait for the results. Adam's friend, James, keeps us updated. He's a forensic pathologist and has a network of mates.'

Brian nodded. 'These networks. They're invaluable. Well, at least I wasn't at the Apple Day. No one can accuse me.'

'I'm sure we'll find the culprit.'

'What about this Adam you mentioned. Is he a special friend?'

'Special?' Imogen raised an eyebrow. 'It depends on what you mean by special. He's a really good friend.'

'But no romance?'

She burst out laughing. 'Not at all. Adam's head over heels in love with a friend of mine – Steph.'

'And you? Are you in love with anyone?'

She felt the telltale blush creep over her cheeks. How could she possibly answer that? 'No,' she said, emphatically.

He was smiling his lopsided smile. 'I heard you were involved with a local artist.'

'How did you hear that?'

'I have rumour channels too. It was your under-manager, Michael. He told me to watch my step.'

'The cheeky little—' Imogen laughed. 'Look, Dan Freeman – the artist – and I knew each other at school. When we met up again last year, just after my husband died, it seemed as though... well, I thought...' She stumbled to a halt.

'Ah. Old affairs. They're never the same. People change, especially when they find money and fame. I imagine this Dan is rich and successful?'

'Well, successful. And, yes, I suppose he's well off. His studio is beautiful, but he's not flashy – you'd never know he was almost a celebrity. But his work always comes first. I know whatever we had isn't going to work out.'

Brian's smile was more intoxicating than the wine. 'That's good news for me. Like you, I have no ties. No wife, no girlfriend. I've given up dating. Or at least, I had...' he let the words hang in the air and Imogen's heart raced.

At the end of lunch, he left, promising to call her soon, 'And not,' he added, 'just about the job.'

Imogen's smile lasted for the rest of the day. Perhaps it was true, after all, that when one door closed, another opened.

25

SECRETS

Adam was surprised to find Pierre on his doorstep that morning. 'Good to see you again,' he said. 'Come on in.'

Pierre really looked like his father. The same curly black hair, the same slight stoop, common to so many tall men who spend their lives bending down to talk to shorter mortals.

Moving aside a stack of novels, Pierre sat awkwardly on the comfy sofa. 'I hope you don't mind me coming.'

'Not at all.'

'It's about Dad, you see. I'm worried about him.'

Adam nodded. 'That break-in at the gallery was nasty thing to happen. Especially after—' he caught himself up. Did Pierre know about the note left in the donkeys' shelter? If not, it wasn't Adam's place to tell him.

But Pierre was talking about something else.

'The other day, Dad was showing me his work and I caught sight of a set of drawings of a woman, and Dad snapped the book shut and hid it in a drawer as though he hadn't meant me to see it. I asked him who it was, and he said "the proprietor of the hotel", as though he hardly knew her. And, I recognised the signs. Dad's hopeless with women, you see,' he grimaced. 'Runs in the family, I suppose.'

Adam smiled. 'You too? Is that why you came to England so suddenly?'

Pierre nodded. 'I needed a change. I'd been with the same girl since school, but we broke up, and she couldn't... well, she wants us to get back together, but I really don't. I thought a change of scene would help.'

Pierre's gaze was fixed on his feet. 'I know I'm going to have to tell her. But I'll sort it out. That wasn't why I came here. You see, the other day, after Dad had helped Alfie with his painting, I had a chat with Steph, and she told me Dad and Imogen Bishop had been – well, she called it 'friends' but I think she meant something more than that. You see, my mother used to talk about Imogen Jones, someone Dad was at school with, and *Maman* said he'd never got over her. Steph said that was the same woman, now called Imogen Bishop, the widow who owns the hotel. I thought you might be able to help...'

Adam held up his hand. He didn't want to gossip about Dan with the man's son.

Pierre looked up and laughed. 'Don't worry, I'm not prying into Dad's business. There's something important.'

Adam, relaxing, nodded for him to continue.

Pierre fidgeted in his chair. 'It's like this. In recent months, when I talked to him on the phone, Dad had sounded happier than he had for years, but now he's like a bear with a sore head. I wondered if I could help, because it's been hard for him since Fay's death.'

Adam's jaw dropped. 'Who's Fay?'

'I suspected you didn't know.' Pierre said, shaking his head. 'Fay was Dad's girlfriend. She died, and Dad blamed himself. Now, he thinks he's toxic to women. I've tried to talk to him and I know my mother has, but he won't listen.'

Not even a saint could let that pass. 'Now you have to tell me the whole story.'

Pierre hesitated. 'You won't tell anyone?'

'I don't think I can promise that. This isn't a confessional and I'm not a priest. If Dan's done something illegal, I'll have to act on it. I used to be a policeman, you know.'

'That's why I wanted to talk to you. You see, something terrible happened to Fay, a woman Dad was, well, I guess he was in love with her. She died and Dad got the blame.'

'A murder?' Adam half rose to his feet, dreadful suspicions crowding into his head.

Pierre waved both hands at him. 'No, no. He wasn't even there when she died. It was a car crash. I mean, literally a car crash. She was speeding and she drove her car off the road.'

'Why would that be Dan's fault?'

'They'd quarrelled, I think, and she'd been drinking. She drove off in a temper. That's all I know – Dad's never talked about it. But people said he'd caused it. Not the police – just people. And he felt guilty. Ever since then, whenever he meets a woman he likes, he quarrels with them. I think it's because he won't let himself get too close.'

Adam took off his spectacles, polishing them on a soft cloth from his pocket while he thought about that. Maybe Pierre had put his finger on something. He'd noticed, but not understood, the gradual tension building between Imogen and Dan that culminated in their brief but brutal quarrel on Apple Day. Pierre's explanation made sense.

'So, what do you want me to do?' he asked, amid the familiar sinking feeling that crept up on him when someone asked him to investigate. 'I'm retired from policing, you know.'

'But you're famous around here. You solved the murder at the hotel, and then there was the racing murder. I thought you might look into Fay's death, and maybe prove to Dad he wasn't to blame. It wasn't as though they'd even been seeing each other for very long. They'd been friends for a year or two and then got together for a couple of months. It would be great if you could put Dad's mind at rest.'

Adam groaned. 'You know, I came here for some peace and quiet, just running a country pub.' He paused. 'Let me think for a moment. I'll make coffee.'

He played with his coffee machine. He'd never make a barista, but he could produce a decent cup of medium roast. As he carried the cups to the table, his door opened.

'Hello?' Adam breathed more easily as Steph arrived. It felt like a lucky escape.

'Oops, sorry,' she said. 'I didn't know you had company.' Pierre had risen. 'You both look serious.'

Pierre looked from one to the other. 'I need to be off,' he said. 'Can we talk again, Mr Hennessy?'

'Gosh.' Steph looked startled. 'Am I interrupting business?'

'Not at all.' Pierre edged towards the door.

Adam said, 'If I'm to help you, and I'm not promising anything, Steph needs to know about it.'

Pierre sat down again. 'But no one else.'

Adam shook his head. 'Dan, of course.'

Pierre winced. 'I don't really want him to know I'm interfering, in case it comes to nothing. And definitely don't tell Imogen Bishop. Dad would murder me—' he stopped, blushing like a schoolboy. 'Sorry, that was a stupid word to use.'

Steph made herself comfortable next to Adam on the sofa, her arms folded. 'This all sounds very exciting, so I think you'd better fill me in on the details. What on earth has Dan done that you don't want Imogen to know about? And, since the two of them aren't talking anyway, I don't see that we need to tell her anything. Unless we have to later, of course.' She stopped talking. 'You know what I mean,' she finished with a grin. 'We won't make promises.'

Adam looked at her, her face animated. 'I give in,' he said. 'Tell us the whole story, Pierre, and we'll see what we can do to help.'

26

THE PAST

'It all happened years ago, when Dad was living in London,' Pierre said. 'He'd only just started to do really well. Until then, he'd earned a living by teaching in one of those expensive boarding schools. You know, the ones that rich people who live in cities send their kids to.'

Steph and Adam nodded, waiting.

'Well, he met one of the teachers at the school and they got close after a while. She taught sports science.'

Steph chuckled. 'A sports teacher? Dan?'

Pierre rewarded her with a brief smile, but soon his brows knitted together again. 'She was a nice lady. I met her, once or twice, and I thought they might be happy. Dad really enjoyed being with her. His pictures had started to sell soon after his first exhibition down here in Camilton, and the commissions began to pour in. I wondered if Dad and Fay may have talked about getting married, although he never told me. I just had a feeling, you know?'

'But something went wrong?' Adam suggested.

Pierre looked away. He seemed almost embarrassed. 'You know I told you about the drawings of Imogen Bishop?'

Adam nodded. 'I'll fill you in later,' he said to Steph.

'Well, there's a whole book of them dating right back to when Dad was at school with her.'

'I was there, too,' Steph put in.

'Really? Small world.' Pierre grinned. 'And you?' to Adam.

'No such luck.'

Steph said, 'I remember that Imogen and Dan liked each other but they never got together and Imogen went on to marry Greg. Which was a mistake, by the way – but that's another story. Get back to Dan and Fay. I've never heard anything about her.'

Pierre laughed. 'I don't expect you knew about my mother and me, either.'

'Not quite true – Dan mentioned you both, but no details.'

'Dad hates people knowing his business – any kind of business. He gives loads to the Donkey Sanctuary and other charities, but he got mad at me when I told my mother. He thinks it's boasting to tell anyone about the good things you do.'

Steph smiled. 'You're right. He brought Smash and Grab to the village Spring Fair and donated one of his pictures that paid for most of the Village Hall roof.'

Pierre flashed a grateful smile, but Adam said, 'To get back to your story...'

'I think I can guess,' Steph said. 'Fay found the drawings of Imogen and thought Dan was cheating on her.'

'That's it, in a nutshell. She was at the studio; they had a row, and she went off in a huff. Then a few days later the police called round and told Dad she'd died later that night.'

Adam had heard stories like that so many times during his police career. 'When she crashed the car,' he guessed, 'had she been drinking?'

'That was the funny thing. She'd only had one glass of wine with Dad, but after the crash, the post-mortem found she had over twice the legal level of alcohol in her system. And there was a smashed bottle of whisky in the car.'

'So, she must have bought a bottle and drunk it after her row with Dan,' Steph surmised.

'She had plenty of time. She left him at about six in the evening and, according to the police, she stayed at home for several hours before leaving again later. She had the crash just before midnight. But Dad believes it was his fault – she sat at home, drinking because she was upset. She even left a letter that said he'd let her down. He thinks he killed her.'

Adam whistled. 'No wonder he feels bad.' He caught a sharp glance from Steph. 'Not that it's his fault, of course.'

'Of course not,' Steph scoffed. 'No one could possibly blame Dan.'

Pierre heaved a long sigh. 'Well, I think someone did.'

'What? Who?' Steph demanded. 'I mean, has something happened?'

'When Dad stuffed the drawings back in his drawer at the studio, while I was there, he left a corner sticking out. He didn't notice at the time and neither did I until later. Then, out of curiosity, I took a quick look while he was in the kitchen.' He shifted, uncomfortably, in his chair. 'I didn't mean to spy on him, really, but I was curious. Dad's so secretive.'

Steph patted his hand. 'Don't worry. I'd have been on to it like a shot.'

'Just like a journalist,' Adam pointed out.

Pierre shot Steph a grateful look. 'Anyway, I looked in the drawer and saw a scrap of paper scrunched into the corner.'

He paused, biting his lips, as though reluctant to finish the story.

'Well?' Steph encouraged. 'What did it say?'

Pierre pulled out a biro and scribbled on the back of a Wine Society brochure on Adam's coffee table: SEE HOW IT F...

He swivelled the paper so both Adam and Steph could read it easily. 'The paper was torn, so I don't know what else it might have said.'

Steph's mouth dropped open. 'What does it mean?'

Pierre shrugged. 'I've no idea, but I'm guessing it says, "See how it feels." Like a threat, maybe. But I don't know where it came from.'

'I knew about it,' Adam said, relieved to find he no longer had to keep it secret, as he'd promised Dan. 'Remember, I told you Smash escaped from Dan's field and went missing for a couple of days?'

'That's right,' Steph remembered. 'He was missing on Apple Day. But what does that have to do with this?'

Pierre was frowning, 'One of the donkeys was lost? Dad never told me that.' He thumped his fist on the arm of the chair. 'And that proves I'm right. Someone's trying to frighten Dad. Or worse; to teach him a lesson.'

Adam shook his head. 'Hold on there. The note might not have anything to do with Fay's death.' Although, it was the only clue so far to Smash's mysterious disappearance.

Pierre was leaning forward, excited. 'Of course, it does.'

Steph put in, 'Someone took the donkey in revenge. But then, they brought him back?'

Adam thought for a moment, and then spoke very quietly. 'Which means, I'm afraid, that it's a warning shot. I don't think it's the end of the matter. I think that note is a threat, there's more to come and I'm beginning to worry that Dan may be in danger.'

'We need to warn him,' Steph said.

Adam said, 'I'm sure he's well aware what that note means. I know he's added extra security cameras around the studio.'

'So, we don't tell him we know?' Steph said.

'I know you're itching to help,' Adam said, 'but we need to

respect Dan's wishes. If he wanted us to know the story, he'd have told us.'

Pierre's brow furrowed. 'We can't just sit by and do nothing.'

'Certainly not,' Adam said. 'I'm not suggesting that. We do what we can. Pierre, how long are you staying?'

'I was planning to leave in a couple of weeks, but my next assignment won't begin for another month. I was thinking of travelling around the UK, but that can wait.'

'In that case, you keep an eye on him and look out for any funny business at the studio. Meanwhile...' Adam fell silent, thinking hard.

Steph said, 'We need to know more about Fay. Her family, and so on. I suppose you don't have details like those?' She looked to Pierre.

'Sorry, I don't know much about her at all.' He shrugged. 'You know Dad. All he told me was that she was an Australian who'd come to England, liked it and stayed, becoming a teacher. Nothing about Dad's feelings for her, of course.'

Steph rolled her eyes. 'Like a clam. Just like Imogen. They're the perfect pair.'

'They won't be,' Adam pointed out, 'unless we help Dan get over this tragedy. It's clear it haunts him. Although,' he shot a stern look at Pierre, 'you must understand that any facts we uncover may not help Dan. You've only heard his side of the story and it's all a bit sketchy. He may not be the innocent victim we're supposing. Finding the truth will mean the real truth, not one we choose.'

'But we'll try,' Steph insisted. 'Adam always fears the worst. Take no notice, Pierre. Remember, I've known Dan longer than you, Adam, and I trust him completely. Whatever happened to Fay, I know it wasn't his fault. But, if we don't help, he'll give up on Imogen, thinking he's some kind of toxic influence on women. And that will break her heart, no matter how she tries to pretend she doesn't care.'

Noises from the bar alerted Adam. 'The lunchtime rush is about to take off.'

'In that case,' Steph said, 'it's time to eat. My tummy's been rumbling for the last half-hour and I'm meeting Rose in the bar. She's coming in to see you, Adam. You'd forgotten, hadn't you?'

Adam, brick red, blustered a little. This would be the first time he met Steph's daughter, who was currently staying in Steph's Camilton cottage, busily applying for jobs in publishing. He'd been excited and nervous in equal measure, but Pierre's visit had pushed it right out of his head. 'Also, my old mate, James, and his wife are coming, too. They're moving into the area.'

Steph said, 'And James is a forensic pathologist and all-round useful bloke. Maybe he can help.'

Adam had an idea. 'Pierre, maybe James can help us track down the details of Fay's death. He has a web of contacts all over the country. Stay and eat with us. He loves a mystery almost as much as Steph does, although his wife's not so keen. She thinks they're coming to the countryside because James is taking early retirement. She says she's heard enough about gruesome death to last for the rest of her life and she's planning quiet daily walks on Ham Hill.'

'In that case,' Pierre observed, 'Lower Hembrow might not be the best place for them to live.'

27

ROSE

Pierre's eyes were out on stalks as Steph's daughter joined them. A student in her second year of university, Rose was a slightly taller, but otherwise easily recognisable, replica of her mother.

James Barton and his wife arrived at the same time.

'Moving day in three weeks,' James said, as Adam set a pint of Hook Norton bitter in front of him.

'And we haven't even started packing up the house,' his wife added.

James took a long drink. 'That's grand,' he said. 'And, by the way, we were right about the poison angle for your Joe Trevillian's death. There were traces of Amanitin, the toxin found in Death Cap mushrooms, in Joe's body.'

Adam nodded slowly. 'Autumn's the time for fungus. But Joe's a countryman. He wouldn't pick one by mistake, even if the Death Cap's difficult to recognise.'

'Which it is,' James agreed.

Adam's face was screwed into the frown that meant he was thinking. 'It's almost certain, then, that someone slipped it to him. And so the mystery is, how? It must have been before Joe showed up, apparently drunk, at the Apple Day because he wasn't there long enough to drink anything. No one else died – although there were a few sore heads the next day, I remember.' He nodded towards the ever-present group of young farmers.

James lowered his voice, a great effort for a man with a resonant bass-baritone. In a kind of stage whisper, he said, 'Joe could have been poisoned at any time up to a couple of weeks before his death.'

Steph nodded. 'He was already behaving oddly when he arrived. We all put it down to his being drunk, but thinking back, he could already have been feeling the effects of whatever that poison is. How does it work?'

'It killed him by destroying his liver,' James explained. 'He would have been sick and had diarrhoea when he had a first dose, but that could have improved. He probably thought it was a stomach upset and when he felt better, assumed it was all over, but all the time, his liver was deteriorating.'

'Which means,' Adam groaned, 'anyone he met in the last few weeks could have poisoned him, if not with a steak and mushroom dinner, with crumbs in his food or drink. But no one knows where he went when he left The Plough on the night he disappeared,' he added, thinking back. 'He said he was going home – but he didn't arrive.'

He went on, 'Joe came here for a drink, grumbling about his wife and mother-in-law. He calmed down, left and disappeared. That was the last anyone saw of him until Apple Day.'

'You know,' Steph said slowly, 'we've all heard the gossip about Joe being pally with Maria. He might have visited her when he left.'

'Good point,' Adam agreed. 'Which means a visit to Maria is on the cards. And, James, there's another thing.'

He glanced around, checking he couldn't be overheard.

Just then, Terry came across. 'Fancy a drink?' he said to Rose and Pierre.

'Well...' Rose hesitated.

Steph said, 'Go on. Enjoy yourself. You don't want to sit with us old folks. We just need Pierre briefly for some – er – local business.'

'I'll be over in a minute,' Pierre said to Rose. 'Save me a seat?'

James said, 'Now, what else can I do for you with my amazing sleuthing skills.'

His wife laughed. 'You mean, by asking a buddy,'

'Exactly'

'Do you know every pathologist in the country?' Steph asked.

'Just about. It's a small world.'

'And, I know you like a challenge.' Briefly, Adam explained that they were looking into a death that happened years ago. 'So, while I get more drinks in, I'll leave Pierre to fill you in on the details.'

* * *

Next day, James phoned Adam, sounding delighted with himself. 'Mission accomplished,' he said. 'I phoned the pathologist who dealt with the crash in London, and what he told me was most interesting. Apparently, the woman in question had at least twice the legal driving level of alcohol in her body. So, no wonder she crashed.'

Adam nodded. That confirmed Pierre's account.

James went on, 'And there was no evidence of anyone else being involved. She hadn't been wearing a seat belt, so when the car hit a concrete pillar sideways, she was flung half over the back seat. She finished up lying in the gap between the driver's and passenger's seats. The police did a forensic sweep of the car, and there were plenty of fingermarks, but they all matched people she knew well; Dan, her family, a bunch of her friends and a few old boyfriends that the police interviewed. They all had watertight alibis. One of the girlfriends had been out with her that morning, shopping, but no one else except Dan had seen her since lunchtime.'

'So,' Adam said, 'was Dan investigated?'

'He was, but there was no evidence against him.'

Adam was thoughtful. 'Pierre says he blamed himself for her death, but that's natural, as they'd quarrelled. If the police thought Dan had a motive, they'd have looked more closely at him, but if there's no evidence, they can't do anything.'

James agreed. 'The case, my mate tells me, is still open, but no one's working on it. It's gone cold.'

28

EXHIBITION

The exhibition at the Camilton Gallery was due to continue as planned. Henry, the gallery owner, had refused to cancel. 'Only one painting damaged,' he'd said, 'and the rest are fine. It's almost a lucky break, in fact. We'll get the insurance money – that includes you, of course, Dan. Your contract's watertight – and the publicity will be worth its weight in gold.' Every inch of his well-fed, corpulent body quivered with glee and he rubbed pudgy hands together. 'That was a great spread in the *Camilton Gazette*, especially with your son's photos of the remaining works. Brilliant idea, that.'

'I suppose you didn't set it all up?' Dan had suggested, with a smile. Henry was always on the lookout for a profit, but far too canny a businessman to risk getting on the wrong side of the law.

'I almost wish I had, but the police went over my movements with a fine-tooth comb. I think they wanted to lock me up and throw away the key. But I showed them my email to you and, luckily for me, that proved you came on the wrong date. It's a good job you're a cotton-wool-brained artist.'

Dan had defended himself. 'If I hadn't shown up the burglar could have broken into the storeroom and we might have lost the lot. Was there anything more from the police? They haven't told me much, as it happened on your premises.'

Henry had shrugged. 'They're getting nowhere – they've too many other fish to fry with this murder in Lower Hembrow.' He'd pursed his lips. 'I suppose the two aren't connected?'

'I don't see how.' Should he have mentioned Smash's disappearance and the threatening note? But neither of those things were linked to Joe's murder. Dan hardly even knew the man. The police weren't going to put precious resources into chasing someone unknown whose tricks hadn't even reached stalker level. Burglaries and mild damage to property were hardly priorities in these days of county-line drug-smuggling.

Henry had moved on. 'At least we know the burglar alarm works. Our visitor triggered it when he broke a window at the side of the building and climbed through. You wouldn't have seen it from the car park and the back door. The police are convinced it was a one-man job, as there was so little damage.'

'Just many wasted hours of work on the painting.' Dan had clicked his tongue. 'It wasn't one of the best, fortunately. Strictly commercial, to entice more owners of expensive buildings to commission house-portraits.'

'These will make you a fortune,' Henry had said. 'Rich people love to buy paintings that glorify their lifestyles. They'll be beating a path to your door.'

* * *

Dan's trusty alarm system woke him early on the day of the exhibition.

'Pierre,' he yelled. 'Get out of bed. We need to get to Camilton. I want to make sure Henry's assistant hasn't rehung any of the pictures in the wrong place. I know he was dying to move the

Haselbury House canvases into the big room and I don't want that faux-Georgian pile with its pretend Palladian pillars taking centre stage.'

Pierre grinned. 'Don't panic. The paintings of The Streamside Hotel will be front and centre – you made your feelings about that pretty clear to Henry.'

'It's a fine building,' Dan was short, but he knew Pierre was right.

They climbed into the old white van, a couple of lesser paintings in the back. 'In case,' Pierre said, 'the others all sell out – which they will – and you need replacements.'

After they'd inspected every aspect of the exhibition and Henry had insisted they'd find a space for the paintings Dan called, 'my second-rate reserves', Dan relaxed. At lunch, Henry toasted Dan with champagne. 'I'm only in this business so I can drink with the clients,' he said, his round face beaming with anticipation. 'Everyone we invited is coming, so it's going to be a great event.'

Dan wandered through the gallery, his heart in his mouth, suddenly beset by terrible foreboding. How could anyone want these mechanical, unlovely daubs? What if no one came, or the critics hated the paintings, or – and this was the part that made his breath stop in his chest – what if Imogen came and thought they were rubbish? Dan would know, from her face. She was hopeless at hiding her feelings.

Still, there was nothing more he could do. It was time for the gallery doors to open.

Adam was first to arrive. He strolled among the paintings, hands clasped behind his back, nodding, saying hardly a word. Dan followed him. His nerves were twitching, for Adam knew enough to tell good work from bad.

Finally, he approached Dan and held out his hand. 'These are amazing. You've brought your subjects alive.'

To Dan's relief, a steady stream of visitors soon followed, and the level of excitement rose as the free champagne flowed. A pleasing number of 'sold' red dots appeared on the paintings.

Pierre was thrilled. 'I'm basking in the glow of being your son,' he confessed, 'but I don't much like the look of this character.'

He nodded towards Roger Masters, the owner of Haselbury House, who was approaching fast.

Rose tapped his shoulder and Pierre's eyes lit up. 'Right, Dad,' he grinned. 'I'll see you later.'

'Well, well, not bad at all.' It was too late for Dan to avoid Masters. 'Very impressive show,' he said, unconvincingly. 'I can't afford the painting of Haselbury myself, of course – but maybe it'll go to a good home. The administrators are selling the place, you know, contents and all.' He grunted, angrily. 'For half what it's worth. And most of that will go to creditors. But then, times are hard, aren't they?' Dan felt a perverse pleasure. Imogen had told him the man had been a pest when she'd worked with him. At least he'd never get his hands on Dan's painting.

Surreptitiously, Dan sketched the faces of the visitors, enjoying the contrast between the regular art-gallery set and his friends from Lower Hembrow.

But Imogen wasn't there. Had she chickened out? Or maybe she just wasn't interested.

The earliest visitors had left, and fewer than half the canvases remained unsold, when she finally arrived. Forgetting, just for a moment, that they were estranged, Dan hurried towards her. 'Imogen? Thank you for coming.' He caught his breath at the warmth of her smile. She glowed with happiness. Was he forgiven?

'You're the artist?' A smartly dressed man appeared at Imogen's side and Dan's heart sank. This stranger, annoyingly handsome, was the cause of Imogen's good mood, then. 'Imogen tells me you're famous,' the fellow said.

Imogen, blushing, introduced Brian. The two men shook hands. Brian gripped Dan's hand in one of those strength contests Dan thought belonged in the boardroom, not in an art gallery.

'Can't stay long,' Brian said. 'We just came to see The Streamside Hotel pictures. I'm working with Imogen on redeveloping the outbuildings there.'

'I'd heard,' Dan said coolly.

'Brian's running the project on the old folly, for me.' Imogen's voice wobbled. 'We're just about to start work on the foundations.'

Dan forced himself to be polite. 'You'll be leaving the façade as it is, I hope?'

Brian waved a hand vaguely at Imogen. 'This lady has perfect taste. She won't let anything good be destroyed. But, if you'll excuse us, we'll whisk round, and I'll be off. Places to go, you know. Adam Hennessy's giving Imogen a lift home.' He turned and squeezed Imogen's arm in a warm, proprietorial gesture. Dan longed to land a punch on his self-satisfied face.

Imogen blushed. 'I want to see everything,' she said.

Resolutely refusing more champagne, Dan spent the next hour talking politely to prospective purchasers, wishing the whole business would end so he could go home. These events took so much energy – more than the painting itself. He'd love to get back to his studio, put his feet up, pour a glass of wine, if Pierre hadn't drunk it all, and think about his next steps. He'd be glad never to see the likes of Roger Masters again.

He felt a touch on his shoulder. 'Imogen?'

Her eyes glowed. 'It's wonderful. Everyone's loving your work and, what's more, they're buying it. I'm so pleased for you.'

For a moment, she was the old Imogen and Dan's heart set up a hopeful drum beat. He never should have let her go. What a fool he'd been. Maybe it wasn't too late to try again, after all?

'Has your friend left?' he asked, politely.

'Brian? Yes, he's gone up to London to see an aging parent. He's very kind to his mother.' The warmth in her voice brought Dan's hopes crashing down. This Brian was clearly more than just a contractor.

Sick at heart, Dan turned away to sweet-talk a buyer.

The guests left, at last. Pierre took Rose off to dinner in town and Adam ushered Imogen out of the gallery.

'Terrific exhibition,' Adam said. 'Coming to The Plough to celebrate?'

As Dan hesitated, his phone rang.

'Mr Freeman?' The voice sounded heavily official. 'Detective Constable Stanley here. I'm afraid there's a problem at your studio. Can you get home?'

Dan's heart lurched.

'Problem? What do you mean?' He held his breath.

'A fire, sir. I'm afraid there's some damage.'

'The donkeys?' Dan blurted out.

'Donkeys, sir? The ones in the field, you mean?'

'Yes. Two donkeys.'

'Nothing wrong with the – er – donkeys,' DC Stanley spoke slowly and clearly. 'But the building – well, I'm afraid it's been rather badly damaged, sir. You'd better come over, straight away.'

Dan raced from the gallery, pausing only to grab Henry's arm. 'Got to go. It's an emergency.'

* * *

Imogen and Adam were already outside, chatting happily. Imogen was half in, half out of the car as Dan appeared at a run.

She turned. 'What's the matter?'

But Dan just jumped in the white van, revved the engine and screeched on two wheels down the road.

'Get in,' Adam said, and Imogen obeyed. In seconds, they were speeding after Dan. 'Something's wrong,' he said.

'You think?' Imogen breathed, pressed forward against her seat belt as though that would make the car go faster.

They shot along the main road, keeping Dan's tail lights in sight and following as he turned onto the narrow lanes leading to Ford. 'He's going home.'

Finally, they followed the van into the lane leading down to the studio.

Imogen sniffed the air that filtered into the car, and coughed. 'I smell smoke.'

'And no one else lives down this lane.' Adam spoke grimly.

They turned the last corner to a scene of chaos.

Smoke billowed around the building, shrouding the fire engine parked across the entrance to Dan's studio in a grey haze. A fire hose pumped water from the vehicle towards the house, where a side section had collapsed in a pile of bricks and charred wooden beams. A single tongue of flame spurted up from the scorched remains, crackling wickedly. The firefighter holding the business end of the hose aimed a torrent of water into the heart of the inferno. Steam and smoke hissed, disappearing into the blackness of the sky as the flame flickered and died.

Adam drew up alongside Dan's van, as Dan slammed the door and sprinted towards the house.

A huge yellow-coated firefighter stuck out his hand, stopping him in his tracks. 'Sorry, sir. It's not safe. Is anyone in there?'

Dan shook his head. 'No one.'

Silently, Imogen and Adam joined him, gaping at the sight.

'Best check, anyway.' One of the team, in full breathing kit, strode through the ruined front door into the wreckage of the studio.

After moments that seemed like hours, he emerged and pulled off his helmet.

'Clear,' he shouted.

Pungent smoke polluted the air.

Dan turned and ran through the gate and across the paddock.

'Smash and Grab,' Imogen gasped, and charged after him, arriving just as he emerged from the shelter. 'They're safe,' he said, tersely. 'They're upset, but they'll be fine. The smoke didn't reach the shelter.'

'Oh.' Imogen stood, aghast. Dan's face was chalk-white, his eyes as deep and dark as coalmines.

'But it looks as though the studio's gone.' He pointed and Imogen turned to look at the right side of the house. Dan's treasured studio was ruined.

Imogen stepped towards him, her arms out. 'I'm so sorry,' she murmured into his shoulder.

Gently, he took her arms and set her aside. 'I need to see the damage.'

'You won't be able to go inside. It's not safe.' She drew a breath that ended in a sob. 'All your work.'

He smiled, a ghostly caricature. 'Most of it's at the gallery.'

'But, the easels and paints and things? Even if the fire didn't get everything, the water will ruin it.'

He shrugged. 'They're just things. Replaceable. No one's hurt.' He groaned. 'Except for my sketchbooks in the drawers. Years of work, there, all spoiled.'

'They may be okay,' Imogen said, longing to help but not knowing what to say. No sheets of paper could possibly have survived the fire. 'When it's safe, we can go and look.'

Dan's shoulders lifted in a hopeless shrug and he moved away, towards the wreckage of his lovely home.

Imogen turned at a touch in the small of her back.

Grab had ventured out of the shelter, looking for company.

Imogen felt in her pockets. 'I'm sorry, Grab. I haven't anything for you.' Since she'd stopped coming to see Dan, she no longer filled her pockets with treats. She buried her face in the softness of the donkey's neck. 'What will he do, Grab?'

A leaden weight seemed to fall on her shoulders. He'd go. He wouldn't stick around after this. Smash had been stolen, one of his paintings destroyed, and now the studio was wrecked. Slowly, reality sank in and Imogen straightened up. This was no accident. Dan was careful, he never left lights on or the stove alight. Someone had set fire to his beloved studio. Deliberately.

Sick to her stomach, she gave Grab a final scratch behind the ears and traipsed after Dan, back to the house. He stood beside Adam on sodden ground, gazing gloomily ahead.

A car screeched to a halt. Adam turned, 'Steph? And Rose?'

Dan looked, 'And Pierre.'

Dan and his son talked with one of the firefighters. The sky was dark, but Imogen could see Pierre's face clearly as it turned from a bright red flush, paling to ghostly white with shock. He took his father's arm.

'There's nothing we can do here, until it's light tomorrow,' he said.

The firefighter agreed. 'We'll just secure the place where we can. No point in inviting burglars,' he said.

Imogen, Adam and Steph stood in a tight group as the others joined them. 'Come to the hotel, both of you,' Imogen said to Dan and Pierre. 'Stay as long as you like.'

29

CONFESSION

Next morning, Adam phoned Imogen. 'I'm paying a visit to our friend, Maria,' he said. 'Will you come?'

'I certainly will. Half the village suspects Joe was having an affair with her.'

'Have you spoken to Dan this morning?' Adam asked, as they walked through the village.

'I saw him having breakfast with Pierre,' she said. 'He looked terrible, but – well, he didn't say much. Pierre told me they're going back to the studio today, to see what they can salvage from the fire.'

Adam took a breath. It was way past time Imogen knew about all Dan's troubles, in his opinion, and it was clear that Dan wasn't telling her everything.

At the news of the threatening note, she looked near to tears. 'I wish I'd known,' she muttered. 'I wasn't at all sympathetic about Smash – and then, his ruined painting, and this terrible fire. What a mess it all is. If only—' she stopped abruptly.

Adam suspected she was thinking about their relationship. Was it too late for them to sort out their differences? He wondered what Steph would think.

'We do have one lead,' he said, and told her about Fay's death. 'I'll be talking to James' friend in a couple of days. I'm hoping he'll shed a little more light on it.'

They knocked at the door of Maria's small, thatched cottage situated at the end of a terrace, near the shop, 'Just a moment, my darlinks,' she called. Imogen, despite the horror etched on her face at the news of Dan's woes, managed a tiny smile. Only Maria pronounced 'darlings' as 'darlinks'.

Maria's heels clacked smartly on the wood floor and in a second, the door flew open. 'My dear Adam and Imogen, I saw you coming and hoped you would visit me. No one seems to come near, these days.'

Despite the four-inch stilettos, Maria's customary footwear, she looked a little less glamorous than usual. Adam couldn't pinpoint the difference. Then Maria patted her hair. It was wet and pulled back into some kind of bun affair on top of her head, and she wore no make-up. Was she suffering a little from Joe's death? Had there really been something between those two?

'I was just coming out of the shower,' Maria explained, with a touch of defiance. 'I have lunch with a friend in an hour.'

Imogen, walking into the tiny front room, said, 'We don't want to hold you up. Are you coming to The Plough?'

Maria hesitated. 'Not today, I'm afraid. Are you missing me, perhaps? I will call in this evening.' She peered at Adam. 'Have you heard about the fire, over at Daniel Freeman's place? Such a shock. I hear the poor man's moved into the hotel, now.' A spark of her usual wicked spirit flickered in her eyes as she glanced at Imogen. 'With you.'

Imogen said, 'His son's staying there as well.'

'But we wanted to talk to you about Joe.' Adam returned to the point. 'The other day Terry and his mates were talking in The Plough and they said Joe was selling off some of his land. Now, we know you're friendly with Jenny Trevillian. She sings in the choir with you.' In fact, Adam had never seen Maria waste her time chatting with Jenny – her target had always been Joe – or, indeed, any other man in the vicinity.

But his approach worked.

Maria heaved an enormous sigh and pressed her hand to her heart. 'My heart breaks for Jenny,' she said. 'A widow, like me. And with all those children. How many she has to care for. It's no wonder Joe never had money to spare.'

For Maria, the love of money held second place to her enjoyment of men's admiration. Sometimes, Adam suspected, it took the lead. He'd never seen a penny of the money he'd lent her when she was new to the village.

Imogen smiled. 'I know that you and Joe had a special bond, as well.' Somehow, she made Maria's blatant man-hunting sound romantic.

Maria sank gracefully into a chair. 'We were soulmates,' she sounded like a tragic heroine. 'I adore Jenny, but she doesn't – didn't – understand Joe. A man does, after all, have appetites.'

Imogen smiled, warmly. 'And were you on his menu?'

Adam blinked, expecting a blast of anger, but Maria gave a tinkly laugh. 'We were very good friends,' she said. 'I comforted him when he was distressed.'

'And,' Adam said, 'that included having him in your house, when he left Jenny.'

'Oh,' Maria gave a little squeak. 'No, no, I mean...' she looked from Imogen to Adam. 'I mean...'

'No point in denying it,' Adam said. 'His wife used her phone to track him.'

Maria fanned a hand in front of her face, gave a little wriggle and sat up straight. 'Well, you've uncovered our little secret. Joe and I were, as I've said, very good friends. When he was at the end of his tether, he came here for comfort.' She broke off, 'Jenny is not a very comfortable lady, is she?'

Adam kept his voice steady. 'She was his wife.'

Imogen joined in, 'Didn't you feel the least bit bad – stealing her husband?'

'Oh, my dear. I wasn't stealing him. No, no. I just borrowed him now and again.'

As Imogen raised her eyes to the ceiling, Adam said, 'We're not here to judge. But we want to know how you kept him out of sight for a week, until he returned to Lower Hembrow on Apple Day.'

Maria gave a tinkly laugh. 'No, you have it all wrong. You see, Joe and I were – er –friends for a long time, but we no longer needed to...' she stopped, one hand poised delicately in the air. 'To – you know...'

Imogen said, 'You mean you were no longer his mistress?'

Maria shrugged. 'When I said we were just friends, I was telling the truth. No, his, er, needs were met elsewhere.'

'So, he didn't stay here, in your cottage,' Adam said, trying to make sense of this tangle. 'He left that night. Tell us where he went. It's important.'

Maria's lips were set in a thin line.

'Unless you want to be blamed for his murder,' Adam pressed.

'Do come on,' Imogen said, impatiently.

'Oh, very well,' Maria said. 'I promised Joe I wouldn't tell, but, I suppose, now he's gone...' and for the first time, a shadow crossed her face.

She does care, Adam thought. Despite all the drama. His voice was softer as he said, 'You can tell us, now.'

Maria's head went up and she tucked a strand of hair behind one ear. 'Her name is Christine Brennan. She lives in Camilton. I don't know the address. I never met her.'

'We can track her down. But we need you to tell us what happened, that night.'

'Joe came here from The Plough. He was furious with Jenny – they'd been quarrelling about money. You see—'

'We'll come to that in a moment,' Adam said. 'What happened here?'

'I told Joe I'd finished with him.' She shrugged. 'I know, it sounds bad, but he hadn't wanted me for months. He just used me when he wanted to get away from home, and I'd had enough of that. I told him to get over to his fancy woman.' She pulled out a tiny lace handkerchief and raised it to her eyes. 'We had words,' she said, and dabbed at her eyes, 'and he went.' She swallowed. 'But he left his phone.'

They were getting to the truth at last. Adam let out a long breath as she went on.

'He'd always been careful before, leaving his phone at home. But he used it to call Christine,' she spat the name angrily, 'he asked her to come and fetch him – meet him up by the Church so no one saw – and he dropped the phone under my table when he left. He was rather angry with me, I'm afraid. He left in a hurry.'

'Two domestic arguments in one night,' Imogen whispered in Adam's ear.

Adam said, 'So you got rid of the phone?'

'I took out the – what do you call it? – the SIM card, crushed it and threw the phone into the rubbish. I didn't want his wife on my doorstep, making a scene.'

Adam hid a wry smile. Maria enjoyed scenes – but only the ones she manufactured herself.

After a long pause, Adam changed the subject, satisfied with Maria's account. 'We heard Joe was in financial trouble,' he began. 'Did you know about that?'

'Ah yes, but he had a plan.' Maria's face cleared and she tucked the handkerchief back into a pocket, suddenly pleased with herself. 'I suggested it to him. He had land to sell and he wanted his mother-in-law to buy it back. The farm had been in her family, you know, but she wouldn't agree. So, I suggested a better idea.' She leaned confidentially towards Adam and Imogen, her eyes bright. 'I introduced him to my friend, Roger, at Haselbury House, who was looking for land to buy.'

'What was he going to do with it?'

Maria swallowed. 'I don't know if I should say any more...'

'You can't stop now,' Imogen said.

Adam nodded. 'Joe's dead, don't forget, and his killer's still free. You owe it to him to tell us about this deal. It may be important.'

Maria looked from one of her visitors to the other, her eyes narrowed. 'I introduced them.' She dropped her gaze, and squirmed in her chair, her cheeks turning pink. 'Roger Masters talked about rearing thousands of chickens. He was going to build some enormous henhouses. He says the market for poultry is huge and growing bigger by the week. He had links with supermarkets, you see.'

Imogen was aghast. 'But that would mean using prime dairy land; the Trevillians have their herd of pedigree Jerseys on there. I bet Joe didn't tell his wife what he was up to and it's a terrible idea. For one thing, big chicken factories are the worst polluters of waterways in the country.'

'According to talk in The Plough,' Adam said, 'purebred cattle are unprofitable, these days. Vegans won't eat meat at all, and plenty of folk have turned away from cows' milk products. They prefer oat milk, now. Joe could sell the land to Roger at a huge profit, sell the Jerseys, pay off High Acres' debts and get his family back on their feet.'

Maria tossed her head. 'But, in any case, the deal fell through. Haselbury House went out of business before Roger could buy the land. Poor Joe was at his wit's end just before he died, not knowing where to turn next.' She rose majestically to her feet. 'And now, I don't want to be rude, but I have to dry my hair and put on my make-up.'

As she left with Adam, Imogen said, 'So, there was some shady deal going on behind Jenny's back. Joe was seeing Maria and this woman, Christine, but it sounds as though money's a more likely motive for his murder. He was trying to make some by selling off the farm's best pasture, and Roger Masters wanted to cram in thousands of chickens for a quick profit. I hate the sound of that. And if Haselbury House hadn't gone broke, the plan would probably have gone ahead.'

Adam nodded. 'I think we need to pay a visit to Haselbury House in the next few days – before it's sold and Masters disappears.'

30

HOTEL

'I need a word with you,' Dan said, grabbing Pierre's arm as he headed out to the hotel garden, Harley bouncing happily in his wake.

Pierre had the grace to blush. 'I promised to play with Harley,'

Despite the gloom in his heart at the loss of his home, Dan managed a laugh. 'You promised who? Harley?'

'Yeah, look at him. He wants attention. And I want to take photographs.'

Dan waved an arm in a gesture that encompassed the hotel and its grounds. 'And he doesn't get enough fuss from all the staff and visitors who play with him? He's the most popular dog in Somerset.' Dan caught sight of his son's grin, realised he was being led down a rabbit hole in his son's attempt to cheer him up, and changed tack. 'We can talk and throw sticks at the same time, can't we?' he said.

Pierre nodded, 'Come on, then. Let's go.'

The air in the garden felt sharp, an autumn breeze blowing gold and red leaves from the trees, so they swirled in circles on the grass. The local weather forecast predicted a gale later that day.

'Isn't this wonderful?' Pierre said, kneeling to take shots of

Harley. 'I mean, it's dreadful about your place, but the insurance will cover the fire, and you can rebuild. It's a good job we both had our laptops with us and your paintings were all at the gallery. And this is a seriously comfortable hotel. No wonder there are all those celebrity photos in the foyer.'

Dan turned away. Pierre was right – or he would be, if the studio wasn't the one place Dan had poured his heart and soul into, that had been, and still was, his haven, where he lost himself in art and forgot the mess he'd made of his life. He even, sometimes, managed to put his past out of his mind; his broken marriage, Fay, who'd died because of him, and Imogen who he'd loved all his life and, finally, through his own stupidity, lost.

'Hey, Dad,' Pierre's voice cut into his gloom. 'Sorry. That sounded a bit... callous, maybe?'

Dan turned back. 'Just a bit. But you're right, in principle. It's just – well, it's my home, you know, that's been destroyed. It's where the heart is, as they say.' He struggled to keep his voice level.

'When I was a kid,' Pierre said, looking through the camera lens at Harley running towards them, carrying two sticks in his mouth at once, 'you told me people are more important than places, and so it didn't matter that you were in England while I was in France.' Dan looked at his son's face. Pierre was no longer joking. 'And you were right. My friends envied me. Most of them came from families who stayed together, bickering and having French *affaires*, but when you came to see us in France, we all had a great time. I could never sleep the night before you arrived. It was like Christmas. And I don't mean because you brought presents – although they were very welcome.' Pierre chuckled, good humour resurfacing, 'Even *Maman* enjoyed your visits. She said she needed a dose of your English *sangfroid*. Which means "cold blood" of course, but she meant it as a compliment. It put all the arm-waving, duplicitous French husbands into perspective. She said you were too honest and authentic for the two of you to stay together.'

Dan, taken aback, dropped the stick he'd taken from Harley. He'd always thought Elise despised him for leaving. He grinned at his son. 'Thank you for that. But now, I want to know why you told Adam Hennessy about my past. He confessed he'd heard all about it.'

Pierre, with a shrug and a roll of the eyes, said, 'I told him because he wants to help you and he's a detective. I know you wouldn't ask him for help yourself, and I think you're wrong.'

'You do?'

'I do.'

Dan let that sink in. 'Advice from my son – that's something I never expected.'

The tension broke. Pierre said, 'Face it, Dad, I'm an adult, and you're an ageing Brit with a stiff upper lip. And I need to get on with these photos. An English autumn light beats any other I know. Hey, I have an idea...'

'I haven't forgiven you, no matter what good ideas you have.'

'I can live with that. But you see the folly over there, near the boundary?'

'Yes,' Dan's response was guarded. What was Pierre up to?

'You know that's where Imogen's planning to have her craft studios?' Dan nodded cautiously, wondering where this was going.

Pierre grinned, just as he used to when he was a cheeky boy, playing *Maman* off against his father during Dan's visits to France. 'What if I take some photos, do a kind of "Work in Progress" series? If I send a few to a local magazine – you know, that *Country Life*-type publication – I might get a commission. There's plenty of interest in The Streamside Hotel. I can sell a great story.' He counted on his fingers. 'It was taken over last year after the sudden death of a local councillor, there was a murder in the grounds, the brand-new high-end gardens opened – and now there's been another murder in the same village as the hotel. It's all terrible, but irresistible.'

Dan nodded. 'Maybe you should collaborate with Steph Aldred,' he suggested. 'She did a feature before Apple Day – that was before Joe's death, of course.'

Pierre's eyes gleamed. 'Ah yes, Rose's mother. Brilliant idea, Dad. If Steph could interest the nationals as well, maybe I could get a big enough commission to stick around for a while. I might even stop scrounging off you. Just think of the publicity for the hotel. Someone should make a film about it all.'

Dan rubbed his chin, infected by Pierre's enthusiasm. 'For now, let's start with your photos. And don't forget, Joe was a local. Everyone knew him. And his children are heartbroken. Try not to treat the tragedy as a photo op.'

Imogen intercepted Dan as he headed back towards his room in the hotel. 'I wanted to catch you alone,' she said.

He stopped, turned, and smiled, but his eyes were troubled. 'Here I am. And thank you for taking me in. I'd be on the streets, otherwise.'

Embarrassed, she laughed. 'What nonsense. But I wanted to help.'

'Well, I'm grateful. What can I do to earn my keep? I mean...' he reddened. 'I'll pay my way, of course. I just meant can I help you at all? Do you need a waiter?'

'I'm not going to take advantage of you, Dan.' She steeled herself. 'I'm sorry I was unreasonable that day – Apple Day – when you were late. I was selfish and thoughtless and I wish I'd known about Smash. I didn't listen.'

He shrugged. 'No problem.'

There was a long pause. Imogen bit her lip. Was this really the sad end of their relationship? Her heart trembled at the thought.

She was about to explain that she knew about the note, and about Fay's death, but Dan spoke first. 'I'll be out most of today – the insurers are coming to the studio and I'll need to show them around. Depending on what they offer, I'll decide whether to rebuild. And I have unfinished business. I need to know who's after me.'

'Any ideas?'

'Just the note, so far, left when Smash was taken. The gallery burglary could be a whole separate thing, aimed at Henry, not me, but destroying my home was meant to hurt. The firefighters think the blaze was started with a firebomb, thrown through a window. With all the new security cameras, I may get a look at the culprit, although I imagine he'll be well hoodied up. But a glimpse of a car would be something. I'll be looking at the footage today, at the police station.'

'I wish I could help.'

He shrugged. 'There's nothing for you to do. The police are involved now.'

Was that all he was going to say? Clearly, he didn't trust her. Well, that told her all she needed to know.

She shot a glance at her watch.

He grinned, although the smile didn't reach his eyes. 'Busy day for you, too?'

'The consultant wanted to meet about the craft studios.' She could put Brian off if Dan needed her.

'Good for you,' Dan said. 'You're making a great success of this place.' He took her hand. 'I'll always be rooting for you, you know.'

He let go and Imogen's hand fell to her side. 'Thank you...' She couldn't say more. Her chest hurt too much. She turned away before Dan could see her tears welling up, but she felt his eyes on her back as she scurried into the office. Emily was busy elsewhere in the hotel, so she could spend a few minutes alone, gaining control of herself.

Her coffee grew cold as she sat, thinking.

Finally, she reached for her phone. She tapped in a number and waited, barely breathing, until it was answered.

'Brian,' she said. 'I find I'm free today, after all.'

31

LUNCH

For an hour or so, Imogen and Brian clung to the pretence that today's meeting was essential to the craft studio project. They pored over the plans in a business-like way and strode into the garden, muffled in hats and gloves. 'I've worn my thickest socks,' Brian said.

'Harley,' Imogen called. 'Are you coming out?'

Harley stood, head on one side as though considering his options, but just then Michael, the deputy manager, crossed the foyer. Harley grinned as only a happy, healthy dog could grin and bounded across to beg in front of Michael.

'Doesn't he like the cold?' Brian asked,

Imogen laughed. 'Michael's his new best friend. He's been teaching him tricks. There's an agility course just behind those trees over there and Harley's brilliant at it. Next year, we're going to enter him in the county show. Also,' she chuckled, 'it uses up his energy.'

Brian looked relieved. She could see he was no dog lover, but nobody was perfect.

They strolled towards the river. 'This hotel's in a lovely place,' Brian said. 'The gardens are spectacular.' He pointed at the bench by the river. 'What's the plaque for? A memorial?'

Imogen hesitated. She hated telling the story.

'It's all right. I don't want to be nosy,' Brian said.

'Nonsense. I'm being silly. You see, we had an orangery here and my husband died in it. I'm sure you've heard the story. Everyone in Somerset knows it.'

'But I'm not local. I'm from London.'

'So, what are you doing down here?'

'It's restful,' he said. 'I was tired of packed tube trains and crowded streets. I have no ties in this country so I can live where I like, and I chose Somerset. The company I work for have a branch of the business near here.'

'Good choice,' Imogen said. 'And, to answer your question about the bench – my husband was murdered, and I couldn't bear to see the orangery every day, so I had it removed. The plaque is for him. We'd grown apart, but he still deserves to be remembered.'

'I'm sorry,' Brian said. He turned and his eyes were warm on her face. 'That must have been terrible for you.'

'It was, but it's over, now. And I reconnected with some old friends over it all. And found new ones. So I have Greg to thank for that.'

'Friends like that odd little sleuth over the road?'

She laughed, 'Adam? He's the brother I never had.' Brian seemed to be checking she wasn't romantically involved. 'See, you do know a bit about the area,' she said, covering her sudden confusion.

'I have a distant cousin living nearby. We don't really get on – he thinks I'm a stuck-up townie.'

'With a nice clean Barbour jacket,' Imogen teased.

'True. I bought it after my last visit here – I was chilled to the bone.'

'It will wear in. It'll soon be as crumpled and muddy as the others around here,' Imogen said, 'and you'll look like a local. But it's almost lunchtime. Shall we have something to eat?'

'How about going somewhere away from the hotel? No prying eyes?'

Imogen's heart was pumping. 'Well – yes, why not?'

'And not The Plough, where your friend will be watching our every move. How about climbing up Ham Hill? There must be a superb view up there, and I hear the pub at the top is great.'

* * *

After a thoroughly satisfactory lunch in the Ham Hill pub, Imogen insisted on returning to the hotel.

Brian said, 'No need to worry about the craft studio project. The planning's all done and the contractors will be rolling in next week. Wednesday, I told them. Let's get Bonfire Night out of the way. Will you have a display here?'

'No way,' Imogen said. 'I hate fireworks and so does Harley, and the hotel's run more than enough events this year. But there will be a big bonfire and firework display nearby at the village hall. I'll show up for jacket potatoes and baked beans once the noises stop.'

'You know, you could give Harley a sedative.'

'I will, but I want to be with him. And he can listen to Classic FM. They have a special programme of soothing music for animals.'

'Seriously?'

She nodded. 'It works, as well.'

'Is anyone welcome to the event?'

'Of course, if you really want to come. I mean, people will have a good time, but I think it will be low-key this year. It's so soon after Joe Trevillian's death. We haven't even had the funeral yet as the body hasn't been released. Local people dialled down some of the worst of Hallowe'en the other night – you know, the ghoulies and ghosties stuff – out of respect for Joe. Although we still had every single child in the village calling at the hotel, begging sweets for Trick or Treat.'

'It's a ghastly time, between someone dying and the funeral. Like a limbo.'

'Exactly.' She shivered. He looked grim. Had he lost family recently? 'Is your family still around?' she asked.

'I've been alone in the world for years,' he said, brightening up. 'I only have to think of myself.'

'Me too.'

'Apart from your dog.'

As they left the pub, she shivered. 'It's getting colder, I think we're in for a hard winter. Oswald says so.'

'Your trusty old gardener?'

'You know him?'

'Not really. I've heard about him. Quite the aging retainer, isn't he?'

As they walked, Brian put his arm lightly around her shoulders. Imogen couldn't resist snuggling into his body.

'Is there,' he asked, 'any reason why I shouldn't ask you out properly? You know, apart from you being the boss, and all.'

'Hardly your boss. You consult for your company. We can do what we like.'

'In that case,' he said, pulling her closer, 'may I formally ask you to dinner next week?'

His face and its lopsided grin filled Imogen's vision. She could even see the tiny lines around his eyes. 'That would be lovely,' she said. It was such a relief to be with someone so uncomplicated. She pushed away the image of last night's fire and Dan's stricken face. It was time for a new beginning.

32

HASELBURY HOUSE

'Look, we're almost there,' Imogen said the next day, as Adam drove them towards Haselbury House. 'And we haven't yet decided how to approach Masters about his links with Joe.'

'I think we need to frighten the socks off him,' Adam said grimly, pulling up in the car park.

They climbed out and walked through the deserted, now-defunct ticket office. No more visitors here for a while. 'I suppose Masters will be moving out soon,' Imogen said.

Adam took a moment to admire what he could see of the grounds. 'You did a good job here. The gardens look beautiful.'

'I was glad when the project finished, to be honest,' Imogen said. 'I started it before I inherited the hotel and my head was spinning while I was working on it. And working with Mr Shady didn't help. He gave me the shivers. I'm sorry to hear of anyone going broke, but it couldn't happen to a more deserving man.' She looked up. 'And here he is.'

'Imogen, good to see you again,' Roger Masters said, with a perfunctory handshake. 'Who's this you've brought with you?' His smile reached nowhere near his eyes. 'I was surprised to get your message, but you're welcome, of course. You saved Apple Day when we had to pull out. Family emergency, I'm afraid.'

'That was such a shame,' Imogen said innocently. Surely, he was aware everyone knew his business had failed because of bad management. 'But your planning made everything work. We just supplied the space and everything transferred. I'm sorry to hear you're leaving the area. I hope your family are well.'

'Storm in a teacup,' he said. 'The wife and I are going back up to Leeds to get away from all these cold-blooded Southerners – present company excepted, of course.' He folded his arms. 'Now, what can I do for you? I can't give you much time. It's moving day tomorrow.'

Masters shifted from one leg to the other, darting quick glances at Adam and looking away.

Adam said, 'It must be difficult for you, leaving your home. We won't keep you long, but Joe Trevillian was a friend of ours and we need to see if you can help us. We heard you had some kind of a business deal going on.'

Masters frowned.

Adam continued, 'You probably know he disappeared for a few days before he died, and we've been trying to find out where he went. Maria Rostropova said you might have an idea. She said Joe was planning to sell some land to you.'

'Yes, he approached me wanting to sell, but it all fell through.'

'Did Joe back out?'

The man's lips were a thin line and Imogen could see droplets of sweat on his forehead. He didn't like this line of questioning.

Adam pressed harder. 'You were planning some development, I believe?'

'Maria told you that, did she? Hah. She would. That lady, I'm afraid, has a big mouth, and she seems to be determined to drop me in it.' He took a step towards Adam. 'I know perfectly well who you are, by the way. You're the local do-gooder, ex-policeman, fighting crime because the idiot police couldn't find their way out of a paper bag.' He folded his arms across his chest. 'I've given you enough time, if that's what you came to say. You can get off my land, now. It's still mine until tomorrow.' He pointed a finger in Adam's face. 'And hear this. Joe Trevillian and I had no deal, nothing on paper, and the local planners gave me the run-around for so long, all the deals on the table fell through. I've lost my livelihood as a result, gone bankrupt, can't start another business and the wife won't talk to me. Satisfied?' His piggy eyes squinted at Imogen. 'So, you can both turn around and leave, or I'll be fetching my old shotgun before the administrators for the business sell that as well.'

'You don't know anything about Joe's death?' Imogen asked, deliberately turning the knife.

'Just clear off. I've talked to the police and they're satisfied I had nothing to do with it. You can look elsewhere for someone to blame. Maybe start with that wife of Joe's, always on his back, moaning. Poor man was just trying to keep her sweet and look what happens. I wouldn't mind betting she topped him herself.' He turned away, shouting over his shoulder, 'And now, Mrs Bishop, get yourself and this interfering specky four-eyes off my land.'

33

JOE

On Monday morning, Adam called in at the hotel soon after the breakfast rush had ended, just as Imogen crossed the foyer. 'Hey, I hoped I'd catch you again. I forgot to ask about your building project,' he said.

She blushed. 'Brian says the council are willing to move fast, as the old planning permissions my father drew up are still in place and they don't anticipate opposition to the studios from local residents. It's not as though we'll be putting anyone out of business. So, he's busy getting the contractors geared up.'

Harley, catching sight of Adam, dashed across, tail aloft, excited to see one of his favourite people.

'Hello, old fellow.' Adam fed him a treat.

'Do you know, I believe he still loves you best,' Imogen complained. 'Even though everyone here makes a fuss of him.'

'He's a fine animal, for a dog,' Adam said, mischievously. 'And does Brian like dogs?'

The blush deepened. 'Well, he says he likes Harley, although Harley's not so sure. He growled at him the other day. Brian's a bit of a townie and I think he's nervous of animals.'

Adam burst out laughing. 'Well, he's come to the wrong part of the world, although I can't blame him. I felt like that when I first arrived. In his case, I suspect it's the human company that attracts him.'

'Well, he does get on well with Emily – what? Why are you laughing?'

'You know perfectly well Brian makes twice the number of visits here he needs for the project, and Emily isn't the attraction.'

'I don't know what you mean.'

'Just don't let Dan see him around.'

Her smile faded. 'Nonsense. Dan and I are friendly again, I'm pleased to say, and that's all. He's too... too busy with this horrible business of the fire, and the donkey, and the threat. He's renting a cottage on the edge of the village. It has a small paddock and Pierre's helping him move over there today. He had to hire a horsebox for the donkeys.'

'Does he need our help?'

She shook her head. 'You mean, about the fire? I asked, but he's leaving it to the police. They've been very helpful...' her voice faded away at the look on Adam's face.

He said, 'They'll do their best. But we need to keep a lookout. Whoever's been targeting Dan is getting dangerous.'

'They haven't attacked him. Just his home,' she argued.

Adam wagged his finger at her, his eyes flashing fiercely behind his glasses. 'They know how to hurt him most – his donkeys, his paintings and his home. And the fire's a pretty drastic escalation. The perpetrator's getting more successful and more vicious. It's a worrying sign.'

Imogen bit her lower lip, frowning. 'At least Dan and Pierre are staying in the village. It's safe here. People watch out for each other.'

'Relatively safe, I suppose,' Adam conceded. 'I'm just saying, Dan should take care. Until we know exactly what's behind this vile campaign, we don't know what might happen next. We're guessing it has some connection to Fay, but we don't know for sure.'

She shook her head, stubbornly. 'You're overreacting. Nobody's been hurt. The donkey arrived home safely, the painting at the gallery was vandalised while the place was empty, and Dan's home was attacked while he was out.'

He left it there. 'Tell Dan to take care, anyway. Now, I dropped in because I'm hoping you'll help me out.'

'Any time.' Imogen looked relieved that he'd changed the subject.

'Will you come and visit Jenny one more time with me? I've had an idea about Joe.'

Her eyes lit up. 'You have? Brilliant. With all this worry about Dan, I'd almost forgotten about poor Joe. Just give me a minute to talk to Emily – we've some VIPs coming in tonight so I need to be sure everything will be running smoothly. Not that she needs my input, really. She ran this place alone when my father died, and she's taught me most of the little I know. Still, we like to pretend I'm in charge.'

Adam hid his worried frown as she left.

* * *

Jenny was at home alone when Imogen and Adam arrived. Adam nodded at her in approval as she opened the door, dressed this time in clean jeans and a neatly pressed blouse. It looked as though she was keeping her promise to stay sober.

'I'm going to an AA meeting in Camilton, in a couple of hours,' she said, confirming it.

'Good for you.'

Jenny smiled shyly and Adam caught a glimpse of the attractive young woman she used to be.

'Everyone's been very helpful,' Jenny went on. 'Helen's been wonderful, and you, too, Imogen, and, well, everyone, really.' She led them through.

Adam looked around. The living room was spotlessly tidy.

'Are the children all at school?' Imogen asked.

'Even Harriet – she's at nursery – and Hermione,' Jenny said. 'In fact, Hermione's been such a help since that day you were here. But she misses her dad terribly. I think he was closest to her.' Tears welled in her eyes. 'Oh, dear, I'm sorry,'

'No, not at all,' Imogen said. 'It's very hard for you.'

'I wish I'd been kinder to Joe,' Jenny confessed, sitting and waving the visitors to the sofa. 'I took him for granted, you know. I wish he could come back, just for a while, so I could tell him that I... that I loved him. Despite everything...' She wiped her eyes and sat up straighter. 'And I haven't even offered you a cup of tea...'

Adam shook his head. 'Don't you worry about that. You're on your way out and we don't want to hold you up, but I need to ask you something about Joe.'

'I won't say a word against him,' she said, suddenly fierce. 'I did enough of that when he was alive. Maybe if I'd been more understanding, he would have stayed...'

Imogen started to say, 'I'm sure he knew how you felt,' but Adam broke in.

'That's what I wanted to ask. You see, I know this is hard for you, Jenny, but if we're going to find the truth, I have to ask some awkward questions.'

Jenny nodded, her lips set in a straight line.

Adam continued, 'is it true you had a quarrel, that evening he left?'

She started to shake her head, but Adam held up a warning finger.

'No one's judging you or him. We just need to know.'

Jenny's gaze drifted from Imogen to Adam, avoiding their eyes. 'We did have a... a bit of a barney, yes, but we often did. You know that?' she turned to appeal to Imogen.

Imogen stayed silent. Adam had a reason for his questions. When he was interested in a case, there was no mistaking his experience as a detective. He knew how to get the answers he needed and he clearly had something in mind now.

'Who was with you?' he asked.

Jenny gulped. 'Just the children. Well, Shona was about to go out, and Hermione was in her room – I'd grounded her because she'd stayed out past midnight the night before. Donald and Irene were squabbling about some computer game in the kitchen and... and the two youngest were in bed – at least, my mother was putting Jack to bed. The baby was already asleep. She's a good sleeper, bless her. The best of them all. Donald was worst—'

Adam interrupted. 'And the quarrel was about?'

She sighed. 'Joe was doing some stupid deal with Mr Masters over at Haselbury House. Or, at least, he was trying to, because my mother didn't want to buy back any of our land and we were almost going broke. But the deal wasn't working out. I... I gave Joe a piece of my mind about things during dinner.'

'Did he leave after you ate dinner?'

Jenny seemed to gather herself together. 'I know what you're asking,' she said, 'The police told me he ate some poisonous mushroom. Death something? But it can't have been here – we all ate the same food. Shepherd's pie, it was.'

'Did Joe have anything different from the rest of you?'

She shook her head. 'Only a glass of Butcombe beer. But he only took a few mouthfuls, then we were arguing, and he slammed his glass down on the table in a temper, spilling most of the beer. Then, he calmed down a bit, put on his coat and went to The Plough.' Her eyes filled again. 'And that was the last time I saw him alive.' She looked at her watch, 'I'm sorry, but I have to get over to Camilton for this meeting. I mustn't be late—'

Adam and Imogen stood up.

Adam said, 'You know it was poison from a Death Cap mushroom that killed Joe. Do you know how the poison works?'

She was silent.

'You do, don't you, Jenny?'

Dumbly, she nodded. 'I googled it. It can take days or weeks. It attacks the liver and that slowly poisons the whole body until everything shuts down.'

Adam said quietly, 'That evening, after Joe ate the shepherd's pie, he was sick, wasn't he?'

She bit her lip but failed to stop it from trembling.

'Come on, Jenny,' he said, more quietly. 'There's no point in telling lies. Forensics will show us what we need to know. He was sick, wasn't he, before he left? The police will check.'

'I cleaned it up.'

He shook his head. 'You may think you did, but there will be traces.'

Jenny, dull-eyed, said, 'Then, he went to the pub,' in a monotone. 'And then home with that woman. That's what happened. He'd always had a bit on the side, ever since we were married.'

He looked her in the eye. 'The police will track down the woman.' He didn't tell her that Maria had given the name. 'And in any case...'

Jenny shrugged. There were no tears, now. 'It didn't matter where he went,' she finished for him.

Imogen was puzzled. Was Jenny confessing?

'No,' Adam nodded. 'It didn't matter, did it? Because Joe was already under sentence of death.'

Jenny stood tall, drawing her shoulders back. 'You think I killed him?' Her eyes flashed. 'Well, you're wrong. I was angry, we fought, and he left. I knew nothing about any Death Cap mushrooms. I never pick fungus – it's far too dangerous.'

'But you know who does, don't you?'

She stared at him, her face crumpling. 'N-No. Not...' she gave a sob. 'It can't be that – it must have been that woman in Camilton...' She fell silent.

'Imogen and I are calling the police,' Adam said. 'It's time for Joe's killer to confess. Isn't it?' Jenny was shivering, her face deathly white. Adam turned towards the door. 'But, before the police come, Imogen and I will leave you for a moment or two. We'll go outside while you compose yourself.'

34

THE TRUTH

'What are you doing?' Imogen stammered as he guided her out of the front door. 'You can't leave her alone. She'll do something to herself.'

Taking her arm, he led her to the car. 'No, she won't. She won't do anything that might hurt the children.'

'Well,' Imogen exploded. 'I think killing their father might have hurt them just a bit.' The sarcasm in her voice cut through the cold air. 'You think it was her, don't you?'

Adam didn't reply. He unlocked the car door. 'We're taking a drive.'

Giving up, Imogen slid into the passenger seat. 'Where are we going?'

'You'll see.'

He started the car, slid it into gear and drove off. Imogen, looking back at the house, saw the curtain twitch.

'It's not far,' Adam said.

Sick at heart, Imogen closed her eyes. 'It was the shepherd's pie. So, if it wasn't Jenny, it must have been one of the children. Shona, or Hermione? Did they poison their father? I can't believe it. Those two both loved him. Where are we going?'

'You'll see in a moment.'

The drive was short.

As Adam turned into the driveway, Imogen realised where they were.

'What are we doing here?'

Without a word, Adam left the car and rapped at the door. Imogen followed, and for a long moment, nothing happened. Then, the door opened.

'Mrs Little?' Adam said.

Jenny's mother smiled at him, arrogant as ever.

Adam pushed the door further open. 'Too late?' he asked.

The woman nodded. 'It's the best way. I don't want the children to know.'

Imogen felt the gears in her brain click into place at last. How could she not have seen it before. 'You? You killed your son-in-law? But why?'

'He was no good, everyone knew that.'

Adam was stern. 'He was good enough to marry Jenny when she was pregnant with someone else's baby.'

She clicked her tongue. 'You can't keep secrets hereabout. I should have known. They've all been laughing at us all these years, haven't they? Edwina Topsham and all the rest. Everyone chortling behind our backs.'

'No one was laughing, Mrs Little,' Imogen's hackles rose at the slur on her friends,

The older woman gave a twisted smile. 'Joe wasn't a bad man, at first, but oh, he was stupid. So very stupid. My husband and I divided up our farm and gave him half. We set him up for life, but he couldn't keep it going. Didn't have the gumption. My daughter suffered because of him – he was always in the pub, or if he wasn't, he was with one of his fancy women. And then, he expected me to buy back the land at some ridiculous price. How could I manage a big farm, with my husband dead? Joe never could see beyond the end of his nose.' She heaved a deep sigh. 'When I refused, he tried to sell off the best land in High Acres for some get-rich-quick scheme – land that my husband's family had nurtured for years. Joe didn't care about that. He'd let the farm go to rack and ruin and he set out to trash my husband's memory and sell the family land for factory farming chickens. It was the last straw.' Her face was pale, yellowish. 'I couldn't protect my Jenny. She's suffered so much over the years, trying to keep everything going on the farm while Joe played around. No wonder she turned to drink and made a few mistakes with the accounts.'

She gave a hollow laugh.

'I've put that right for her. I'm broke, now, of course, but Jenny and the kids will be okay. She'll have all the land, and she'll make a go of it, without that man holding her back.' She heaved a heavy sigh. 'I suppose I might as well tell you the rest. I'd been out mushrooming, earlier that week, before Joe ran away like the coward he was. I've seen those Death Caps in the fields before, always in the same place, every autumn. Beautiful things, they are. I picked them, dried them and ground them into a powder. Then, I made the shepherd's pie and took it round. We all had dinner together. Joe still had a chance, then, if he'd have listened to me. I was willing to compromise.'

Imogen said, 'The mushroom wasn't in the pie?'

'No. I wouldn't risk Jenny or the children eating it. I asked him, one more time, if he would change his mind and give the land back to me. I wasn't going to pay for it – we gave it to him in the first place – but for Jenny's sake I was willing to pull in my horns, employ a manager and muddle through. But Joe just laughed in my face.' Her mouth twisted. 'He said the deal with Masters had fallen through but he'd find another. He wasn't going to let me cheat him. Me, cheat him? When it was our land to start with?' She snorted. 'Jenny begged him to agree, but he shouted at her and that was when I made up my mind. I said, "Well, there's no arguing with some. I need a drink."

I went out into the kitchen and poured glasses of wine for me and for Jenny, put them on a tray, found a beer in the fridge, poured it into a glass and mixed a handful of Death Cap crumbs into it.' She was grinning, pleased with her own cleverness. 'When I took the drinks back, Jenny and Joe were still arguing and Joe drank half the beer down in a couple of gulps.' The skin of her face was drawn tight, showing the outline of her skull. She smiled, bleakly. 'He shuddered a bit, said the beer was too cold and went on nagging at Jenny. Finally, she shouted at him to get out of her sight and he went into the bathroom, threw up, came back a bit calmer, grabbed his coat and left the house. Off to the pub, as always.'

Adam said, 'And later, he went to see Maria. He must have been feeling ill, but he hoped she was going to help him. You can't imagine her nursing anyone, our Maria, even a boyfriend. I suppose that's why he moved on to Christine, his long-term mistress in Camilton.'

Imogen finished piecing things together. 'Jenny tracked his movements and knew where he'd gone, but she thought he'd soon come home as he always did, because they loved each other underneath all the worry about money and the quarrelling.'

'She's better off without him,' Maggie Little insisted. Her hands were shaking and sweat broke out on her upper lip.

Imogen gulped as the terrible truth dawned on her. 'You... you've eaten the mushroom yourself?'

Maggie Little wiped her brow. 'Of course I have. My work is done. My job was to look after Jenny and her children and that's what I've done. No one will miss me. I'm old, anyway and my husband's gone. What's left for me?' She smiled at Imogen, her eyes like shards of ice. 'Jenny rang me when you left. She told me you were on your way and that gave me time. I'd kept some of the crumbs, in case I needed another dose for Joe.' Imogen shivered. Maggie Little posed as an upright, respectable woman, but behind the mask she was a wicked, calculating killer. She showed not an ounce of regret for killing her daughter's husband – the father of her grandchildren.

Joe's killer turned narrowed eyes on Adam. 'You knew what I'd do, didn't you? That's why you talked to Jenny first, and you made sure she realised what I'd done, so she could phone to warn me.'

Adam's normally mild eyes glinted like steel behind his spectacles. 'I needed to be sure. I knew you had nowhere to run. By the way, I rang the police, I think I can hear them arriving, right now.'

Her hand was at her mouth, her face ghostly green, but she was smiling. 'But it's too late.' With a triumphant laugh, she rushed from the room.

Imogen said, sadly. 'She's being sick. But she'll die, anyway?'

Adam nodded. 'It will take time, as it did for Joe. It's a terrible way to go, but it feels fair that she chose the death she inflicted on Joe. She'll feel better for a while, but there's nothing that can be done about her liver. It will all be over in a couple of weeks.'

Imogen was thinking aloud. 'Jenny saw that Joe had been ill before he left the house. She didn't think much of it – she must have been sick herself, often, with all her drinking. She knew he had affairs – with Maria and with this Christine in Camilton. She told herself it must have been one of those two who poisoned him. I suppose she couldn't let herself believe her mother would do such a thing. She just shut herself off and retreated into more alcohol. No wonder she was drunk that day we visited – she didn't want to accept the truth, but deep down she knew her mother was capable of anything.'

Adam nodded. 'Her mother, who loves her, and in her twisted way still imagines she did the right thing. She thinks she's saving the children from knowing what she did by killing herself.'

'But they're not stupid. Shona and Hermione will put two and two together, even if Jenny pretends their grandmother's dying from a stroke or a heart attack or something. Besides, I think Jenny will want to be truthful. She loves her children too much to lie to them.' Imogen shook her head as the doorbell rang. 'Here are the police,' she said. 'What a mess – and all, I suppose, for love.'

35

REX

The Plough was hot and steamy that evening, even though the air outside was sharp.

'Likely be a frost, tonight,' Oswald said. 'We spent the day bringing them young citrus plants into the greenhouse. It's this time of year when I miss the orangery.'

Terry, already on his second pint, said, 'I heard the hotel pulled it down after the Missis's husband was found in there, dead as a doornail.'

Oswald glared at the upstart. 'You mind your business, lad. That was a tragedy.'

'Seems like this village has plenty of them,' Terry shrugged. 'When I've finished my apprenticeship, I'm off back to the Southeast. It's safer, there.'

His mates sniggered.

'You won't be able to afford a house there,' Oswald said. 'You'll be sorry if you leave. This is the best county in the country.'

Ed was frowning into his glass. 'That was a bad business, though. Joe Trevillian, murdered by his own mother-in-law. It's like a bad joke.' The news of Maggie Little's admission into hospital, following her confession to poisoning Joe, had travelled around the village like wildfire.

'It's not in the least funny.' Rex slammed a bottle down on the bar. 'Those kids are in a state, losing their dad like that, and then their grandmother. And Shona has to look after them all, with Hermione out at all hours drinking, and Shona not daring to tell her mother.'

'All right,' Adam said, raising his voice. 'Let's calm down. Joe's funeral's on Wednesday, and while you're all in here, you'll show some respect to his family.' He nodded to Rex and muttered, low enough to keep it from the other customers, 'We don't need you, tonight. You get over and see Shona. She could do with some support. And tell her we'll all come to her dad's funeral, with a big do in The Plough, if she'd like that.'

Rex didn't hang about. With a quick, 'Thanks, Boss,' he was gone.

Terry had seen the exchange. 'Rex has got a thing for that Shona, you know,' he jeered. 'It started at the Apple Day.'

Then maybe one good thing had come out of that day, at least, Adam hoped.

Oswald chuckled. 'That Rex is a sucker for a damsel in distress. It's high time he settled down with a nice sensible girl like Shona. She's made of strong stuff is that one, like our Mrs Bishop over the road.' He sighed into his glass. 'I thought Mrs Bishop had found someone worth keeping with the painter chap, but it looks like that's all over. Polite to each other, that's what they are, and neither of them happy.' He shook his head, sadly. 'I don't know what's wrong with folk, these days. My wife and I have been together for fifty years and never had a cross word. Well, not many,' he raised his voice as the young farmers hooted. 'You have to take the rough with the smooth, that's what you young 'uns don't understand...' his voice trailed off as he swallowed the last of his glass of scrumpy.

The door swung open, letting in a blast of chilly night air, and Steph stepped inside, bright as a robin in a brown coat and red hat, returning from a long day's shopping with Rose. 'It's cold and wet out there, and the wind's getting up. I think we're in for a proper storm before long.' She shivered as she looked around the bar and kissed Adam on the cheek. 'And watch what you say because I passed Dan on his way over and he looks like he needs a drink,' She whispered in Adam's ear.

Sure enough, Dan arrived, coat collar turned up against the wind.

Adam offered, 'Beer, cider, or something stronger?'

'Anything will do.' He stared down Terry's gaze and groaned. 'A morning with the police and an afternoon with the insurance claim adjuster. It's enough to drive anyone to drink.'

Oswald moved away, sitting by the fire with Arthur, a retired lorry driver, even older than the gardener himself. The two, heads together, concentrated on putting the world to rights over more cider, while Adam, Steph and Dan gathered at one end of the bar, Dan holding a glass of beer.

Steph squeezed Dan's arm. 'Have the police come up with anything about the fire?'

'From the cameras? Not really. They caught a glimpse of someone, but whoever it was had a hoodie pulled over their head, of course. There's a shot of the car, but the licence plates were obscured. There was tape or something all over the registration number. But at least it proves someone else started the fire and not me. That lets me off the hook with the insurers.'

Terry raised his voice. 'Some folks have all the luck. Free money for them as don't need it.'

Dan blinked at the force of Terry's anger.

Adam said, 'Ignore him. He's fishing for a fight. His boss was in at lunchtime and told me Terry's on a final warning. Late in the mornings, hungover, and missing half the time.' He raised his voice, 'I reckon you've had enough to drink, young Terry. Get yourself home and don't cause trouble.'

Ed said, 'I'll take him. I've not had much,' but Terry shoved himself up, rocking the table so his mates had to grab their drinks, and pointing at Dan.

'If you knew what I know about Mr Nice-guy Dan Freeman, you'd not be so quick to have him in here.' Terry squared up to Dan. 'Yeah. You kept it all quiet, didn't you?' He swung round, unsteady on his feet. 'Wanted for murder, he was.'

The Plough had fallen silent, all ears on Terry. Dan took a step towards the young farmer. 'Just you watch your mouth—'

'Who's gonna make me? You? Stick to killing women, why don't you, Freeman?'

Dan, with a face like thunder, took another step, his fist clenched.

In a flash, Adam slipped through the hatch in the bar and grabbed him from behind just as Ed caught at Terry's arm. 'Leave it, mate. Come on home.'

Terry struggled, but his heart wasn't really in it. His satisfied grin told Adam he'd made his point.

Adam jerked his head towards the door. 'Out you go. There's enough trouble in this village without you making more.'

As the lad left, smirking at his mates, Dan shrugged off Adam's arm. 'Sorry about that,' he said. 'I don't know what came over me. I'll get out of here.'

Steph rested her hand on his shoulder. 'Don't be ridiculous. Terry's drunk. He's just looking for a fight. He's got hold of the story somehow – you know – about Fay.'

Dan was breathing hard. He looked around the bar. 'And everyone knows, now?'

Adam slipped back behind the bar. 'I've no idea how the news got out, but it travels fast around here. Believe me, no one here thinks you're responsible for your girlfriend's death.'

Dan glanced around the bar, but the drinkers all looked away. 'I'm not so sure.' He gulped down his drink. 'I'll get some sleep.'

'Things will look better tomorrow,' Steph said.

Dan grunted. 'Doubt it,' he said, pulling out his wallet.

'It's on the house, Dan,' Adam said.

Raising a hand in thanks, Dan left.

Another silence fell for a split second before the drinkers in the bar could keep quiet no longer and launched into a torrent of excited gossip.

'Can't you shut them up?' Steph pleaded.

Adam shrugged. 'It's a free country. Folk come here to let off steam. But this business with Dan isn't going to go away. I wonder how Terry got wind of the story.'

Steph ran a finger around the rim of her wine glass, making it sing. 'Not from any of us, but I bet someone leaked it to the press. Look on the internet. It will be there now, and in the dailies tomorrow.'

Adam thought about that. The campaign against Dan was hotting up in the most unexpected way. 'I don't know who's behind this vendetta,' he said, 'but they're not giving up, are they?' He fell silent for a moment, thinking. 'I wouldn't have thought Terry was the kind of bloke to read the news, though.' He collected an armful of glasses to wash. 'We need to know the whole truth about Fay's death if we're going put an end to this vicious campaign. And I know who I can ask.' He reached into his back pocket, pulled out his phone and, with a nod to Steph, headed next door to the living room to track down old contacts.

At the door from the bar, he paused, listening, as Steph tapped a glass for quiet and raised her voice. 'I just want to remind you all that it's Bonfire Night tomorrow. I hope you've all helped build the

Bonfire outside the village hall. The vicar will be lighting it at 5.30 p.m. I'm sure all you "guys" will be there.' She paused as a mass groan echoed through The Plough at the pun. 'We'll be open before, during and after the official event for those of you who can't stand fireworks and loud bangs.'

'Yeah, better tell Terry to stay safe at home with Mummy,' someone mocked.

'On the subject of loud noises,' Steph added, 'the vet asked us to remind you to keep your pets safe. Imogen tells me they're hoping to put Harley in a soundproof room with a soothing radio programme.'

Ed shouted, 'He's crazy at the best of times,' to general laughter.

Steph finished, 'See you all tomorrow and don't forget to bring your sparklers.'

What a girl. What had Adam ever done to deserve her?

36

FAY

Next morning, Adam took the London train, watching the green fields of Somerset, lashed with wind and rain, disappear into the distance. He'd begun by phoning James's pathologist friend and after a lengthy series of calls, during which he ardently wished he still had access to HOLMES, the national police computer, Adam had eventually tracked down a member of the Metropolitan Police he'd once worked with on a training day at the Police College, helping young officers improve their interviewing skills.

His contact barely remembered the Fay Harman case but knew one of the officers involved and gave Adam his number.

George Ellis, it turned out, was happy to help. 'I only remember it because it was my first case after moving into CID. Get over here and I'll dig out the details and give you whatever I can remember. Over lunch for which you'll be paying, naturally.'

Resigned to the hit on his wallet, Adam spent most of the journey googling press reports of Fay's death. There was very little to find. A fatal car crash involving a woman in her late thirties who'd been drinking wasn't likely to make the daily news.

During their expensive dinner in London, George, a tall, thin, bespectacled Detective Chief Inspector with a serious manner, was able to add a little detail. 'The forensics were definite – she was well over the limit and alone in the car. The coroner's inquest gave the usual verdict, accidental death while under the influence of alcohol, and that would have been the end of the case apart from her brother's evidence.'

Adam's ears pricked up. This was new information.

'Yes, he was quite a bit younger than Fay. He wanted someone blamed for her death and he fixed on her boyfriend. That's the Daniel Freeman you mentioned. The painter fellow. The brother showed us a letter she'd written to him on the day of the accident but not posted. In those days, folks still sent letters. Hardly any texting then – amazing to think of that, now. Still,' a rare smile spread across his face, 'I got one of my staff to dig out the file and send me a photo of the note, for which you owe me one of those elaborate desserts I see on the trolley over there.'

While George tucked into a hollow chocolate orange filled with orange mousse, pistachio sponge and chocolate, Adam read the note on his phone. His heart sank. It was damning.

'Dear Little Bro,' it said. 'I've had enough. We went out to dinner yesterday, and I was sure he'd propose, but he didn't. He's never going to. I think he's cheating on me. He just wants what he can get and I hate him...'

'But she didn't send it?' Adam said.

'No. Look, she didn't even finish her sentence. Must have thought better of it. It's embarrassing, telling your brother that your boyfriend didn't propose. I suppose she realised she'd feel a fool when she'd calmed down, so she threw the note into the waste-paper basket. We told the brother it was irrelevant. He wasn't best pleased, but there was nothing we could do. There's no name, you see. The brother said the letter referred to your friend, Dan, but there's no proof of that.'

Adam sat in thought. It looked as though the brother was the most likely suspect for the campaign against Dan. 'What's the brother's name?' he asked.

'Terry.'

* * *

Adam, aghast, emailed Dan. 'Terry could be Fay Harman's brother. Keep an eye on the little blighter.'

Dan read the email, head in hands. In his mind, he travelled back to that dreadful moment the police came to tell him Fay was dead. He'd been distraught. Horrified. Unable to take it in, at first. Then, a few days later, the police had returned to show him the letter.

'I don't understand,' he'd told the young constable. 'We never got as far as discussing marriage. Why did Fay think I was going to propose? We did have a quarrel that evening – I've never denied it – but it was just about pictures of... of an old friend of mine.'

Even now, years later, Dan couldn't make sense of it all. He'd thought Fay had understood he wasn't the marrying kind. He'd told her all about his first wife and that he wasn't keen to repeat that mistake, and she'd laughed, telling him she was just looking for fun, and was happy with things as they were.

But apparently, that hadn't been true.

In fact, when Fay saw the sketches of Imogen, she'd hardly seemed jealous. They'd had a brief row and she'd fled, but it hadn't been their first quarrel, or their biggest. Dan had expected her to come back, as she so often did, and they would make up. Everything would have gone back to normal.

But that note told Dan he'd completely misunderstood what Fay wanted.

The shock had hit him like a punch in the gut.

She'd died because of him.

Every time he thought about it, an old, familiar burden of guilt settled on his shoulders, pressing him down until he could barely breathe.

He'd fatally misunderstood his relationship with Fay. He'd had no idea she wanted to marry him. She'd expected him to propose at dinner the day before and when he didn't, and she caught sight of the pictures of Imogen, she'd been so devastated she'd got drunk and crashed her car. The accident happened at the end of her street, so she could have been heading anywhere. Dan was sure she'd been on the way to see him; to patch up their quarrel.

He would never forgive himself.

And now Terry was in the picture, calling Dan a killer. Terry, the young farmer. Was he really Fay's brother? Adam pictured Terry, imagining him with fair hair, like Fay's. The name was different, but that was common these days when a marriage broke up and the father remarried.

Fay was Australian, Dan remembered, although she'd come to England when she was young. Dan tried to recall the things Terry said, for clues. He swore a good deal and said, 'Good on yer,' and 'I reckon,' but so did plenty of Englishmen.

But it was possible. She'd mentioned a younger brother, living on the other side of London, but Dan had never met him.

Dan hardly even knew Fay's friends. She kept her life in compartments, as Dan did. It was easier, that way. No baggage. That had been one of the things he'd liked about her – no ties, no ex-husband, her parents both sadly dead. She'd seemed to be as free as a bird, and that had appealed to Dan.

Terry had not made contact at the time of her death. He must have been at her funeral, but Dan hadn't recognised him. The crematorium had been full of her friends and Dan had kept at the back, out of sight, slipping in when no one was looking and leaving as soon as possible, feeling he had no right to be there. He hadn't approached anyone else – what could he have said? Her few friends thought he'd been the cause of her death, and they kept away from him.

He'd sent flowers and set up an annual donation to her favourite sporting charity – football for refugee girls. It had made him feel better, just a little, to know he'd helped someone in Fay's stead.

But her brother had been nursing his anger all these years and looking for revenge. Maybe he'd recognised Dan's name – the name of a successful artist, holding exhibitions and selling his work. Terry must have hated that. Once he discovered Dan was in Somerset, had he followed him, finding work as an apprentice on a local farm?

Dan shivered at the thought of such hatred directed at him.

But what could he do about it?

He had no idea.

He checked the time. He'd agreed to join Pierre, tonight. His son was determined to extract every moment of fun from Bonfire Night. 'I've never been here on the fifth of November before,' he'd pointed out. 'We don't have Guy Fawkes in France, but judging by the accounts I heard in The Plough, I've been deprived of burnt fingers, fireworks that fizzle and bonfires that won't light.'

'That about sums it up,' Dan had said, 'and the kids love it. Out in the dark, eating burnt marshmallows and staying up late. I imagine you've seen the guy they've been dragging round the village for the last few days? Although actually it's a female, I believe.'

'Looks remarkably like the local head teacher, I've been told. And those boys told me I had to give them a pound.'

Dan had laughed. 'It was only "a penny for the Guy" in my day.'

'Inflation,' Pierre had grinned. 'Also, it's my last few weeks in

Lower Hembrow. The article I've been working on with Steph Aldred about The Streamside Hotel is almost done, and I'm off back to France soon. The guy I worked with in Africa's got me a commission in Morocco, so I'll be sweating in the heat while England's covered in snow.'

'Snow?' Dan had scoffed, trying to ignore the ridiculous ache that hit his chest at the thought of losing Pierre. 'Half a centimetre if we're lucky. And that'll only happen if this wind drops. At least it hasn't turned to a gale yet, so the bonfire's still on target.'

Now, he closed his laptop with a snap. He'd find time to talk to Terry before going to the police. The boy was Fay's brother and Dan didn't blame him for being angry, but he'd gone too far.

37

BONFIRE NIGHT

The wind dropped at last, enough for Helen Pickles and the village hall committee to agree with the police that the grand lighting of the bonfire could go ahead.

As darkness fell, the village gathered outside the hall and watched, breath held as Helen lit the fire. The wood stuttered at first, damp from recent rain, but at last it caught fire and, with a series of pops and crackles, sparks leapt skywards and one log after another burst into flame.

At the top of the bonfire, the new head teacher's effigy caught fire, tilted, toppled and, finally, with a resounding crash, crumpled into the flames.

The head teacher, standing with her husband and children, grumbled, 'Maybe next year they'll choose another guy. I don't want to be the annual villain.'

'It's meant as a compliment, I think,' her husband said. 'I expect they'll put you in the stocks or something at the next Spring Fair as well. I gather that's what happened to their last headteacher.'

'And now,' the vicar's voice boomed out through a megaphone, 'We'll light the fireworks. Please keep well away from the roped-off area. We've never had a Bonfire Night accident in Lower Hembrow and we don't want to start now.'

The first firework, a Roman candle, sparkled and fizzed, and the crowd oohed and aahed in excitement. Soon, Catherine wheels flashed in dizzying circles while rockets screamed and exploded overhead. On the ground, anxious parents lit sparklers and hovered as their children wrote their names in the air.

Steph arrived with her daughter. 'Rose and I have been serving in The Plough, but there are only a couple of customers at the moment. Rex and Shona volunteered to hold the fort. They seemed to like having the place to themselves.'

Pierre and Rose moved a few paces away, to get a better view of the display, but Dan hardly noticed. He'd caught sight of Terry with his mates. Terry clutched a plastic pint glass in his hand, and judging by the shouts and scuffles with his mates, it wasn't his first.

Dan took a deep breath and stepped towards the lads. 'Barrington,' he called.

Over his shoulder, Terry shouted, 'Who wants me?' and looked round, his face eery in the bonfire's light.

In that turn of the head, the familiar profile, Dan recognised Terry's likeness to Fay. How could he have missed it before?

'You're Fay's brother.'

Terry's lip curled. 'Half-brother,' he said. 'Same mother, different father. I'm Terry Barrington. My sister was Fay Harman.' He took a step towards Dan, hands clenched, menacing in the flickering light. 'And don't you dare even say it.'

He lunged for Dan's jacket.

Dan dodged and Terry tripped. Ed, nearby, turned in time to catch his friend as he stumbled. 'Watch out, mate,' he said, shocked.

The last of the fireworks burst above them in a cascade of red, white, and blue sparks.

'This man...' Terry's voice seemed to echo in the sudden hush. 'This man killed my sister.'

A sea of faces, ghostly pale in the waning light of the bonfire, turned and stared.

Steph laid a restraining hand on Dan's shoulder as Ed tugged at Terry's arm, 'Don't be daft, man,' he urged. 'Leave it. This is Dan Freeman. The artist. You've got a bee in your bonnet.'

Terry shook off his friend's hand. 'I know who he is,' he growled.

Ed appealed to Dan. 'Sorry about this, Mr Freeman. Terry's had a bit too much to drink.'

Suddenly, the weight of those years of guilt threatened to overwhelm Dan. He stepped back, wearily. 'I know what you think, Barrington. You imagine Fay died because of me. But her death was an accident. I wasn't with her at the time. I didn't know she'd been drinking. I'd never have let her drive like that...'

Dan's voice trailed away.

He was wasting his time. Hatred and grief were contorting Terry's face into a grotesque mask.

Dan shook his head. 'You loved her. I know that, and I suppose kidnapping Smash was revenge. At least you didn't hurt him. But you didn't stop there. My painting, my studio? You burned down my home...'

'What?' Terry's eyes widened with fear. 'I've never been near your place,' he muttered...

Steph slipped between the two men, her arms outstretched. 'That's enough. Let's go over to The Plough and sort this out. Everyone's watching and the children don't need to see grown men fighting. You should both be ashamed of yourselves.'

* * *

Steph led the way to The Plough, her hands in her pockets so no one could see them trembling. Terry and Dan followed meekly, the young farmer's friends close behind, anxious not to miss any action.

Only Rex and Shona were in the bar, cleaning and tidying in anticipation of the post-firework rush of customers. Wayne was busy in the kitchen.

Steph glared at the young farmers and waved them to empty tables. 'You keep out of it.' They sank into their seats like naughty schoolchildren.

She pushed Dan and Terry into chairs and sat in front of them, her elbows on the table, her eyes narrowed. 'Right then. Who's going to go first?'

Neither spoke.

'Terry? Do I have to call the police? Criminal damage is serious.'

'I didn't do it.' Terry had sobered up. 'I mean, not the studio. I wouldn't do that.'

'Why don't you just admit it?' Dan asked.

Terry's friends stirred. A couple rose to their feet.

Steph snapped, 'Sit down the lot of you and grow up.'

Rex and Shona had been watching from behind the bar. Rex crossed the room in two long strides and stood behind Dan. 'No fighting allowed in here.'

The young farmers subsided.

Steph said, 'Terry, if you didn't firebomb the studio, who did?'

Terry leaned back in his chair and shrugged. 'No idea. Not me.'

Dan's face was like thunder. 'But the rest of it?'

'The rest?' Terry shot a look at his friends, but no one helped him out.

'The rest,' Dan said, through gritted teeth. 'The donkeys and the paintings.'

Terry scowled. 'Okay, I borrowed the donkey. Just to... well, to teach you a lesson, I suppose. I didn't mean any harm – I don't hurt animals. It was a spur of the moment thing – I was passing Ford late the night before Apple Day, on my way back from here. I was in the truck from our farm over in Misterton – I'd taken some sheep to a new owner and stopped for a beer with my mate who works there. I saw the track leading to your place.'

He sighed. 'I guess I'd had too much to drink. It seemed like a good idea at the time. I kept the donkey at our place over the weekend – my boss and his wife were away at a family wedding somewhere up north and I was in charge. To be honest, once I sobered up, I didn't know what to do with the donkey. The boss was due back on Monday, so in the end I drove him back in the middle of the night.'

Dan's lip curled. 'Just wait until your boss hears what you get up to when he's away.'

Steph said, 'I heard you were already on a warning. You'll be looking for a new job.'

Terry's face turned brick-red. 'I didn't mean any harm. I just wanted you to feel bad. That's why I wrote the note – so you'd know how I felt when I lost Fay. I didn't do nothing else. And I didn't do nothing to no pictures.'

Steph exchanged a glance with Dan. The denial rang true. Terry wasn't the sharpest knife in the drawer. She could easily imagine him acting on impulse after too many beers, but he'd never manage to plan the burglary at the gallery or the attack on Dan's studio without getting caught.

Terry made a noise like a hiccup, half-laugh and half-sob. 'I wanted to punish you. Fay was my big sister. If it weren't for you, she'd still be here.'

Dan looked him in the eyes. 'You think I don't know that? That I don't wish every day that it never happened? That I know I let her down?'

Terry's lip trembled. 'She was like a mother to me,' he said, dashing the back of his hand across his eyes. 'I wanted you to know how it feels – losing something you care about. But I wouldn't have hurt that donkey. Or torched your house.' Tears dribbled down his face. He wiped his nose on his sleeve.

Steph breathed a sigh of relief. 'I think maybe we need to hear the full story,' she said.

Between sniffs, Terry explained. 'Fay was my half-sister. We had the same mother, different father, and that's why our names were different. Fay came here from Australia when I was ten, and Mum and I followed her. Dad had gone off with someone else, by then.'

'You and I never met?' Dan frowned.

'She was much older than me. She looked after me when Mum died and found me a flat in London. Then, after she... she died, the police showed me the letter.' He pointed at Dan. 'It was all your fault she died and I wanted you to suffer, but I got scared. I left you alone, after. The police might... Well, I'd had a bit of trouble in the past. Not much – just a fight or two. But I didn't dare get into trouble again.' He pushed hair out of his eyes. 'I backed off.'

Steph looked at Dan. He was nodding, sadly. 'I can understand,' he said. 'I never forgot Fay, you know. I never will. But it was all a misunderstanding. She was a great girl, but I'd never even thought about marrying her – I had no idea she had it in her head. I'd known her for a while, but we'd only got together a few weeks before she died.'

'Nah. That's not true.' Terry eyes blazed again. 'She said she'd been with you for months.'

Dan was frowning. 'No,' he shook his head. 'Not me.'

Steph said, 'Look, it sounds like there's been a misunderstanding, but we can't sort it all out tonight. The question is, if you didn't set fire to Dan's studio, Terry, who did?' She looked around at the sea of puzzled faces. 'I wish Adam were here,' she said. 'He'd sort it out. Or Imogen. By the way, where is Imogen?'

Dan shrugged. 'No idea. She doesn't have to tell me what she's doing.'

Exasperated, Steph rolled her eyes.

Ed joined in. 'I saw her earlier. She was with that smooth guy she's been going around with, but they were leaving the bonfire. They looked pretty smoochy. I don't know his name.'

'Brian Arbogast,' Dan's head jerked round to look at Ed.

'Arbogast.' Terry repeated.

'Yeah, that was it,' Ed said. 'Funny name, don't you think?'

Terry rubbed his cheek. 'I've heard it before.'

Steph said, 'He's a consultant with that firm of developers, Newbury, Smith and Harnsworth.'

Terry's eyes stretched wide open. 'That's it. I knew I'd heard the name. I met him once, in London. With Fay.' He looked Dan in the eyes and swore. 'Arbogast. I remember, now. He was at her flat in London once when I went round.'

* * *

In the long silence that fell after Terry's words, images from the past whirled through Dan's brain; Fay's occasional absences, her drunken accident and, finally, that letter to Terry. She hadn't mentioned a name; just 'him'. Dan, and everyone else, had assumed it was Dan she meant.

In a single moment of clarity, like a bubble bursting, Dan felt the guilt fall from his shoulders.

Fay hadn't been referring to Dan at all. She'd been cheating on him with Brian Arbogast all the time they were together and even her brother hadn't realised the truth.

Dan saw his own shock mirrored in Terry's eyes.

'Sorry, mate,' Terry said, awkwardly. 'About the donkey and that—'

'Never mind that,' Steph interrupted. This was no time for more explanations. 'If Brian Arbogast's responsible for this vicious campaign, he's dangerous. And he's gone off alone with Imogen. We need to find them.'

Terry said, 'But where have they gone?'

'Emily might know,' Steph suggested. 'She was talking to Imogen earlier, while they watched the fireworks.'

Wayne poked his head out of the kitchen, startling Steph. She'd forgotten he was still there. 'I saw them too, y'all,' he said. 'I was there with Emily while The Plough was quiet. I couldn't resist your British Guy Fawkes Day. Kinda like the Fourth of July, what with the fireworks and all.'

Dan was already on his way to the door. 'Where did they go?'

'I heard them say Ham Hill. Brian wanted to go look at the stars, when the weather cleared. He said y'all can see them better up there than most places in England—'

But Wayne was talking to himself. Dan had already left at a run, and the others were close behind.

Dan charged down the road to his dilapidated rented van in the village hall car park, fighting through the press of villagers wandering in the opposite direction as they left the display, chattering and laughing. He threw the door open, started the engine and rattled through the narrow lane winding up towards the hill, tracking along a bridle path until the hedges drew closer and there was no more room for the van.

With an exclamation, he leaped out and raced up the hill on foot.

Behind him, more car doors slammed, but Dan couldn't wait for the others to catch up.

He prayed that, for once, he wouldn't be late.

38

STARS

Imogen could hardly believe her luck, that evening. After all the heart-searching over Dan's on-off attitude, it was wonderful to be at Bonfire Night with the handsome, attentive Brian by her side. She noticed plenty of envious looks from other women, but Brian only had eyes for her.

Emily, passing by with Wayne, stopped to whisper, 'Having a good evening, Boss?'

Imogen laughed. 'And you?'

Emily grinned. 'Wayne's just going back to cook, and I'm on my way back to the hotel, to check on Harley.'

Imogen wondered which of them was happier. For a moment, she felt a pang of sympathy for Rex. But hadn't Adam said he was seeing Shona? So, everyone in her small circle was happy.

Except, of course, for Dan. 'As if he even cares.' She shook her head, as though shaking him away, and turned back to Brian.

'Fancy a walk up the hill?' he suggested. 'Look at the stars?'

'In the dark?' She thought a moment. 'Why not? I have a torch and I could use some exercise.'

Brian walked fast and she was getting breathless, trying to keep up. 'Hey,' she said. 'What's the hurry?'

He stopped walking and laughed into her eyes. 'I can't wait to get up there and see Somerset below and the stars above. It'll be romantic, don't you think?'

'Well, we have all the time in the world,' Imogen said, as they climbed higher, but he was in no mood to slow down. 'Romance is lovely,' she panted, 'but not if I have a heart attack on the way.'

'I have a surprise for you when we get there,' he said.

'Oh.' Imogen was half-intrigued, half-anxious. She wasn't keen on surprises. 'What is it?'

He reached into his expensive leather backpack and pulled out a bottle of champagne. 'Wait until we get to the top,' he said.

He was right about the view. They stood close together when they reached the summit, finding a spot as far away as possible from the hilltop pub.

Imogen pointed at the lights in the village. 'The bonfire's still burning. And I can see people on their way home. All those children, having a wonderful time. Look...' A handful of tiny sparklers still waved cheerfully in the dark.

They stood for a long while, close together, watching. Imogen could smell Brian's aftershave, lightly musky. His arm was very close to hers.

Slowly, the bustle below drew to an end. Someone doused the final embers of the bonfire and Imogen shifted her gaze up to the sky.

'You can't see many stars after all,' she observed. 'There's too much smoke. But I don't mind. It's like so many bonfire nights when I was a child, and my mother was still alive. Was it like that for you? Did you walk to school next day—'

'With the smell of gunpowder still in the air? Yes, I did. Even in London.'

Brian's arm slipped around her waist, drawing her close. She breathed a sigh of bliss. 'London,' she said. 'I can't imagine living there – so much noise and dirt.'

'I was born in the suburbs. I lived there while I was growing up, and started work there. But I'm beginning to think Somerset is my spiritual home.' He pulled her around to face him and his hands travelled up to her face, gently cupping her cheeks. He'd slipped off his gloves and his hands felt warm and soft. 'You're very beautiful,' he said.

She waited, hardly daring to breathe. Her eyes closed in delicious anticipation of their very first kiss. Her lips parted.

Brian pulled away.

She whimpered softly, disappointed.

He laughed. 'It's time for the fizz, first. Let's sit down.'

They sat close together on a rock, for the grass was still damp. Imogen's heart thudded. She hoped he couldn't hear it.

He pulled two plastic champagne flutes from his pack and balanced them on the ground.

'You've thought of everything,' she said.

'Always do.'

His voice had changed. Puzzled, she tried to read his face in the darkness. Was something wrong?

But he was smiling into her eyes again. She'd imagined that edge in his voice.

'Wait for the pop,' he said.

But the cork slid out, noiselessly.

Imogen laughed. 'You've done this before,' she said, as bubbles spilled onto the grass.

She grabbed the glasses and fielded champagne, the liquid fizzing up to the rims.

Brian held his drink up in the air. 'To you, and me,' he said, 'and a future together.'

Her heart pounding, Imogen raised her glass in a toast. 'To us,' she whispered.

The champagne flute hovered for a moment as she smiled at Brian. Was this the beginning of a wonderful new relationship? The promise of happiness at last?

She touched the glass to her lips.

But before she could take a single sip, she heard a shout. 'Don't drink it,' and the glass was dashed from her hand.

* * *

Imogen swung round, furious, clambering awkwardly to her feet.

'Dan?' she shouted, beside herself with fury. 'How dare you?'

Dan said nothing. Instead, he stepped past her, swung his fist and landed a punch squarely on Brian's chin.

Brian toppled sideways from the rock to the ground.

'Leave him alone,' Imogen cried, horrified, grabbing Dan's arm. 'What d'you think you're doing? Are you crazy?'

He shook her off, as Brian struggled to his feet, grabbed Dan's jacket and, with a swift motion, headbutted his nose.

Dan growled and aimed a punch at Brian's ear.

Brian reeled back.

Dan's punch missed. He staggered forward, almost losing his balance.

Brian threw a punch of his own, panting with effort, and caught Dan's nose again.

At that moment, Steph, Terry and Ed arrived.

Ed and Terry grasped Brian's arms from behind while Imogen and Steph pushed Dan away.

Dan gasped at Imogen, 'You didn't drink, did you?'

She shook her head, too shocked to speak.

Dan took her shoulders and pulled her close. Blood gushed from his nose. 'I thought I'd be too late,' he said.

'Too late for what?' Imogen pushed him away. 'Why did you follow us here – Brian and I were—'

'Brian Arbogast,' Steph interrupted, 'set fire to Dan's studio and vandalised his paintings.'

Brian struggled, but Terry and Ed held him fast.

Terry said, 'It's all over, mate. They know the whole story.'

'Story? What story?' Imogen looked from Brian to Terry, confused.

Brian writhed in Terry's burly grip. 'I'm not your mate,' he grated.

Terry and Ed exchanged a glance. Ed gave a nod and, one on either side, they marched Brian away down the hill.

Imogen was shaking. 'I-I don't understand?' she said. 'Will someone please tell me what's going on?'

Dan took off his coat and wrapped it around her shoulders. He pressed a handkerchief to his nose.

'You're shivering,' he said. 'It's shock. Are you sure you didn't taste the champagne?'

'Not a single drop.' She nodded, slowly, trying to understand. 'Do you think there was something wrong with it?'

'Possibly. Although it sounds a bit melodramatic,' Dan said.

'But why?' Imogen wailed. 'Why would Brian want to...?' she didn't want to finish the thought.

'We'll take the wine and the glasses to the police for testing,' Steph said, stuffing them in her bag. 'But first, let's get Imogen back to the hotel before she freezes.'

Imogen said, 'And you have to tell me what's been going on. Brian and I were just looking at the stars, and...' She stared at Dan. She'd no idea he could fight like that. She felt a twinge of secret pride. Two men fighting over her – who'd have thought it? But why? 'We need to look at your nose,' she said. 'Is it broken, do you think?'

'Just a scratch,' Dan said. 'But I've dripped blood all over my coat.'

* * *

Holding a handkerchief to his nose, Dan led Imogen down the hill, Steph close behind.

Imogen drove them to the hotel in his van. 'You're in no fit state to drive,' she pointed out, almost bursting with the need to understand what had happened.

Soon, the whole party were back at the hotel. Steph and Dan took Imogen up to her rooms, leaving Terry and Ed, with the silent, sullen Brian firmly under their control, to call the police. 'Don't let him out of your sight,' Dan warned.

'If there's really poison in the champagne, Brian will be arrested for attempted murder,' Steph said, her eyes wide with excitement, 'as well as criminal damage to the studio.'

'But, why would he... he try to kill me?' Imogen said, weak with shock as the full implications of Brian's actions hit her. 'I thought...' she stopped talking, trying to understand.

She took a long breath. She was safe. Dan was here, on the sofa with her, his nose red and swollen, one arm protectively around her shoulders.

Slowly, the horror of the events on the hill drained away.

She touched Dan's face with gentle fingers.

'You need a doctor.'

'I'll live,' he said. 'It's not broken. Look, I can wiggle it.' The demonstration brought tears to his eyes.

'Have some paracetamol, at least.' She fetched tablets and water and settled down again, beside him.

Steph's phone beeped. Imogen jumped like a nervous kitten.

'Here,' Dan left her side, opened her precious art deco drinks cabinet and poured a stiff gin and tonic. 'You need this. In fact, on second thoughts, I think I need one too.'

Steph said, 'Adam's arrived back at The Plough, so I'll leave you two together, if you're sure you don't want a doctor?'

Dan and Imogen hardly noticed her leaving.

* * *

Adam and Steph were alone in The Plough next morning, clearing up after the night before. 'You seem to have had quite an evening,' Adam said, as Steph recounted the Bonfire Night events. 'I'm sorry I missed all the excitement. I had a useful day, though, piecing things together with the DCI in London. That's why I was so late getting back on the train.'

Steph threw the final empty bottles from the last table into a bin and flopped onto a nearby chair. 'I suppose Brian is one of those men who use women, one after the other, but never truly loves them.' She shivered. 'I suppose he was always able to sweep women off their feet if he tried, like he did Imogen. I bet there's been a trail of broken hearts behind him.' She smiled at Adam. 'I'm glad you're not like Brian.'

Adam drew up a chair next to hers, leaning his elbows on the table. 'Are you suggesting I don't sweep women off their feet?' he said, only half-joking.

Steph's face was serious. 'You're very special, Adam. Everyone who knows you thinks you're wonderful and I'm the luckiest woman in the world to have you by my side.'

'By your side?' Adam cleared his throat. This was no time for cold feet. 'Do you think we should make that permanent?'

'Make what permanent?' Steph's eyes twinkled. 'Me sitting by your side?'

His ears throbbed. It was now or never.

He slid off the chair, dropped to one knee on The Plough's cold flagstones, took a long breath and said, 'Steph Aldred, will you marry me?'

She knelt down, took both his hands in hers and smiled into his face. 'Of course I will, you foolish man. And get up, for goodness sake, or you'll have rheumatism in your knees.'

Leading him through into the cosy sitting room, she pulled him onto the sofa and snuggled down in his arms.

'I can't believe it,' he murmured in her ear. 'I thought no one could ever love me.'

'Idiot,' Steph said. 'I bet you never asked anyone.'

'Just once,' he said. 'When I was young. She laughed at me.'

'So you let a stupid woman spoil your life for years? And I thought you were the clever one. Now, stop talking and kiss me.'

And, obediently, Adam obliged.

* * *

Much later, Adam made coffee for them both.

'Where were we?' Steph asked. 'I mean, before—'

'We were wondering what makes a man like Brian turn to murder.'

'So we were. I mean, if he was so angry at Dan, why turn on Imogen? It doesn't make sense.'

'Revenge. The most chilling emotion in the world,' Adam said slowly. 'Once you realise Brian has a giant ego, you can see how it happened. Fay left him by dying in the car crash. He couldn't take any blame for her death – that would ruin his self-image – and so he told himself it was Dan she referred to in her letter. It followed, then, that he would set out to punish Dan. And he was willing to take his time. I bet he obsessed about it for years. He tracked Dan down, and discovered that he lived in this part of the world, near Fay's brother. He persuaded his firm to put in a bid for renovating the old folly and they sent him as their consultant. If that hadn't happened, you can be sure he'd have found another way to reach Dan, eventually.'

'He could certainly sell anything to anyone – like those second-hand car salesman types on *The Apprentice*,' Steph said.

Adam sipped coffee. 'Brian got to know Lower Hembrow, found out about Dan's relationship with Imogen and Terry's stupid act of spite and started on this mad vendetta. It must have seemed a perfect revenge, and once he'd begun he couldn't stop. He became more and more obsessed. It's just as well you and Dan figured it all out and saved Imogen's life, because he definitely meant to kill her. He confessed, you know, once the police arrived. He'd heard about Joe's death and the Death Cap poison. He saw that as a good, safe way of committing a murder. It was easy for him to look up the fungus and search around the countryside until he found one to put in the champagne glasses. It didn't matter which glass Imogen took – they both contained poison and he had no intention of drinking from them himself. It would have been easy enough to spill his drink on the grass. He didn't need to resort to a fair fight to take his revenge. He wouldn't want to get his hands dirty. He's no action man.'

Steph chuckled. 'Unlike Dan. You should have seen him in action on the hill, last night. And Terry came up trumps in the end, although he's still an idiot. I hope he decides to stay in Somerset, and his boss gives him another chance. Like Oswald told him, there's no better place to be and Dan's a forgiving type. I reckon young Terry can find a way to put things right if he keeps on his best behaviour. Maybe a stint or two mucking out those donkeys for free and a decent apology to his boss. There's good in him somewhere. Once he lets himself get over the circumstances of his sister's death, he'll want to talk about her with Dan. It would do both of them good.'

Adam said, 'I wish Dan and Imogen would sort themselves out and get together. I'm finding being engaged a most enjoyable state, and I think it's well past time they tried it.'

'So do I. And judging by the way those two were looking at each other when I left them last night, it won't be long before they join the club.'

* * *

Steph had no idea that Dan and Imogen had talked long into the night after she left, close together on Imogen's sofa, Imogen's head snuggled on Dan's chest.

'I'm so sorry,' he said.

'About Brian? No need to be. I was a fool. I thought you and I were finished, and it was my fault for being so unreasonable when you were late on Apple Day. You see, I'd made it into some kind of test of... of your feelings.'

'And I failed, spectacularly,' he sighed.

'But it wasn't your fault. I should have listened to you.'

'I'm not surprised you'd had enough. I've been selfish. Over the years, I'd become used to the idea of being by myself. My first marriage hardly lasted for ten minutes and then Fay happened. I was so sure her death was my fault. That I was kind of toxic; I couldn't deal with the kind of relationship other people managed.'

Imogen pushed her glass across the table for a refill. 'I should apologise, too. All I thought about was myself – you know, my hotel and my garden, and being independent and so on. And I was angry, because I felt you didn't care enough, so when Brian came along with all his flattery and dinners—'

'And his perfect timekeeping.'

She laughed. 'I can't believe I was so shallow. And there you were, with your painting ruined, and your home destroyed. And now your nose is a mess.'

He grinned, and pulled her closer. 'I only lost things. None of them matter. And my face will recover. You know, I've been thinking about my life since Pierre arrived. He's better at living than I've ever been. He doesn't care about money or fame. He's just trying to make a difference with his photos and I'm going to take a leaf out of his book.'

'Oh?' Imogen sat back, frowning. 'How do you mean?'

He laughed, awkwardly. 'I've realised I love teaching even more than producing my own work. Or, at least, I love it more than painting what other people want to buy. I mean to experiment a little; try other styles, less commercial stuff. I have savings, a boost from this latest show and the insurance from the studio and I can teach for a while. Alfie brought his mate, Donald – you know, Shona's difficult teenage brother – to our second lesson. We were in the village hall, with some kind of step-dancing crashing away in the next room – and I got the biggest buzz from it all. In fact, I shall have to tell Adam and Steph their plot to get me to Lower Hembrow has worked, although I don't think they were planning anything as drastic as burning down my house.'

'The folly conversion was their idea, you know, but it's a good one. I suppose Brian only wanted to be part of it so that he could get close to you and think of ways to get at you.'

'And he's no fool – he found the worst thing he could do to me was to hurt you – or worse.'

Imogen shivered. 'The man must be unhinged.'

'He must have been tracking me for a long time,' Dan said. 'I think he even paid for that photo of Pierre's in the local paper, to get my son here, maybe planning some kind of revenge through him.'

'What a twisted man,' Imogen said. 'But at least he didn't hurt either Pierre or me in the end. In fact, you were quite the knight in shining armour, tonight, rescuing me like that. I'm very sorry about your face.'

He laughed. 'That's the last time I get into a fight. I'm far too old. And it won't be needed, now Brian's with the police.' He frowned, thinking, but suddenly his brow cleared. 'I won't be rebuilding the studio. The cottage I'm renting on the other side of the village is fine for now – there's even a paddock that the donkeys like. I'll sell the studio land for someone else to build on.' He cleared his throat. 'Where I go next, will depend—'

But Imogen had interrupted. 'Do you know, I've been thinking something similar. About me, I mean, not you. I don't want to live in the hotel any more. I want a place where I can cook and clean, with a little private garden of my own...' She stopped talking, 'Why are you laughing?'

Dan shook his head and she bit her lip.

'I'm doing it again, aren't I? You were telling me something important and I was just thinking about me. I'm so sorry. What were you saying?'

'Well, as it happens, I was going to ask if you'd be interested in living in a little cottage on the other side of the village, with a donkey paddock and a tiny garden – for a while at least.'

Tears started in Imogen's eyes. 'Really? In your cottage with you?'

'With me. And Smash and Grab. Until we can build something permanent.' He hesitated. 'I have to start over, and I can't imagine a better way to begin.' He took a breath, as though steeling himself for the next words. 'You see, although my paintings were safe, I lost all my sketches in the fire.'

Imogen hesitated, watching his face. 'Were they very precious?'

To her amazement, Dan blushed like a schoolboy. 'They went back years, starting when we were at school.' He shrugged, as though trying to hide his feelings, but he couldn't quite meet her eyes. 'In fact, most of them were of you,' he muttered.

'Me?' she said blankly. 'When we were at school?'

'They weren't very good,' he said, with an unconvincing laugh.

Imogen sat quite still, hardly daring to breathe, while the implications of what he was saying sunk in.

At last, Dan said. 'Say something, please. Are you angry that I kept secret drawings of you?'

'Angry?' She frowned, amazed. 'How could I be? For so many years, I've...' She swallowed, struggling to get the words out. She gulped. 'I've always loved you. But I thought it was all one-sided.'

He shook his head. 'Not at all. But I've never been able to put my feelings into words. I draw, instead. Those sketches – for years, when we lost touch, they were all I had left of you. And now they're gone.'

'But I'm still here.' Gently, she kissed his forehead. 'I wish I'd known. I thought you were losing any interest you had in me. When we quarrelled at the Apple Day – and that was my fault, for not listening to you – I made up my mind it was hopeless, and you'd never want me the way I always wanted you. I thought I should give up and move on. And then Brian appeared and I latched on to him.' She held his head, looking into his eyes, her heart pumping. 'I think that, deep down, I wanted to make you jealous.'

'Well, you certainly succeeded in that.' He sighed. 'Every time I tried to do better – to ring you on time and remember dates – I messed up. I thought I just didn't have what it takes to make a woman happy. I thought about my marriage, and the mess I'd made of it, and then...' he hesitated. 'And then, there was Fay.' His voice shook as he said the name. 'I was never in love with her, and

I'd thought she was just with me for fun. But when she died, I thought I'd let her down, although I didn't understand how. I thought we'd understood each other, but I'd been wrong. After that, I didn't dare get too close to you. I couldn't bear to let you down, too. So when we quarrelled on Apple Day, I thought I should leave you alone.' His eyes twinkled. 'Even if you did end up with a loathsome slime-bag like Brian Arbogast.' He took her hand. 'But I nearly got you killed, as a result. You would have been paying for my stupidity.'

She pointed an accusing finger at him. 'Don't you dare imagine Brian's attack was your fault. I'm a grown-up – like Elise, your ex-wife. Fay was an adult, too, and Brian Arbogast is a psychological mess and a danger to anyone who crosses him.' She smiled at the relief in his eyes. 'You don't have to fix everyone's lives,' she went on. 'Just enjoy yours. Although, I hope that it will include me.'

Dan pulled her closer. He smelt deliciously of woodsmoke and fresh air as his lips touched Imogen's, tenderly at first, then with more urgency, and she gave herself up to the joy of his embrace. For at last, after so many years of doubt, no shadow lay between them to hinder their sheer delight in each other.

Slowly, she pulled her head away, searching his face with her eyes. 'You were saying something about your cottage in the village?'

'I asked if you'd share it with me, while we found somewhere bigger. Where Harley could join us.'

Imogen laughed aloud. 'I can't wait. And, once Adam and Steph have chosen their kittens, maybe we'll ask Jenny to give us one as well – to keep Harley in order.'

'Whatever you want, is yours.' He swallowed, biting his lips. 'But we don't want the village gossiping about us, do we?' he said.

'What do you mean? I don't care what people say – oh.' She broke off as Dan reached into his pocket and pulled something out. 'What's that?'

'I've had this with me for a while,' he muttered. He coughed. 'I'm making a mess of this, aren't I?'

Imogen grinned, pretending she didn't understand, hardly able to believe this was really happening. 'A mess of what?' she teased.

He showed her the box. 'I've had this in my pocket since Apple Day.'

Imogen took it with fingers that trembled. She flipped it open, saw the ring and gasped. 'A sapphire. My favourite stone...'

'Well, that's great,' Dan said, removing the ring from the box. 'But I-I wanted to ask you...'

She waited, not daring to breathe.

'Will you marry me?' he finished.

She laughed aloud. 'Of course I'll marry you.'

As he slipped the ring on her finger, a broad smile spread across Dan's face, crinkling his eyes.

Imogen touched his cheek. 'We've been such idiots,' she said. 'And we've got so much wasted time to make up for...'

Dan took her in his arms. 'Then, let's not waste any more time talking.'

AUTHOR'S NOTE

As a chill arrives in the air, the days grow short and the leaves begin to fall, autumn reigns in England, where *A Harvest Murder* is set.

As I began researching the background to the story, I realised how much tradition and how many happy memories are tied up in the season so often overshadowed by the exciting run-up to Christmas.

Harvest:

The fun begins with the Harvest Festival, held on the Sunday nearest the Harvest Moon which is the full moon in late September or October. In *A Harvest Murder*, the festival falls in the middle of October.

Traditionally, the hard work of the summer in the fields is over. The crops are gathered in, the grass stops growing, and the farming community enjoys a moment to take a breath and celebrate the year's largesse.

I find something touching in Harvest songs. While 'We Plough the Fields and Scatter (the good seed on the land)' was a favourite when I was at school, I'm almost as fond of my memory of my children singing the cheery 'Cauliflowers Fluffy' in their schools.

Many places in England also celebrate with a Harvest Supper, an evening of food and entertainment for the whole local community.

Apple Day:

A newer arrival on the autumn scene is Apple Day, begun in the UK in 1990 by Common Ground, a Dorset-based charity aiming to connect people with nature. It's designed to mark the importance of the humble apple in all its varieties – and there are over seven thousand different types of apple in the world.

In Somerset, the Apple Day idea's been taken up with enthusiasm. After all, we make arguably the best cider in the world. On the weekend nearest to 21 October, Barrington Court held their most recent Apple Day weekend in 2019, before Covid-19 struck.

As it's a recent tradition, the celebrations can include anything orchard or apple-related – although too much scrumpy, the strongest, roughest kind of cider, is probably best avoided.

Hallowe'en:

Hallowe'en follows on 31 October, the day that began as Samhain, a kind of pre-Christian celebration more like our harvest festival, but recently it's been linked to All Soul's Day when the ghosts of the dead were expected to rise up and connect with the living world.

Nowadays, Hallowe'en, in a tradition largely imported from the United States of America, allows children to dress up in scary costumes and visit homes to trick or treat, demanding sweets from householders in order to avoid a trick.

In some parts of the country, trick or treating built on the tradition of Mischief Night, when children played supposedly harmless trick on adults.

In order to spare householders who prefer not to open their doors to crowds of children, there's a generally agreed rule at Hallowe'en that you place a pumpkin carved with a face, and with a lit candle inside, outside your door to signal that you want to take part and have remembered to build up your supplies of treats.

Bonfire Night:

Bonfire Night, or Guy Fawkes Night on 5 November, is traditionally an evening spent around a roaring bonfire with a Guy burning on top, while fireworks light up the sky. The 'Guy' effigy is based on Guido Fawkes, one of a group of Catholic conspirators who, in 1605, attempted to blow up the Houses of Parliament in London and the Protestant James I of England, who was also James VI of Scotland.

The plot failed and the conspirators were caught, but the fun of Bonfire Night lived on, with toffee apples and gingerbread, hot potatoes, sausages and toasted marshmallows to stave off the November chill, while children waved burning 'sparklers', the sparks lasting just long enough to leave a trace of the first letter of a name in the dark sky.

I remember chanting the old rhyme at school when I was a child:

Remember, remember, the fifth of November.
Gunpowder, treason and plot.
I see no reason why gunpowder treason
Should ever be forgot

Children would, until recently, build their Guy out of old

clothes stuffed with straw or rags and wheel it around in a cart for days before Bonfire Night, begging adults for 'a penny for the Guy' so they could buy fireworks.

Nowadays, children can't buy fireworks in the UK and the Catherine wheels, bangers, rockets and Roman candles are restricted mostly to safe communal displays. But, in some places, the old tradition of burning a Guy, sometimes an effigy of a politician, remains.

Classic FM, a UK radio station, provides a programme of suitably soothing music designed to help your dogs or other pets relax and ignore the scary bangs and crashes of the night.

ACKNOWLEDGMENTS

While the world's been in hibernation, suffering from the pandemic, I've counted myself lucky to be a writer. I can write anywhere so long as I have a computer or at least a pen and paper. Although it's been hard to get out and about for 'real' research while lockdowns came and went, in this book I've been able to use many of my own very happy memories of autumn celebrations.

In many ways, autumn's my favourite time of year, full of conkers, festivals, log fires, fireworks and spectacular autumn leaves. My husband and I even married in November and still celebrate if we can with a few days relaxing in the countryside.

I hope you've enjoyed reading *A Harvest Murder*, and I'd like to thank everyone at Boldwood Books for their help in producing the story, especially Caroline Ridding, my long-suffering editor.

And thank you to my grandchildren for keeping me up to date with the latest Hallowe'en costumes – Toothless? Unicorns? – and my children who, by taking part in Harvest Festivals at school, introduced me to the everlasting earworm that is 'Cauliflowers Fluffy'.

MORE FROM FRANCES EVESHAM

We hope you enjoyed reading *A Harvest Murder*. If you did, please leave a review.

If you'd like to gift a copy, this book is also available as an ebook, digital audio download and audiobook CD.

Sign up to become a Frances Evesham VIP and receive a free copy of the Lazy Gardener's Cheat Sheet. You will also receive news, competitions and updates on future books:

https://bit.ly/FrancesEveshamSignUp

Discover more about the world of Frances Evesham by visiting boldwoodbooks.com/worldoffrancesevesham

ALSO BY FRANCES EVESHAM

The Exham-On-Sea Murder Mysteries

Murder at the Lighthouse

Murder on the Levels

Murder on the Tor

Murder at the Cathedral

Murder at the Bridge

Murder at the Castle

Murder at the Gorge

Murder at the Abbey

The Ham Hill Murder Mysteries

A Village Murder

A Racing Murder

ABOUT THE AUTHOR

Frances Evesham is the author of the hugely successful Exham-on-Sea Murder Mysteries set in her home county of Somerset. In her spare time, she collects poison recipes and other ways of dispatching her unfortunate victims. She likes to cook with a glass of wine in one hand and a bunch of chillies in the other, her head full of murder—fictional only.

Visit Frances's website: www.franceseesham.com

Follow Frances on social media:

facebook.com/frances.evesham.writer

twitter.com/FrancesEvesham

instagram.com/francesevesham

bookbub.com/authors/frances-evesham

Boldwⱺd

Boldwood Books is an award-winning fiction publishing company seeking out the best stories from around the world.

Find out more at www.boldwoodbooks.com

Join our reader community for brilliant books, competitions and offers!

Follow us

@BoldwoodBooks

@BookandTonic

Sign up to our weekly deals newsletter

https://bit.ly/BoldwoodBNewsletter